Love's Lifeline

Love's Lifeline

JULIAN T. WESTWOOD

BiblioSky

Copyright © 2025 by Julian T. Westwood

All rights reserved.

The right of Julian T. Westwood to be identified as the author of this work and has been asserted by them in accordance with the Copyright, Designs and Patents Act 1988.

No part of this publication may be reproduced, distributed, or transmitted in any form or by any means, including photocopying, recording, or other electronic or mechanical methods, without the prior written permission of the publisher, except as permitted by U.S. copyright law. For permission requests, contact [include publisher/author contact info].

The story, all names, characters, and incidents portrayed in this production are fictitious. No identification with actual persons (living or deceased), places, buildings, and products is intended or should be inferred.

Published by BiblioSky – A Division of Skyward Media & Publications

Book Cover by BiblioSky

Illustrations by Troy Wilson

Editor Hayley Willens

2nd Edition 2025

Dedicated to my dear mother, Tania,
who passed away last year.
Love and Miss You Always, Mum

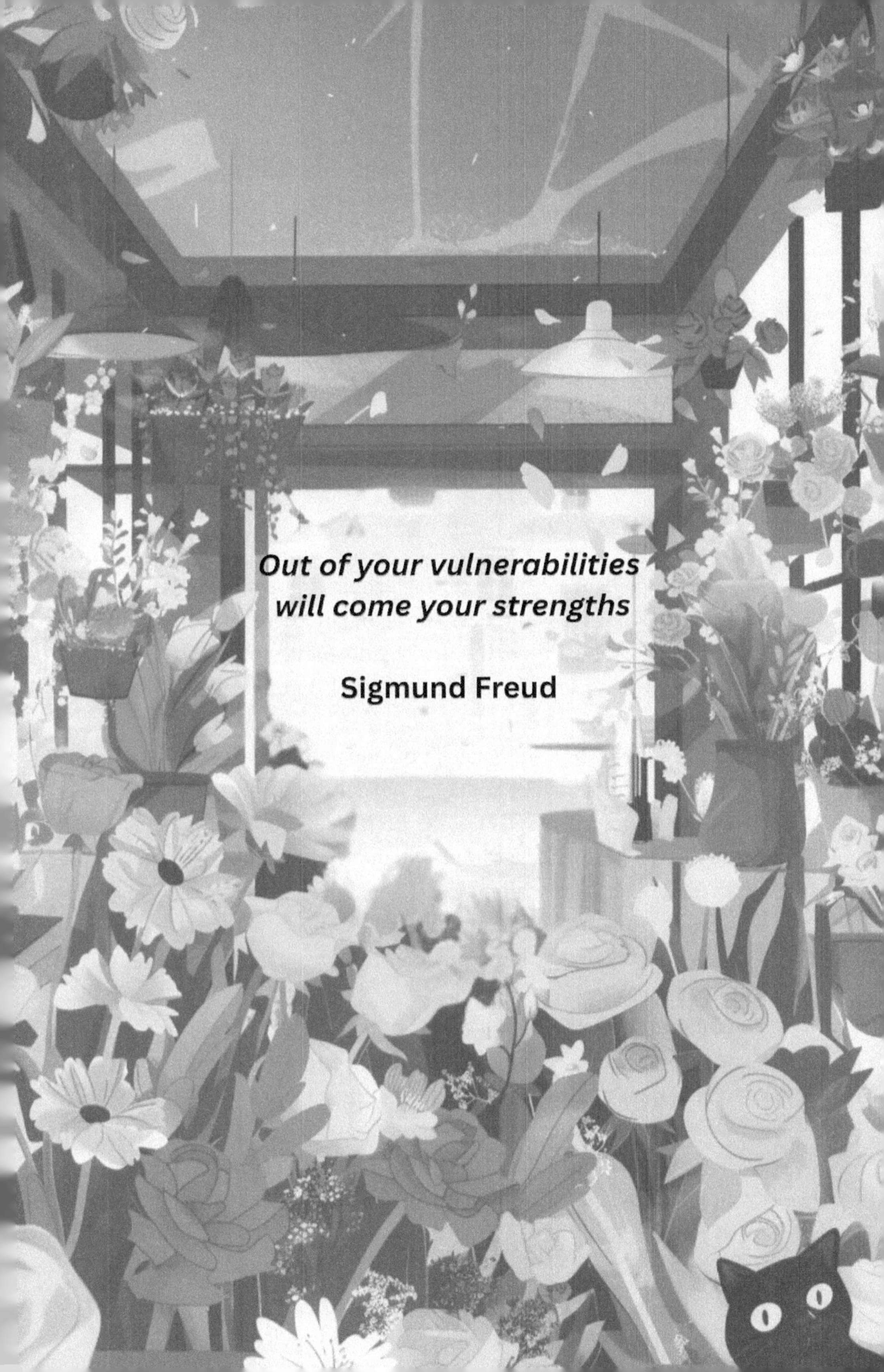

Out of your vulnerabilities
will come your strengths

Sigmund Freud

Chapter 1

Morning light streamed through sheer drapes, casting soft patterns across the Persian rug in Dr. Reginald "Reggie" Fitzwilliam's office. Freud, the British Shorthair, settled into his miniature leather armchair with his usual dignity as the first clients of the day arrived.

The Mitchells took their usual positions on opposite ends of the three-cushion leather couch. Sarah dabbed at her eyes with a tissue while John crossed his arms, his jaw set. Debussy's gentle notes floated in the background—an intentional choice Reggie often made to ease his clients into calm.

A crack appeared in Sarah's voice as she confessed, "He doesn't understand me anymore." "It's like we're speaking different languages."

John shifted in his seat. "I try, but nothing's ever good enough."

Reggie watched as Freud rose and padded to the space between them, settling with the quiet authority only a cat could command. Seeing the cat, Sarah smiled subtly.

"My impression is that you both feel under appreciated." Reggie leaned forward, adjusting his silk tie. "Sarah, you're seeking understanding, while John, you're feeling inadequate despite your efforts."

Sarah's shoulders relaxed slightly. "I just want him to listen without trying to fix everything."

"Sometimes I don't know what else to do," John admitted, uncrossing his arms.

Freud stretched, his paw touching John's leg. The tension in the room shifted as John unconsciously moved closer to pet the cat.

"Let's talk about what listening means to each of us," Reggie offered, noticing Sarah's body language directed at her husband.

As the session progressed, the physical gap between the Mitchells narrowed. Sarah's hand found John's, their fingers intertwining.

"I never thought about it that way before," John murmured, squeezing his wife's hand.

When the session concluded, the Mitchells left walking closer together than they had in weeks. Reggie settled in behind his desk, a pen poised over his notepad. Freud returned to his chair, assuming an identical posture to his owner's, golden eyes fixed on the closed door.

Reggie glanced at his cat. "Well done, old chap. Though I suspect you're rather better at this than I am."

Reggie stepped out of his office, adjusting his burgundy tie as the Mitchells approached Pam's desk to reschedule. The reception area hummed with the gentle buzz of phones ringing and fingers tapping on keyboards. A fresh arrangement of native flowers——waratahs and kangaroo paw——brightened the space, their vibrant colours drawing the eye away from the stack of his latest bestseller, *Love Without Walls: Building Bridges in Your Relationship*, displayed prominently on the corner table.

Freud had claimed his favourite spot on the window ledge, methodically grooming his grey coat in the late morning sun. His peaceful routine halted mid-lick as Dr. Cassandra Linton's clicking heels announced her presence.

"Another happy couple, Reginald?" Cassandra's voice carried across the reception area, sharp enough to cut glass. Her blonde hair caught the sunlight as she paused by Pam's desk, her gaze sliding from the Mitchells to the pile of the doctor's books.

Freud stood up, showing obvious dissatisfaction with Cassandra's presence. He gracefully moved away from his sunny spot, his tail swaying as he walked between the two practitioners. He deliberately turned his backside towards Cassandra. Glancing at the cat, she remarked, "What's the purpose of having this creature in our workplace? Surely, he has somewhere else to be?" "Freud's an integral member of the team," Pam interjected. "You're the only one who seems bothered by his presence."

"I wasn't aware of your aversion to cats, Dr. Linton." Reggie maintained an even voice, though his fingers unconsciously drifted to straighten his immaculate necktie. "Beautiful day, wouldn't you say?"

Cassandra scoffed, irked by the suggestion she disliked cats. "That's not the issue - I simply question the appropriateness of having one in a professional environment." Pam and Reggie shared knowing looks. "We, that is, the team believes that Freud's presence creates a therapeutic atmosphere, and the majority supported his residency," Reggie explained. "Though you made your opposition quite clear."

Pam's phone trilled again. "Dr. Fitzwilliam's office. How may I help you?" She juggled the receiver while checking the appointment book. "Yes, actually we have a cancellation this Thursday...."

"Your waiting list must be growing by the day," Cassandra remarked. "All those couples desperate for the famous Dr. Fitzwilliam's expertise on matters of the heart."

The Mitchells finished booking their next session, Sarah's hand still linked with John's as they headed towards the exit. Reggie noticed how Cassandra's gaze followed them, her eyes giving away the calculations being made behind her professional mask.

"Success leaves clues, doesn't it?" She gestured towards his book display. "Though I've always wondered...how does one become such an expert on love without experiencing it firsthand?"

Freud's tail twitched more vigorously, his posture rigid as he maintained his strategic position between the two doctors.

Reggie settled into his leather desk chair, the familiar creak a comfort after the morning's intense sessions. Through the window, Paddington's skyline stretched beneath a clear autumn sky. He spread his morning case notes across the polished mahogany surface, each page filled with his precise handwriting.

Freud claimed his afternoon spot on the wide windowsill, his grey form stretched luxuriously in a patch of sunlight. The cat's golden eyes fixed on Reggie with that uncanny perception that sometimes made him wonder who was analysing whom.

"The Mitchells made remarkable progress today." Reggie reviewed his notes, pen tapping against the paper. *"Classic case*

of love languages misalignment. Once they understood how differently they expressed affection...."

A face-down silver frame caught his eye - his parents at his graduation, his father's arm stiff around his shoulders, his mother's smile fixed for the camera. He turned back to his notes.

"Three couples back on track this week." He made a few additional observations in the margin. *"The Hendersons' breakthrough about their communication patterns. The Parnell's working through their trust issues. And now the Mitchells reconnecting."*

Freud's tail swished; his expression distinctly unimpressed.

"What? These are significant therapeutic achievements." Reggie straightened his tie; aware he was defending himself to a cat. "My methods work. The results speak for themselves."

Freud stretched, each movement deliberately graceful, before settling into a more attentive position. His stare remained fixed on Reggie, carrying all the weight of his namesake's psychological insight.

"Don't start. Not all of us are as naturally gifted at relationships as you are.

Freud's tail twitched in what seemed like amusement, and Reggie couldn't shake the feeling he was being judged by his own cat.

The afternoon sunlight slanted through the therapy room windows as Rebecca Turner settled into the familiar leather chair. Reggie noted the absent wedding ring, the tissue twisting between her fingers, speaking volumes about her emotional state. Freud shifted in his miniature chair, his golden eyes also tracking the subtle signs of distress.

Reggie maintained his practiced therapeutic posture, one leg crossed over the other, hands folded loosely in his lap. "Tell me more about how you're feeling about these changes."

"Everything I believed about love was wrong..." Rebecca's voice cracked. "Fifteen years of marriage, and he just...walked away. Said he'd outgrown me." Fresh tears spilled down her cheeks. "The thought of dating again at my age——"

Freud's ears pricked forward at the shift in her emotional state. His tail swished once, then stilled.

Reggie leaned forward slightly, his voice gentle but firm. "Dating after divorce can feel overwhelming. It's natural to question your judgment after a significant relationship ends."

"But how do you know when to trust again?" Rebecca dabbed at her eyes. "How do you..." She paused, looking directly at him. "Dr. Fitzwilliam, how do you manage your own relationships?"

His hand moved automatically to his tie, adjusting the perfect Windsor knot. Freud's head tilted, watching this telling gesture with feline intensity. The silence stretched for a heartbeat too long.

"Let's focus on your journey," Reggie redirected smoothly, though something flickered behind his professional mask. "Your concerns about trust are valid, but they're specific to your experiences with——"

"But surely you understand personally?" Rebecca pressed. "Someone who helps others find love must have special insight into their own relationships?"

Freud rose from his chair, padding across to settle beside Rebecca on the couch. She automatically reached down to stroke his grey fur, finding comfort in his steady presence.

"My role is to guide you through your healing process." Reggie maintained his distance, even as his jaw tightened imperceptibly. "My personal life isn't relevant to your therapeutic journey."

"But how can you guide others if you haven't..."

"Rebecca." His tone remained kind but firm. "Your healing isn't dependent on my personal experiences. Let's explore what trust means to *you* specifically."

Freud's purr filled the silence, offering the comfort Reggie couldn't allow himself to give. Rebecca's shoulders relaxed slightly as she continued petting the cat, though her eyes still held questions about her therapist's careful deflection.

As the session ended, Rebecca gathered her belongings, calmer but thoughtful. Freud returned to his post, watching as she made her way to the door.

The latch clicked shut, leaving Reggie alone with his feline companion. Their eyes met in a moment of silent understanding. The cat's tail twitched once, eloquent in its judgment of his human's practiced evasions.

After struggling with the door lock, Reggie arrived home to a darkened apartment. Switching on the lights and setting down Freud's cat carrier, his feline companion went straight to the kitchen, hoping to find food. Reggie set down the leather briefcase, which landed with a soft thud beside the entry table. His shoulders sagged, the weight of maintaining his professional persona finally lifting in the sanctuary of home.

The silk tie loosened with practiced movements; his top button undone as Freud wound figure-eight between his legs. A stack of mail awaited him––professional journals, therapy conference invitations, publishing house correspondence. Bach's "Cello Suite No. 1" filled the space, the automated system sensing his arrival.

In the kitchen, Reggie divided his left-over pad Thai onto a single white plate while Freud supervised from the counter. The cat's own gourmet dinner––wild-caught salmon in Gelée––went into a ceramic dish with "Dr. Freud" elegantly painted on the side. They ate in silence, the city's evening rhythm playing out beyond the glass.

Standing at the window, Reggie watched lights flicker on in neighbouring buildings, each window a glimpse into other lives, other stories. Freud perched on the windowsill beside him, their reflections overlapping in the glass.

His phone buzzed––a message from his publisher. Latest sales figures for *Love Without Walls* had broken records. The old gleam of professional pride flickered briefly within him before dissolving into a familiar hollow ache. Freud's golden eyes met his in the window's reflection, seeing past the successful facade to the loneliness beneath.

The carefully maintained walls crumbled for a moment. Reggie's hand found Freud's soft fur, something he did automatically dozens of times a day. The cat's purr rumbled deep and steady, offering unconditional acceptance. But the moment passed quickly. Reggie straightened, withdrawing behind practiced distance as the city lights blazed brighter against the deepening night.

The study's single desk lamp cast a warm circle of light across scattered papers and leather-bound psychology texts. Beyond the windows, Paddington's skyline sparkled against the velvet night, a constellation of urban stars. Freud lounged in his plush, duck feathered pillow, tail curled precisely around his paws, golden eyes half-lidded but alert.

Reggie's fingers traced the edges of his client files. The day's sessions spread before him like a roadmap of other people's emotional journeys. The Mitchells' breakthrough brought a slight smile to his face; their shift from defensive positions to holding hands embodied everything he strived for in his practice.

His pen paused over Rebecca Turner's notes. Her direct question about his personal life had pierced his professional armour with surgical precision. Even now, hours later, the moment replayed with uncomfortable clarity. His hand drifted to his loosened tie; a habit so ingrained he barely noticed anymore. Freud's ears twitched at the gesture, the cat's attention sharpening as he sensed his human's disquiet.

The laptop's notification light blinked, drawing Reggie's attention. Another email from his publisher, this time a major television network was asking about adapting *Love Without Walls* into a relationship segment on a prime time show. The prospect of such public exposure sent an uncomfortable prickle down his spine. Freud abandoned his pillow, padding across the desk to plant himself squarely on the keyboard.

Reggie caught his reflection in the darkened window——he thought of who he appeared to be, a successful author, renowned therapist, sought-after expert, and so on. The image wavered, revealing something more vulnerable beneath. Freud's paw batted gently at his hand, offering silent support in that uncanny way of his. For a moment, Reggie's carefully constructed walls trembled.

But professional instincts kicked in quickly. He gathered tomorrow's files with practiced efficiency, arranging them in precise order. Freud settled closer, his presence a steady comfort as Reggie moved through his evening routine. Each file represented another chance to help, another opportunity to focus on others rather than himself.

The desk lamp dimmed, leaving only city lights to illuminate the study. Man and cat sat in companionable silence, success and solitude intertwined in the gathering night. Freud's purr rumbled softly, a gentle counterpoint to the quiet rustle of papers and the distant hum of the city below.

Chapter 2

Seated in his leather chair, Reggie carefully reviewed the day's schedule. Each appointment slot represented another opportunity to help, another chance to focus on bettering others' lives. Freud occupied his miniature chair with matching dignity, his grey coat catching the orange glow of the sunrise.

A professional tranquility filled the office—lavender, classical music, and meticulous order reigned. Reggie adjusted his navy silk tie, already flawless, as he reviewed the notes for his first client.

A soft knock disrupted the morning routine. Pam entered, carrying a cream-coloured envelope with elegant letterhead.

"For you, Dr. Fitzwilliam—a special delivery. Marked urgent."

Freud's ears pricked forward, his golden eyes fixing on the envelope with sudden interest. As Pam placed it on the desk, Freud rose and stretched, padding across the polished surface. With deliberate precision, he batted the envelope onto the floor.

"Thank you, Pammy." Reggie retrieved the letter after shooting a look at Freud, noting the television network logo. His stomach tightened as he broke the seal.

It was everything he'd quietly dreaded: a prime-time slot, national exposure, and weekly relationship advice segments.

Freud watched him intently, tail twitching with feline perception. Before Reggie could process the implications, another interruption shattered his contemplation.

"Good morning, Reginald," Cassandra Linton's voice cut through the peaceful atmosphere. Freud's fur bristled visibly as she entered, uninvited.

"Cassandra." Reggie's professional mask slipped into place, though his hand remained on his tie. "What brings you by so early?"

Her sharp eyes caught the network letterhead before he could slide it away. "Oh my, moving to television now? How...commercial of you."

Freud positioned himself between them, tail held high with clear intent. Cassandra's lip curled slightly at the cat's protective stance.

"The network approached me," Reggie replied evenly, though his tie felt even tighter. "Nothing's been decided."

"Of course not." Her smile didn't reach her eyes. "Tempting, though—all that exposure. People hanging on your every word about fixing their relationships." She paused deliberately. "Speaking from experience, naturally."

Freud's low growl perfectly conveyed Reggie's unspoken feelings. He focused on breathing steadily, maintaining his composed exterior while his stomach churned.

"I should prepare for my next client." He stood, a clear dismissal.

Cassandra's heels clicked against the hardwood as she made her way back to the door, each step precise and measured. "Do let me know what you decide. It would be fascinating to see how you handle such...intimate discussions on camera."

The door closed behind her, but the tension lingered. Freud maintained his protective position, golden eyes fixed on the spot where she'd stood.

After a short wait, Reggie collected himself behind his closed office door, preparing to face the reception area. The invitation burned in his jacket pocket like a live coal. He heard the office's busy hum through the frosted glass, knowing what awaited.

When he emerged, his concerns had only deepened. Cassandra hadn't left. Instead, she'd positioned herself by Pam's desk, engaged in what appeared to be casual conversation with Dr. Matthews from the third floor. Having already left, Freud sat majestically atop the reception counter, his tail twitching in obvious disapproval.

"The challenge with television appearances," Cassandra's voice carried deliberately, "is maintaining professional credibility. Some find the spotlight... changes their perspective. Altering their integrity altogether."

Dr. Matthews nodded, though his eyes darted uncomfortably toward Reggie. "Yes, well...."

Reggie kept his face neutral as he checked the day's messages with Pam, but his hand betrayed him, moving to adjust his tie. The invitation seemed to pulse in his pocket, drawing attention like a beacon.

"Reginald." Cassandra broke away from Dr. Matthews, intercepting Reggie once more in the hallway. "We were just discussing your exciting opportunity. Such exposure could be...transformative for your practice."

Freud materialized at Reggie's feet, positioning himself between them with military precision.

"Cassandra, I appreciate your interest in my offer." Reggie maintained his professional tone, though his stomach tightened.

"Of course. We all want what's best for the practice." Her smile didn't reach her eyes. "Though I wonder if your patients might feel...less secure, knowing their therapist is sharing their relationship insights with the masses."

Reggie's years of therapy prevented any change in his expression despite being struck. "Your concern for my patients is touching." Reggie's voice remained steady, even as his tie felt increasingly constrictive. "Though perhaps misplaced."

Cassandra stepped closer, her perfume sharp in the hallway air. I'm bringing this up out of concern for you, Reginald. About the practice. About...professional boundaries."

Before Reggie could respond, Pam's voice cut through the tension. "Dr. Fitzwilliam, your ten-thirty is here early. And Freud's dry food bowl needs refreshing."

The cat took his cue perfectly, weaving between Cassandra's legs in a way that forced her to step back to avoid tripping on him.

"Thank you, Pammy." Reggie nodded gratefully. "If you'll excuse me, Cassandra."

As he turned toward his office, Freud trotted ahead with his tail held high in clear victory. Behind him, he heard Cassandra's heels clicking away, her retreat marked by the sharp staccato of frustration.

Pam caught his eye as he passed, her smile knowing and supportive. The practice might have his name on the door, but it was clear who really kept it running smoothly.

Reggie stood at his office window, the city sprawling beneath grey autumn clouds. The chicken salad sandwich lay untouched next to the invitation; his appetite had vanished. Freud had claimed his usual spot in the patch of weak sunlight that filtered through, his grey coat almost silvery in the pale afternoon light.

The carpet absorbed the sound of Reggie's measured steps as he paced. Three steps toward the door, pivot, four steps back to the window as Freud watched patiently.

Morning television. National exposure. Professional advancement.

He adjusted his tie.

Public scrutiny. Personal exposure. Loss of control.

"The opportunity is self-evident," he muttered, mainly to himself. Expanding our reach and strengthening more relationships....

Freud's tail twitched once, calling his bluff.

The memory unexpectedly appeared—him in his father's dark-wood study, filled with disappointment. "Second place might as well be last place, Reginald. Excellence demands visibility. Leadership requires a public presence."

His twelve-year-old self had stood there silent, the debate team's silver medal heavy in his pocket. A tightness filled his throat which made it difficult to speak. It was the same tightness he felt now, decades later——successful and accomplished and still somehow falling short.

Freud abandoned his sunbeam, padding across the desk to sit directly on the invitation. The cat's purr connected past memories with the present moment.

Reggie's fingers found his tie again, adjusting the Windsor knot. "Not now, old friend. I need to think this through logically."

His phone buzzed, Marilyn's name lighting up the screen. Freud's ears perked forward in approval.

"Your timing is always either terrible or perfect," Reggie answered.

"Which means you're overthinking something." Marilyn's tone carried years of friendship and understanding. "Spill it."

He mumbled "Nothing, really...", his cat's knowing gaze making him stumble. "They've asked me onto breakfast telly. Regular commentary spot."

"So, you're wandering about your study, fussing with your necktie, while Freud silently critiques you."

"He's actually sprawled across the letter at present."

"Clever puss." Her gentle chuckle warmed the line. "What's the real issue here, Reg?"

Silence stretched between them while Freud continued his contented rumbling atop the document.

"Well, perhaps it's the crushing irony of being a renowned relationships consultant who's rubbish at personal connections? I wouldn't want to spoil the mood with my self-deprecating humour.

"I just..." his tone grew hushed. "What happens when they cotton on? The knowledge, the achievements...what if they realise it's merely academic? He helps others with their romantic problems, but can't seem to manage his own love life.

Freud stood, stretching deliberately before walking across the desk to press against Reggie's free hand.

"Oh, Reg... when are you going to realize that your understanding comes *from* experience, not in spite of it?"

His father's voice echoed through him: *Excellence demands visibility.*

The intercom buzzed, Pam signalling that his one o'clock appointment was arriving early. Giving his tie one last adjustment, Reggie projected professionalism as he promised Marilyn a later catch-up.

Freud returned to his miniature leather chair, watching as Reggie gathered himself for the afternoon ahead, the invitation still lying unresolved on his desk.

The late afternoon sun cast long shadows across Reggie's office as he adjusted the psychology texts on his bookshelf for the third time. Perfect alignment of each volume was crucial, their spines creating a seamless line showcasing professionalism and composure.

Freud observed from his leather perch, whiskers twitching as Reggie shifted *Attachment Theory in Practice* a millimetre to the left.

Perfectly controlled environment, perfectly controlled life. How utterly predictable.

His mobile buzzed. Cheryl Penn, his publisher. Reggie's hand moved to his tie as he answered.

"Darling, please say you'll take the television spot," Cheryl's voice, tight with barely suppressed excitement, crackled. "This exposure could triple your book sales."

"Right, because that's exactly what I need – more people examining my competence as I give relationship advice like an automated dispenser of emotional support."

"Don't get snippy with me, Reginald. This is an opportunity..."

"To become a caricature? The bachelor love doctor? Another Dr. Phil... how delightfully ironic." With a tug, he loosened his perfectly knotted tie. Freud's tail twitched in response to the sharp edge in his tone.

A gentle knock preceded Pam's entrance with his afternoon tea. The delicate China cup rattled slightly on its saucer as she approached his desk.

"Not now, Pam," the words came out harsher than intended. "I'm in the middle of something."

Pam froze, tea service hovering. Freud's golden eyes narrowed in disapproval.

"Cheryl, I need to go." Reggie ended the call, shame already colouring his cheeks. "Pammy, I apologize. That was totally unwarranted.

"Rough afternoon?" She set the tea down with practiced care.

"Just my charming personality shining through." His attempt at self-deprecating humour fell flat. His shoulders slumped as he sank into his chair.

Freud abandoned his perch to wind between them, offering a bridge of connection.

"You know," Pam said, scratching behind Freud's ears, "those walls of yours must be exhausting to maintain."

Reggie's hand moved automatically to straighten his tie. "I believe that's rather outside your professional purview."

"Perhaps. But someone needs to say it."

He started tidying his desk, meticulously positioning his pen parallel to his notebook. "I appreciate your concern, but..."

Choosing that moment, Freud deliberately created chaos in his otherwise controlled environment by sprawling across his organised papers.

"Even your cat knows you're deflecting." Pam's gentle observation cut through his defences.

Reggie looked from his scattered work to his cat's insightful stare, then to his perfect bookshelves, which now felt confining. The exhaustion of maintaining his walls settled heavily across his shoulders.

"He does have rather inconvenient moments of insight." The words came out soft, tinged with both humour and pain.

Shadows engulfing Reggie's office marked evening's approach as the last sunlight faded. He methodically sorted client files into precise stacks, each movement deliberate and controlled. The television show invitation remained untouched on his desk, its presence an unwelcome disruption to his carefully ordered world.

Freud perched on the windowsill, his grey form silhouetted against the emerging city lights. Half-eaten digestive biscuits littered Reggie's desk——evidence of his anxiety-driven snacking throughout the afternoon.

The sharp click of heels in the hallway drew both their attention. Freud's ears flattened before Cassandra appeared in the doorway, her calculated, casual pose betraying deliberate timing.

"Working late, Reginald? So dedicated." Her smile didn't reach her eyes. "That morning show invitation. Quite an opportunity."

Reggie's hand moved to his tie. "Did you need something specific, Cassandra?"

"Just offering friendly advice." She stepped into his office uninvited. "Morning television can be quite...exposing. The format favours more...dynamic personalities."

Freud abandoned his windowsill, positioning himself between them with deliberate intent.

"I imagine several of our colleagues would jump at the chance," Cassandra continued. "Dr. Harrison has quite the media presence already."

The mention of his rival sent Reggie's fingers tightening around a pen. "How fortunate for him."

"Your latest book sales have plateaued, I presume?" Cassandra examined her manicure. "Public speaking isn't everyone's strength, dear."

Reggie's carefully maintained composure cracked. "Unlike some, I don't measure success by television appearances and social media followers."

"No need to get defensive." Her smile sharpened. "I'm merely concerned about your...comfort level with such exposure."

"My comfort level?" The pen snapped in his grip. "Perhaps we should discuss your comfort level with other people's success? Or is passive-aggressive undermining just your natural state?"

Freud's tail puffed as Reggie's voice rose, years of carefully buried feelings for his co-worker surfacing.

"You want to psychoanalyse me, Cassandra? Let's start with your transparent attempts to..."

Freud knocked over the pen holder, the clatter breaking through Reggie's uncharacteristic outburst.

Cassandra's smile held triumph as she backed toward the door. "Well, this has been...illuminating. Good evening, Reginald."

Left alone, Reggie began compulsively straightening his desk, shame burning in his chest. Freud watched as he aligned each pen at perfect right angles, his movements growing increasingly frantic.

"Brilliant display of emotional maturity there, old boy. Father would be so proud."

The city lights sparkled beyond his window now, indifferent to his inner turmoil. Freud's golden eyes held judgment as Reggie slumped in his chair, professional mask finally slipping away to reveal the frightened boy still seeking approval.

"Don't look at me like that," he muttered to his feline companion. "I know exactly what I'm afraid of."

Chapter 3

Reggie barely registered the gentle spring morning as his feet carried him along the familiar path to work. Cherry blossoms drifted like snow around him, but his mind churned with the weight of the TV show invitation waiting on his desk.

His key opened the heavy, wooden door of the practice; the usual lavender scent did nothing to calm his distracted mind. He moved past Pam's desk in a daze, his usual morning greeting forgotten as he fumbled with his office key.

"Good morning, Dr. Fitzwilliam," Pam's gentle voice broke through his reverie.

Reggie's blink was followed by a realisation of his impoliteness. "Sorry, Pam. Good morning." He smiled apologetically, trusting her to understand his distraction.

His office was perfectly ordered. The degrees on the wall, the psychology texts on the shelves, and the polished surfaces all showed his precise nature. The invitation sat squarely on his desk—crisp, white, and somehow accusatory despite its innocence.

In his small leather chair, Freud sat regally, his golden eyes intently studying his owner. Reggie's untouched tea sat next to a stack of old photos. These photos, found in his bottom drawer, showed perfect posture and practiced smiles.

His phone's sharp ping jolted him out of his quiet thoughts. The screen flashed with his father's message: "Call your mother, she is worried about you."

Without thinking, Reggie's fingers brushed against his silk tie. Freud's tail twitched, a grey indicator of escalating tension. The Earl Grey, left untouched in its bone China cup, grew cold. Reggie was caught off guard, unsure how he knew.

The blinding lights blazed in his memory. He was eight years old again, standing stiff-backed in his father's production studio. His father's hands were at his throat, tugging at a tie that felt constricting like a noose.

"Excellence demands perfection, son." The words echoed across decades as present-day Reggie began organising his desk items with mechanical precision. He noticed a photo of a young Reggie, impeccably dressed, with a strained smile. With deliberate purpose, Freud rose and padded across the desk, scattering pens like confetti.

The graduation memory surfaced unbidden——standing in his cap and gown, his father's disapproval served as a tangible weight to the otherwise cheerful day.

True success needs public acknowledgment, my son. Psychology? Private practice? You're wasting your potential."

With slightly trembling hands, he organised the scattered pens. Freud abandoned his disruption campaign, moving closer to press against Reggie's arm.

From the past, his mother's voice, the voice of peace, whispered, "Obey your father, my child." He only wants what's best."

Reggie stood abruptly and paced to the window. Dressed immaculately in his bespoke suit, he stared at his reflection, searching for something beneath the surface. His father's top CEO magazine mocked him from the desk, headlines about "Media Empire Legacy" clearly visible. Freud trailed behind, a worried purr vibrating in his chest.

The city sprawled below, already humming with morning activity. Professional success magazines littered his desk——*Top Therapist*, *Psychology Today*, *Breakthrough Magazine*. Everything arranged just so, controlled to the point of suffocation. The childhood photo caught his eye again, the same forced smile he'd perfected over decades plastered across his face.

Freud took decisive action, leaping onto the desk and sending the magazines cascading to the floor.

Reggie's fingers found his tie again, but this time, instead of tightening, he loosened it slightly. The small act of rebellion sent his heart racing.

For the first time that morning, a genuine smile tugged at his lips.

Pam knocked lightly, announcing, "Dr. Fitzwilliam, the first client is here."

The professional mask slid back into place, but something felt different. His tie remained slightly loose, a tiny crack in his perfect composure. Reggie flipped through Michael Bennett's case file swiftly, his eyes catching familiar patterns in the notes. Another high-achieving professional, another demanding father, another perfectly constructed facade. He glanced at the childhood photo on his desk, then refocused on what was happening.

Freud settled into his miniature leather chair, assuming his therapeutic pose as Michael entered the office. The mirror image struck Reggie immediately——another Savile Row suit, another precisely knotted tie. Michael's unconscious change of his collar echoed Reggie's own habitual gesture.

In the corner, the lavender diffuser hummed softly as Reggie pointed to the leather chair. "Please, make yourself comfortable."

Parallel to the rug's design, Michael sat with his shoes neatly aligned. The case notes trembled slightly in Reggie's hands as he observed his client's rigid posture––a reflection too close for comfort.

"The medical practice of my father..." Michael began, voice tight with controlled emotion."It's the legacy of three generations on my shoulders. Nothing else was acceptable."

Upon hearing those words, Reggie's hand automatically went to his tie. His father's study materialised in his mind––dark wood panels, success magazines, disapproving silence.

Freud approached cautiously, his golden eyes fixed on the escalating tension. The cat's movements offered Michael a brief escape from his painful memories.

"Nothing was ever good enough," Michael continued, his perfectly maintained facade cracking slightly. "Every achievement just meant higher expectations."

Reggie's pen tumbled from his grasp, rolling across his neat desk and disturbing its order. His gaze caught the childhood photo again––young Reggie in his first suit, smile never reaching his eyes.

Standing between them, Freud offered silent support as professional boundaries blurred. Michael's voice cracked with suppressed emotion, "I still hear his voice critiquing my every decision."

Reggie resisted the temptation to discuss his experiences; his career and personal honesty clashed. Freud's purr rumbled softly, grounding him in the present moment.

"Sometimes," Reggie offered carefully, "expectations become so ingrained we continue enforcing them long after their original source is gone."

Michael's posture softened slightly, responding to the authentic moment. "How do you break free from that?"

Freud's purr deepened as both men's professional masks began to soften, creating space for genuine therapeutic breakthrough.

"Noticing these patterns," Reggie responded, balancing personal insight with professional guidance. "And choosing which ones still serve us."

While Michael was scheduling his next appointment, steeling himself for a family dinner, Reggie saw his tie was a little loose. Freud returned to his observation post, watching with knowing satisfaction as small victories in authenticity settled into the day's routine.

Picking up his best-selling book off the shelf, Reggie flicked through, bringing momentary relief from the lingering echo of Michael Bennett's session. The glossy pages of *Love Without Walls* felt different now, each carefully crafted chapter carrying extra weight after his own journey through heartbreak and healing.

Freud watched from his miniature leather chair as Reggie's fingers traced the chapter headings––"Trust After Loss", "Building Healthy Boundaries", "The Courage to Begin Again." Words he'd written with professional certainty now held personal truth.

The aroma of Thai food and Marilyn's vibrant energy filled the office as she burst through the door. "Right, that's enough pondering for one day."

Freud abandoned his sunbeam instantly, trotting over to weave between Marilyn's legs as she balanced takeaway bags. Seeing his favourite visitor, his golden eyes lit up, whiskers twitching with excitement.

"I'm actually quite busy with these case notes," Reggie murmured, shuffling papers on his pristine desk without looking at them.

"Mmhmm." Marilyn cleared space on his desk with practiced efficiency, sweeping aside his carefully arranged files. From a folder, a photo fell out: young Reggie, in his first suit, standing rigidly next to his father's desk.

His hand moved automatically to adjust his tie as Marilyn unpacked containers of pad Thai and green curry. "The organisation of those files was done by——"

"By date, client surname, and probably personality type." Marilyn pushed a container toward him. "So, planning to actually eat today?"

Reggie tapped his fingers against his desk. "I had that new client this morning——fascinating case actually. The expectations set by his father——"

"Reg." In Marilyn's voice, one could hear the echoes of their college days, filled with late-night studying and whispered confidences. "You're doing it again."

Freud settled between them, eyes moving from one to the other like a tennis match. As Reggie fussed with his paperwork, the office was filled with the aroma of Thai food.

"The morning show called again," he offered, reaching for safer professional ground. "They are interested in discussing segment topics and——"

"You're still trying to prove him wrong," Marilyn cut in softly.

Reggie's hands froze mid-gesture. "Excellence demands sacrifice, son," his father's voice reverberated in his thoughts. Nothing less than perfection."

His professional walls cracked slightly as he met Marilyn's knowing gaze. She stood by him during his father's rejection of his career, his continuous search for approval, and his difficulty accepting his achievements.

"Remember graduation?" Marilyn asked, pushing the food closer. "When your father said therapy wasn't a 'real' medical specialty?"

As the memory resurfaced, Reggie slumped slightly. His memory lingered on the heavy weight of his disappointment, the awkward congratulations, and Marilyn's spirited defense of his actions.

"You don't have to be perfect, Reg," Marilyn whispered. "No one's perfect."

Freud nudged his hand gently, purring as Reggie's fingers finally unclenched from their tight grip on his pen. A small, genuine smile crossed his face as he reached for the now-cold pad Thai.

His tie loosened slightly as he took his first proper bite of food that day, letting the familiar comfort of friendship ease the constant pressure of perfection.

The next morning, Reggie sat at his desk, staring at the TV show invitation that had haunted him all week. Three messages from his publisher blinked insistently on his phone screen. His eyes drifted to the wall of awards, certificates, and bestseller acknowledgments——each one leaving him feeling hollower than the last.

The gentle tap at his door broke through his reverie. Mrs. Crumble appeared, silver hair neatly pinned back, carrying a tin of her homemade biscuits. Without thinking, Reggie adjusted his already straight pen set.

Freud abandoned his professional stance instantly, trotting over to greet her with an enthusiastic head bump against her ankles. The woman who'd been more of a mother to Reggie than his own mother had always been a favorite of the cat.

"I haven't seen you as much recently," Mrs. Crumble observed, sinking into the client chair with her characteristic ease. "Is this about your parents by any chance?"

Reggie's hand flew to his tie, adjusting the perfect Windsor knot. The air grew thick with unspoken history as his professional mask slipped slightly.

Mrs. Crumble's English rose perfume instantly evoked a rush of memories; many involved him hiding amongst her rose bushes after his father's latest disappointment. The garden had been his sanctuary, a place where excellence wasn't demanded, where simple growth was enough——where it was natural.

His father's voice echoed across the years: "Public success is everything, son. Image is reality." His mother's perpetual silence had cut deeper than any criticism.

The old biscuit sat untouched, crumbling before him; the weight of expectation was too much.

"I can't be what he wants," Reggie whispered, voice cracking. "I've tried. For decades, I've tried."

Mrs. Crumble's eyes held the motherly wisdom of years watching him grow, struggle, and hide behind achievements. Freud settled between them, a warm presence against Reggie's leg.

Mrs. Crumble started, "Can you recall the summer you assisted me with planting those climbing roses?""You were so worried about doing it perfectly."

Reggie paced by the window, the TV invitation seeming to mock him from his desk.

"You told me, sometimes plants need space to grow their own way." Mrs. Crumble's voice carried years of gentle guidance. "Who are you trying to prove wrong, dear?"

Reggie stopped mid-stride, the question hitting home with unexpected force. As he traced the invitation's edge, he realised his lifelong rebellion against his father had ironically led him down the same path of perfectionism he'd always sought to escape.

He reached for the invitation with trembling fingers. Mrs. Crumble's knowing smile reflected in the window as she watched him. Freud's purr of approval filled the quiet office.

Mrs. Crumble finally opened her tin of biscuits, the familiar comfort of shortbread and acceptance filling the air. "Can I get us a cup of tea, dear?" she offered, as she had countless times in her garden all those years ago.

After a long day at the office, his key finally entered his front door, the weight of the day hanging heavy on his shoulders. The briefcase hit the ground near the entrance with a loud thud, unlike him, disrupting his normally perfect order.

Emerging hesitantly from his carrier, Freud sauntered across the room and into the kitchen. The quiet was intense, disrupted solely by the low hum coming from the city beyond his windows. His phone buzzed once more, indicating his mother's third attempt to call him today. He flipped it over, adding to his never-ending list of unanswered calls.

His fingers brushed against something in his desk drawer––an old medical school application, the edges worn with age. His father's precise handwriting filled the margins with notes and corrections. "Excellence in the proper field, son." The words still cut deep after all these years. Reggie's hands trembled slightly as he read them again.

The wall of professional achievements——carefully framed and arranged——suddenly seemed to mock him. Each certificate and award represented another attempt to prove his worth, to justify choosing his own path. Still, the emptiness his father left that day in the study remained unfilled.

The memory surfaced with crystal clarity: standing before the massive mahogany desk, sixteen and trembling with determination, announcing his decision to pursue therapy instead of "proper" medicine. The room was thick with his father's bitter, suffocating disappointment. His mother's silence from the doorway had cut deeper than any words, intensifying the despair he felt.

Something snapped. Reggie yanked his tie off completely, the silk whispering through his collar. He turned the face-down family photo upright for the first time in months. His younger self stared back, already wearing the mask of perfection that would become his armour.

Freud padded over cautiously as Reggie's carefully constructed walls crumbled. The cat's warm presence against his leg anchored him as his mother's latest voicemail finally played:

"Reginald...I should have spoken up back then. Should have supported your choices. I-I'm proud of the man you've become. The people you help. Please call me."

Years of silence had shattered in those few words. Reggie's fingers hovered over his phone, the TV producer's number highlighted on the screen. For once, his professional mask slipped completely as he pressed 'call'.

"Yes, about the morning show position..." his voice carried a new certainty, grounded in something beyond his father's expectations.

The decision voiced, a subtle weight lifted from his shoulders. Freud's approving purr filled the room as Reggie reached for the takeaway menu instead of skipping dinner as usual. His discarded tie remained on the desk; tomorrow seemed clearer now.

The study's oak-panelled walls seemed to close in as Reggie pulled out tomorrow's practice meeting agenda, his reading glasses perched precariously on his nose. Like a sentinel, his charcoal grey suit, perfectly pressed for tomorrow, hung on his study door; a comforting yet confining presence. His tired eyes struggled to focus on the words, which swam on the page in a disorderly fashion.

His laptop screen glowed accusingly, a blank email draft to his colleagues opens with its cursor blinking in silent mockery. Three previous versions lay deleted, none capturing the right balance of professional distance and personal truth. At that moment, Freud decided to lie down on the keyboard, his golden eyes watching Reggie with amused patience.

"And how would you phrase it, old friend?" Reggie muttered, adjusting his collar despite having loosened his tie hours ago. As he practiced his announcement in the study window, his reflection showed him struggling with the word 'change', his voice catching in his throat. He could already picture Cassandra's carefully composed reaction, her sharp eyes calculating the implications.

A leather-bound journal slipped from between two psychology texts as he reached for his reference materials. It was his first therapy journal, its pages filled with earnest observations and idealistic goals. The careful handwriting hinted at a younger Reggie, unconcerned with appearances in his pursuit of healing. His professional mask slipped as he traced the words of his first client notes, remembering the pure desire to help that had driven his career choice.

The meeting points finally began flowing, confidence building with each carefully crafted sentence. His phone buzzed with his publisher's enthusiastic response to the TV show decision, the pieces of his professional and personal life finding a new balance. Show segment notes developed naturally, and as he imagined a different impact, his authentic voice became more powerful.

Marilyn's late call brought welcome interruption:

"You've sent that email yet?" Her familiar directness steadied his nerves.

"Just about to." His admission carried less defensiveness than usual.

"Good. They'll survive the shock of you being human."

As Reggie hit send, his small smile was mirrored in the window. Freud stretched and yawned, clearly ready to escort him to bed. The desk lamp dimmed, casting soft shadows across tomorrow's neatly arranged materials.

Chapter 4

Reggie arrived forty-five minutes early, his footsteps echoing in the silent meeting room. No matter how many times he adjusted it, the projector screen refused to hang straight. A fresh cup of coffee sat cooling on the polished conference table, untouched since Pam had brought it in with a knowing look.

He reviewed the meeting papers for the fourth time, unable to stop himself from searching for imperfections. As he gazed into the darkened window, he noticed his navy silk tie, which was already perfectly knotted with a Windsor knot thanks to his meticulous morning routine, needed another adjustment.

His colleagues started arriving around 8:35 am, their curious looks noticing him already there early. Dr. Cassandra Linton swept in with practiced grace, claiming the front seat with calculated precision. Her perfectly composed expression couldn't quite hide the sharp interest in her eyes. Quietly entering, Pam offered a warm smile, calming his nerves more than he was willing to admit.

Whispers about the unusually early meeting time rippled through the assembled staff. The known surroundings felt strangely charged with expectation. Years of therapy barely masked the tremor in Reggie's voice as he watched their reactions to his email, clearing his throat.

Soft pawsteps announced Freud's arrival through the open door. With his usual dignity, he claimed his observation post by the window. Reggie's wavering confidence was steadied by his presence.

"Thank you all for coming in early this morning," Reggie began, his voice finding its strength in the familiar rhythm of leadership. My email detailed some upcoming changes to our practice.

As Cassandra tapped her perfectly manicured fingers against her leather portfolio, he described the TV show opportunity. The words flowed easier now, confidence building as he shared his vision for expanding their therapeutic reach while maintaining professional integrity.

"But surely," Cassandra's voice cut through the supportive murmurs, "such public exposure risks compromising therapeutic boundaries?"

Although the challenge remained, Reggie's posture had subtly changed. His years of experience and dedication to his profession were evident in his statement: "Boundaries exist to protect our clients—not to limit how far we can reach to help them." His response carried both professional authority and personal conviction."We have an opportunity to destigmatise therapy, to reach those who would likely not step into our offices otherwise."

Unexpected sources provided support. Uncharacteristically, Dr. Thompson spoke in favour of their community outreach programs during the meeting. Even Dr. Chen, their most traditional practitioner, nodded thoughtfully at the proposed protocols for maintaining professional standards while embracing this new direction.

Reggie's authentic consideration of each concern visibly changed the practice's dynamics. He reviewed new procedures, changed schedules, and assigned responsibilities. The path forward materialised through collaborative problem-solving rather than defensive justification.

Pam's understated "Well done, Dr. Fitzwilliam," at the meeting's close, carried more weight than the others' official praise. Cassandra retreated with careful dignity, her calculated opposition having failed to find purchase.

With staff preparing for clients, the office resumed its normal routines. Freud, purring, padded to Reggie's ankles, celebrating a small but meaningful triumph.

Reggie's screen was awash with emails from his publisher, each a stark reminder of approaching deadlines and expectations. His phone vibrated again; it was the fifth text from the TV producer that morning. The carefully organized stack of client files on his desk seemed to mock his attempt at maintaining control.

His hands fidgeted, rearranging the already neat pens and perfectly ordered files. From his leather chair, Freud's golden eyes followed every increasingly frantic movement.

Cassandra entered the room unexpectedly, her heels clicking sharply in the hallway beforehand. She walked in without knocking, her forced smile betraying the dangerous glint in her eyes.

Reginald, the morning shows are already requesting your input. One might think you're becoming quite the celebrity psychologist."

Reggie's collar felt constricted all of a sudden. His fingers moved to his tie, the silk offering no comfort today.

"This isn't about celebrity, Cassandra. This is all about assisting those who need our help.

"Of course it is," her tone laced with doubt. "Though some might question whether a therapist with...personal issues...should be giving public advice."

The room seemed to shrink. Freud's fur bristled as he rose, sensing his human's mounting distress.

My professional choices are not your concern, and neither is my personal life. His words came out weaker than intended, his practiced façade cracking.

Do you not? Psychology Council may object, particularly considering your unorthodox approach.

The tie became a noose. As the walls converged, sweat formed on his temples. His perfectly ordered desk suddenly felt like a cage.

Reggie barely noticed Freud's warning growl as he stumbled to his feet. Years of composure couldn't hold back the overwhelming urge to escape. He barely managed to grab his coat before fleeing his own office.

Rain pelted his face as he burst onto the street, the grey morning matching his internal storm. City sounds blurred into white noise as he pushed through crowds, his breath coming in short gasps.

The cheerful chime of a shop bell cut through his panic. Warm light and the sweet scent of flowers enveloped him as he stumbled into what appeared to be a florist's shop. The chaos in his mind began to settle among the peaceful displays.

"Are you alright?" Her soft voice and gentle green eyes, like the surrounding ferns, matched perfectly. The shop owner approached slowly, as if sensing his fragility.

"I...." His professional mask lay shattered somewhere between his office and here. "No. Not really."

She nodded, asking no questions, simply offering space to breathe. Her quiet presence anchored him as his racing heart slowed.

After a moment, she selected a bright sunflower from a nearby bucket. "For courage," she said, offering it with a smile that held no judgment.

Having taken the flower, Reggie's breathing grew calm. In this moment, with rain drumming on the shop windows and the scent of roses in the air, his carefully constructed walls seemed less necessary.

"I'm Penelope," she said softly.

"Reggie," he replied, leaving off his title for the first time in years.

Her smile widened slightly. "Welcome to my shop, Reggie. You look like you could use a cup of tea."

Reggie gaped at her offer, his professional mask lying in pieces around him. The shop's warmth began to seep through his rain-dampened suit, but his hands still trembled slightly as he accepted the delicate China cup.

"Earl Grey," Penelope said, her voice carrying none of the judgment he'd come to expect. "With a splash of milk."

The familiar smell anchored him to memories of Mrs. Crumble's kitchen and easier times. The tea mirrored a stranger to him; his tie crooked, rain-dampened hair, and his usually flawless composure broken.

"I don't normally..." he hesitated, the usual way he'd deflect seeming silly amongst the natural beauty surrounding them. "Thank you."

Penelope sat in a worn wooden chair behind the counter, giving him space while remaining close. Her calm self-assurance reminded him of his most successful therapy sessions—those marked by genuine connection, not professional detachment.

"The sunflowers always face the light," she observed, nodding toward his still-clutched bloom. "Even on the greyest days."

The simple wisdom in her words penetrated deeper than any of his carefully crafted therapeutic phrases. His grip on the cup steadied as warmth spread through his chest.

"I left my cat," he blurted, the absurdity of his priorities drawing an unexpected chuckle from his throat, "in my office. I just...left him there."

"I'm sure he understands." Penelope's smile was devoid of mockery. "Cats usually do."

Penelope remained in her quiet corner, despite the bell announcing another shopper. Instead, she offered a warm greeting from her seat, her quiet presence a support as Reggie regained his bearings.

While she greeted the newcomer calmly, he slowly savoured his expertly brewed tea. Bubbling with excitement, she gave the customer a perfect flower arrangement, the finest he'd ever seen. Her quiet confidence in her own area of expertise ignited something within him—a realisation of genuineness he had long suppressed. Watching the customer depart, he couldn't resist revealing a weakness.

"I've been advising others to confront their fears for years," he confessed, surprised by his own frankness. "While running from my own."

"Sounds human to me." Penelope's response carried such simple acceptance that his carefully constructed arguments faltered.

The rain continued its gentle percussion on the shop windows, but the panic that had driven him here receded. In its place, something new took root——something that felt surprisingly like hope.

With a heartfelt thank you for her warmth and help to a stranger in distress, he headed towards the exit. "My pleasure," she replied gently. "Come back anytime."

Reggie stood before his office door, sunflower clutched like a shield. His damp suit clung uncomfortably, but the panic had subsided, replaced by a strange calm he couldn't quite explain. The brass nameplate on his door caught the morning light, a reminder of who he was supposed to be.

Pam's relief was palpable as he entered. "Dr. Fitzwilliam! I was about to send out a search party."

Freud materialised suddenly, dodging his legs with unusual worry. The cat's golden eyes studied him intently, as if cataloguing changes.

"I needed some air." His voice sounded steadier than he felt. "Has Dr. Linton...?"

Pam's disapproving tone implied she departed shortly after your departure. "I've moved your eleven-thirty to next week."

The sunflower, with its bright face, stood out in stark contrast to the muted tones of his office. Reggie, in his perfectly organised space, looked for a vase, something he'd never before required.

Pam appeared with his usual tea service, adding a water jug that worked perfectly for the flower. "Shall I hold your calls?"

"No, I'm..." he adjusted his tie, muscle memory returning, "I'm fine now. Thank you."

Freud sat in his small chair, more observant than normal while Reggie tidied his desk. The morning's chaos began to recede, professional rhythms returning.

His phone lit up with messages; most were from the TV show's producer. I was forced to confront reality and make some crucial decisions. Yet something had shifted, the weight feeling different now.

His hand brushed paper in his pocket - a small business card. "Penelope's Petals" in elegant script, green ink that matched certain eyes. The walls he'd spent years maintaining wavered briefly.

Focus returned as he reviewed his afternoon schedule. The next client would arrive soon, needing his full attention. Yet warmth lingered, like sunshine on flowers, making his usual professional distance feel less crucial.

In his leather chair, Reggie reflected on the morning's events. Panic attack in front of a stranger. Complete loss of control. Running from Dr. Linton. Somehow, he felt stronger for it.

His plan was clear: call the producer, set boundaries, and find a balance. The sunflower caught afternoon light, reminding him that even professionals need moments in the sun.

Freud purred approvingly as he methodically organised the afternoon's files. Clients would still arrive, the day would go on, but something essential had changed. Not broken, just...changed.

Though the sunflower looked cheerful, Reggie tried to concentrate on Michael Bennett's file. His own morning vulnerability shifted how he viewed the upcoming session. Despite his usual therapeutic stance, Freud's golden eyes revealed a heightened awareness today.

Michael arrived precisely on time, his tie as perfectly knotted as ever. "Dr. Fitzwilliam." His voice carried the weight of their last breakthrough.

"How was dinner with your father?" Reggie settled into his chair, noting the slight tremor in Michael's hands.

"I..." Michael's professional facade cracked. "I couldn't do it. Couldn't show him the real me."

Freud's ears twitched at the familiar struggle, his attention divided between both men.

"The real you," Reggie repeated softly, his morning's panic attack fresh in his mind. "Tell me about that fear. Why do you feel the need to shelter your true self?"

"What if he sees my weakness?" Michael's words hit close to home. "What if everyone does?"

"Perhaps weakness isn't what we think it is." The words came naturally, born from fresh experience. "Sometimes our greatest strength lies in allowing ourselves to be seen."

Michael's gaze caught on the sunflower. "That's new."

"Yes." Reggie paused, professional boundaries flexing rather than breaking. "Sometimes life reminds us that perfection isn't the goal."

In what way?

"By showing us that vulnerability doesn't diminish our worth." The morning's emotional breakdown unexpectedly led to helpful comprehension, empowering him to move on. "Sometimes our carefully constructed walls protect us from exactly what we need."

Michael leaned forward, his expression changing subtly. "This morning, I almost called my father. Almost told him about the promotion I turned down."

"What stopped you?"

"The same thing that always stops me. Fear of disappointing him." Michael's hands twisted together. "Of not being enough."

"And if being enough meant being real?" Reggie's question carried the weight of personal understanding. "If strength meant showing him who you truly are?"

Freud moved closer, offering silent support to both men as they navigated this new territory.

"I've spent so long being what he expects." Michael's voice cracked. "I'm not sure I know how to be anything else."

"Perhaps that's exactly where we start." Reggie felt his professional expertise deepening with personal insight. "Not with grand gestures, but with small truths."

The session progressed with new depth, both men finding stronger ground through shared understanding. Michael felt his tension ease and his path brighten as he left.

Reggie sat quietly afterward. What was once vulnerability in the morning became therapeutic strength for him, enhancing his capacity to help.

Freud padded across to sit beside him, offering silent companionship as Reggie made his session notes. Each word resonated with authenticity, born from lived experience rather than mere knowledge.

The next session's outline formed naturally, building on today's breakthrough. His therapy methods evolved, shaped by his own personal growth.

Weary but prepared, Reggie settled into his leather chair awaiting his next client. Despite an emotionally draining and vulnerable morning breakthrough with Michael, he felt surprisingly light. The afternoon sun illuminated the sunflower, its petals symbolising surprising refuges.

"Reginald?" A soft tap came with his receptionist's voice. "Your afternoon appointment's cancelled, so I'm happy to mind Freud and bring him to your place later. I'm stuck doing paperwork here anyway.

The feline's attention shifted at hearing his name, amber eyes darting between Pam and Reggie thoughtfully.

"That was really thoughtful of you, Pam." Reggie's response resonated with appreciation."Although I reckon, he's more interested in those special nibbles you've hidden away."

"Fair enough," Pam agreed with a chuckle, getting the cat's bed and placing it under her workspace. "He's weathered quite the day, hasn't he?"

With elegance, the cat stretched, relaxed and calm. He'd been attentive throughout the day, from the early staff gathering through Reggie's anxious episode.

"We both share this." Reggie smoothed his neckwear, more composed than earlier. "I appreciate everything today, Pam."

That's how we support one another. Her words reflected their enduring connection. "Right then, your majesty. Time to let your owner have some peace."

The cat moved to his bed with refined elegance, casting one last evaluating glance at Reggie. Content that his companion had recovered, he nestled into his bed beneath Pam's desk.

Reggie breathed a sigh of relief as they walked away. Despite the room feeling different without his cat, the silence was soothing, not isolating. His attention returned to the golden flower, its vivid petals symbolising how resilience emerged from unexpected sources.

Reggie closed his eyes, relishing the rare peace. No patients to counsel, no professional veneer required, simply the peaceful aftermath of events that had shattered his meticulously ordered existence and mysteriously reinforced it.

Reggie, feeling completely refreshed, faced his final appointment with renewed energy and calmness.

Reggie stood outside his office building, the last client's footsteps fading down the corridor. His tie felt looser, though he hadn't touched it. The sunflower on his desk had done more than simply brighten his office; it had shifted something fundamental in his carefully ordered world.

Before consciously deciding, his feet instinctively carried him toward Penelope's Petals. The evening light painted the wet pavements gold, each step both terrifying and inevitable.

The shop's bell chimed a gentle welcome as he pushed open the door. Surrounded by blossoms, Penelope, with her copper hair glowing in the soft evening light, meticulously arranged roses. His heart performed an unexpected skip that had nothing to do with panic.

"Dr. Fitzwilliam." This morning, Penelope knew who he was, but she stayed quiet. Her smile was welcoming, devoid of any judgment. "The sunflower suited your office perfectly."

"Please, call me Reggie." The words surprised him, his professional facade wavering. "I wanted to thank you. For this morning."

We all require a tranquil moment occasionally. She moved between buckets of flowers with natural grace. "And a friendly face."

"Your shop provided both." His typically precise words seemed insufficient. "I'm not usually so...."

"Human?" His professional detachment crumbled under her gentle ribbing. "I won't tell anyone if you won't."

With surprising ease, he talked about the TV show's pressure, the morning's news, and Cassandra's calculated actions. Penelope listened empathetically, her hands continuously arranging flowers.

"It sounds like you need some more peaceful moments." She selected a stem with careful consideration."The shop's always open. "During regular working hours."

Her laugh wrapped around him like warmth.

"I might take you up on that."

"Good." She moved to the counter. "Now, let's find something to brighten your office for tomorrow. Something that says, 'I'm professional but not afraid of a little joy.'"

As she arranged flowers for him, they talked about the meaning of each bloom, carefully selected for its symbolism. His watch beeped six, reality intruding.

"I should let you close up."

"Same time tomorrow?" she asked. The question held no pressure, just possibility.

"I'd like that." He wrote his number on a business card, accepting hers in return.

As he left the shop, the bell chimed a lingering farewell to the evening. Through the window, their eyes met in shared understanding before he headed toward home.

As Reggie came home, the garden gate creaked a familiar welcome into Mrs. Crumble's haven. Evening light filtered through the rose arbour, casting gentle shadows across the weathered garden furniture. The scent of Earl Grey mingled with blooming flowers, his elderly neighbour's uncanny timing clear in the steaming pot waiting on the small iron table.

"I thought you might stop by." Mrs. Crumble's eyes twinkled as she gestured to the waiting chair. "Especially after such an eventful day."

Reggie sank into the cushioned seat, his professional armour falling away in the garden's embrace. Word gets around rapidly.

"Pam might have mentioned something about an announcement. And a rather hasty exit." She poured tea with practiced grace. "Though I suspect there's more to the story."

As he recounted the morning's events—Cassandra's calculated words, the overwhelming panic, and the surprising safety of Penelope's shop—the warm China cup comforted his hands; he also described the lovely flowers he'd gotten for his office.

"Ah." Mrs. Crumble's knowing smile made him shift in his seat. "And you've visited this shop, how many times?"

"Only for purely professional reasons." His tie suddenly felt tight again. "My office needed..." he found himself struggling to find the right word.

"Joy?" Her gentle suggestion cut through his defences. "Like this garden offered you all those years ago?"

The memory washed over him——a younger Reggie hiding among these same roses, finding peace from his father's expectations in Mrs. Crumble's quiet understanding.

"She has kind eyes," he found himself saying. "Green, like spring leaves."

"Mm." Mrs. Crumble busied herself with the tea strainer. "And does this florist have a name?"

"Penelope." The word carried more weight than he intended. "But my professional position——"

We sometimes need to show our humanity. She reached across to pat his hand. "Fear of vulnerability isn't the same as maintaining boundaries, dear boy."

His resistance surfaced like a well-rehearsed script. The reputation of the practice, the TV show, my clients——

"All deserve an authentic therapist." Mrs. Crumble's wisdom cut through his protests. One who knows healing isn't about being perfect.

The evening air softened around them as truth settled in his chest. "I gave her my number."

"Good." She refilled their cups. "The garden's taught me that the strongest blooms are those that bend with the wind."

Reggie watched the steam rise from his cup, something tight in his chest finally easing. Here, among the roses that had sheltered his younger self, change felt less like surrender and more like growth.

Chapter 5

Facing his wardrobe, Reggie's fingers brushed against his silk ties. The burgundy one spoke of authority, the navy of trustworthiness, but neither felt quite right for this pivotal morning. Freud, his golden eyes assessing his human's uncertainty, sat upon the dresser.

"Your criticism isn't useful," Reggie mumbled, settling on a deep green tie that made him think of eyes he was trying to ignore. The contract from the TV network lay unopened on his kitchen counter, its presence altering the familiar rhythm of his morning.

When he got to the office, he brought in the bright bouquet, a change from his usual simple plants. The producer's call came exactly on schedule. "Dr. Fitzwilliam, about the first segment——"

Reggie's voice was firm, despite his racing pulse, as he declared his therapeutic boundaries were non-negotiable. "We discuss general principles, not specific cases."

"Of course, but——"

"And my practice takes priority over filming schedules."

The precise moment Cassandra appeared in the hallway—as his phone call concluded—challenged his newly formed resolve. "Morning television suits you, Reginald. Though some might question the...entertainment value of proper therapy."

"Morning, Cassandra." His professional mask held, strengthened by yesterday's breakthrough rather than weakened by it."My ethical standards remain unchanged."

His email inbox overflowed with press inquiries, and he found himself drawn back to his work and she scampered away. Local papers wanted interviews, radio stations requested comments, and news shows competed for exclusives. The pressure built behind his temples as he sorted through requests.

The sunflower caught his eye—bright, bold, and impossibly familiar. A quiet echo of green eyes and unspoken warmth. Professional distance wavered as he recalled the warmth of Penelope's shop, so different from his carefully curated office.

Reviewing client notes offered a sense of comfort as he readied for his initial session. Yesterday's vulnerability unexpectedly enhanced his therapeutic insight, blending personal growth with professional expertise.

Pam's arrival with morning tea coincided with Freud claiming his miniature leather chair. "We adjusted your schedule to accommodate the producer's requirements," she announced, her efficiency grounding the morning's chaos.

"Thank you, Pammy." The day's rhythm settled as he reviewed his appointments. The path ahead held challenges, but for once, they felt less like threats and more like opportunities for growth.

The silent phone on Reggie's desk was more menacing than any therapy session he'd ever had. The journalist's number waited in his call log, each passing second tightening his perfectly knotted green tie. Freud maintained his observation post from his leather chair, whiskers twitching at his human's obvious distress.

"This interview's easy," Reggie mumbled, mostly to himself, not his cat. His fingers traced the edge of his desk calendar, each movement precise, controlled, necessary.

A journalist's voice, initially polite, crackled over the speakerphone, soon turning to pointed questions. "Dr. Fitzwilliam, your approach to relationship therapy has gained significant attention. How does your personal experience inform your professional insights?"

Reggie's hand went to his tie without a second thought. "My therapeutic approach draws from extensive clinical research and practice..."

Your perspective must be shaped by your relationship status, surely? The journalist pressed, abandoning subtlety. "Our readers would be interested in knowing how a single relationship expert——"

"My personal life remains separate from my professional practice." His voice maintained its steady tone, though his fingers whitened around his pen. Freud's tail twitched in warning.

The questions continued, each one chipping at his boundaries. Just as the journalist began another personal probe, Pam's voice came through the intercom with perfect timing.

"I'm sorry to interrupt, Dr. Fitzwilliam's next appointment is arriving shortly."

"Of course, just one more..."

"Thank you for your time," Reggie cut in, ending the call with more force than necessary. The silence felt heavy as he released a carefully controlled breath.

From his office window, a glimpse of the florist's sign across the street, bathed in morning light, provided a brief respite. Penelope's Petals seemed to glow, drawing his attention like a beacon. His heart quickened traitorously at the memory of understanding green eyes.

"Reginald, you handle publicity well." Cassandra's voice shattered his moment of peace. She stood in his doorway, uninvited."Though some might question the wisdom of exposing our profession to such...scrutiny."

Cassandra, therapeutic communities, like any other field, are constantly changing. His voice found new strength. "Change doesn't diminish our professional standards."

"No?" Reginald, you handle publicity well. "And what standards apply to single therapists giving relationship advice on morning television?"

"The same ones that apply to colleagues who forget professional courtesy." The words came easier than expected, his spine straightening as he met her gaze. I closed my door intentionally, Dr. Linton.

Cassandra's departure left ripples of tension, but Reggie remained at his desk, the morning's cost settling onto his shoulders. Freud padded over, offering silent support as his human contemplated the price of progress.

The sunflower caught his eye again, its bright petals a reminder of distinct possibilities.

Reggie's carefully maintained control buckled under the intense pressure of the morning's media frenzy. His phone buzzed incessantly, each notification carrying another journalist's probing questions about his personal life. Email alerts flashed across his computer screen with increasing urgency, while his tie seemed to tighten with each passing moment.

"Dr. Fitzwilliam?" Pam's voice carried through the intercom. "Your lunch has arrived. And the producer called again..."

"Yes, that's fine." His clipped tone betrayed the strain. The sandwich ordered from his usual café sat untouched as more messages arrived. Freud watched from his chair, golden eyes tracking every sign of his human's mounting stress.

Pam appeared in his doorway, concern evident in her gentle approach. "Perhaps a brief break would..."

"I don't need a break." The words snapped out harder than intended, sharp enough to make her flinch. "I need people to stop telling me what I need."

His words were barely out when regret overwhelmed him. Pam's hurt expression cut deeper than any journalist's questions. Freud's disapproving stare from his miniature chair spoke volumes about his human's behaviour.

Reggie's reflection revealed the flaws in his usually flawless professional image. Brilliant. Absolutely brilliant. Push away the people who care. His father's voice echoed in his head: *"A Fitzwilliam maintains control at all times."*

His attempted apology to Pammy turned into sarcastic defensiveness. "Clearly I'm excelling at being difficult today."

We all face challenges, Dr. Fitzwilliam. Her understanding somehow made it worse. The phone rang again——another media outlet asking another personal question masquerading as professional interest.

"Dr. Fitzwilliam, about your relationship status..."

"No comment." A slight crack appeared in his voice as he hung up. The office walls seemed to close in, his sanctuary becoming a prison of expectations and appearances. Freud abandoned his post to pad closer, offering silent support as his human's carefully constructed world crumbled.

The next call he didn't even answer, watching it ring with a detached sort of horror. His tie felt like a noose, his professional armour suddenly too heavy to bear.

"Pam?" His voice sounded strange to his own ears. "I apologise for my behaviour earlier. It was unprofessional and unkind. I don't know what's gotten into me."

She appeared in his doorway again, this time with fresh tea and understanding. "Sometimes we all need a moment to breathe, Dr. Fitzwilliam. Even experts."

Reggie stared blankly into the distance. The morning's media frenzy and his harsh comments to Pam left him burdened. His tie constricted with each breath until he couldn't bear it anymore.

His inner voice cautioned, 'You can't stay hidden forever.' The image of Penelope's shop floated in his mind——its warm light, gentle understanding, and those green eyes that saw through every defence.

"I'll be back for my three-thirty," he told Pam, guilt colouring his words. Her knowing smile only made him feel worse about his earlier behaviour.

As he entered, the bell above Penelope's door chimed, a sound both comforting and terrifying. She stood among white lilies, auburn curls catching the afternoon light, hands moving with practiced grace through the stems.

The relationship expert has returned. Her smile reached her eyes, making his carefully prepared professional response dissolve into awkward silence.

"I...." His tie felt wrong, his words clumsy. "I rather made a mess of things today."

"Bad day?" As she casually arranged lilies, his presence became less suffocating.

"I was rather awful to my receptionist." The confession emerged unprompted. "She's been with me ten years, through everything, and I just..."

"Sometimes the people closest to us get the worst of us." Penelope's hands never stopped moving through the flowers, creating order from chaos. "Last week, I snapped at my delivery driver for bringing roses instead of ranunculus. Poor man looked like I'd struck him."

Her admission loosened something in Reggie's chest. "How do you handle it? When the pressure becomes too much?"

"I remember we're all human." She met his eyes then, her gaze steady. "Even experts."

The professional mask he'd worn for so long cracked further as Pammy's words from earlier washed upon him once more. "I'm supposed to have answers. Solutions. Instead, I'm hiding in a flower shop because I can't..."

An elderly customer's entrance, breaking their moment, silenced the shop bell's cheerful chime. Reggie stepped back, walls starting to rise automatically.

"These need homes," Penelope said, indicating the purple flowers after assisting a customer. "Iris - they represent faith and wisdom. Rather fitting, don't you think?"

"Yes, very fitting," Reggie said softly.

"I suspect someone at your office would appreciate these," she stated with quiet certainty.

"You may have a point?" He drifted nearer, pulled in by her gentle empathy.

Smiling, she said, "Tomorrow always comes, no matter how hard today seems."

Their fingers brushed as she handed him the wrapped arrangement. "Same time tomorrow?" Her question carried more weight than simple business.

"Yes," he found himself saying. "Thank you."

Outside his office, Reggie carefully cradled Penelope's iris arrangement. His professional demeanour felt heavier after the calm of the flower shop, though the flowers' fragrance reminded him of gentle smiles and encouragement.

"Pam?" His voice carried none of its usual authority. Her face registered surprise at the flowers, a stark contrast to his typically organised surroundings, as she looked up.

"These are..." he cleared his throat, fighting the urge to retreat into polished phrases, "I behaved abominably earlier."

"Dr. Fitzwilliam..."

"Reggie," he corrected softly. "After ten years, perhaps it's time you called me Reggie when we're not with clients."

Freud emerged from his office, padding over to inspect the flowers with careful consideration before settling near Pam's desk——a silent vote of confidence.

"I'm not very good at this," Reggie admitted, his usual eloquence deserting him. "The personal side. The messy bits. When things feel out of control, I become rather...."

"Human?" Pam's gentle suggestion carried years of understanding.

"A challenge," he conceded with a slight smile. "You've been more than my receptionist for years. Your part of what makes this practice work, and I..." he swallowed hard. "I'm sorry."

Pam took the flowers, her eyes gleaming suspiciously. "These are lovely. From Penelope's?"

"Indeed, she proposed iris for...", He caught himself."Well, that's not important. What's important is that I value your presence here, your loyalty, your...."

"Ability to handle a tough boss?" Her teasing tone eased the moment's tension.

"Precisely." He adjusted his tie, but this time from emotion rather than anxiety. "I don't say it enough, but I couldn't do this without you. Thank you."

The phone's shrill ring interrupted their moment, another media request demanding attention. This time, however, Reggie felt acceptance rather than tension.

"Shall I handle that with our new protocol?" Pam asked, already reaching for their carefully prepared responses.

"Yes, please." He added," And perhaps we could review tomorrow's schedule? I'd value your input on managing the press situation."

Freud's approving purr seemed to seal their reconciliation as Pam arranged the iris in a crystal vase, their purple blooms bringing unexpected warmth to the reception area.

"These really are beautiful," Pam remarked, adjusting a stem. "Penelope has quite an eye for arrangements."

Reggie felt his neck flush with warmth, relieved when the phone rang, sparing him an answer. As Pam fielded the call with practiced ease, he retreated to his office, Freud following with what seemed like amused approval.

The afternoon light caught the iris petals, creating patterns on his degrees and certifications. Not only Pam, but he himself had undergone a change. Perhaps Penelope was right: tomorrow always came, no matter how difficult today felt.

The city lights blurred beneath Reggie's apartment window as he finally loosened his tie, letting it slip from his neck like shedding armour.

He felt the weight of the day's events: the morning's media frenzy, his harsh words to Pam, Penelope's empathy, and the unexpected calm of reconciliation. His reflection caught in the window––less perfect than usual, though he felt somehow more himself for it.

His takeaway sat forgotten on the kitchen counter, the usual evening routine disrupted by the day's emotional expenditure. Below, the city was a comforting tapestry of lights and shadows, usually ordered despite its chaos.

His mother's name flashing on his phone screen sent a jolt of anxiety rippling through Reggie's chest. He stared at it for a moment, half-expecting a lecture or another reminder of how he never quite measured up. With a resigned sigh, he answered.

"Hello, Mother."

He heard the unmistakable shuffle of papers and the echo of voices in the background—his father's curt tone rising. Something about "get to the point" slipped through. His grip tightened on the phone.

"Reginald?" His mother's voice wavered, containing a warmth that caught him off guard. "I saw your interview announcement."

Reggie forced a thin smile, even though she couldn't see it. "You, um... actually saw it?"

A muffled bark of disapproval sounded in the background again, clearly his father. He braced for the usual barrage of criticism.

"Yes, well," she cleared her throat,"your father feels you're engaging in needless risk-taking."Wants me to remind you to present yourself appropriately, about—"

Reggie's jaw became clenched. "Mother, I know his desires."

Though he heard whispers, he couldn't understand them. In the background, a door closing reached his ears.

Quiet. For a second, he pictured her hanging up and returning to her distant politeness. He then heard her voice, gentler than ever before.

"You're braver than I am, Reginald. Facing everyone like that, talking about your work—your therapy and all... That takes courage."

The praise halted him mid-breath. "Mother, I—"

She drew in a shaky inhale. "Your father always demanded perfection. And I let him. I should have... protected you, I suppose."

"Mum?" The childhood name slipped out. Immediately, he felt vulnerable, like a kid again.

Her voice lost the tension. "You built those walls around yourself, darling. I could see it happen, day by day. They looked so familiar... just like mine. I realize now I never gave you the chance to see another way."

Memories cascaded through the line, silent but present: hiding out in Mrs. Crumble's backyard to escape father's rants, the hush around the dinner table, Reggie's first unapproved school project that earned only a scowl.

She continued, voice nearly trembling. "I've never been good at this, Reggie. But I'd like us both to try... to lower those walls."

His breath caught in his throat. This was the closest she'd ever come to an apology—or an admission of her own struggles. Gingerly, he let down his guard.

"Maybe we can figure it out together," he said quietly.

For a few beats, neither spoke. But in that silence, something else bloomed—an understanding, soft and steady, starting to fill the spaces where only demands and distance once reigned.

"Yes, darling," she whispered at last. "Perhaps we can."

After hanging up, Reggie stood at his window, processing the day's seismic shifts. He remembered Penelope, her green eyes, gentle wisdom, and quiet acceptance of his flaws. His professional mask felt different now, less like protection and more like habit.

The approaching TV appearance made him nervous, yet his apprehension was different this time——less about presenting the perfect image and more about making a real connection. A subtle but significant shift had occurred, much like the initial fracture on a long-frozen lake.

Freud settled beside him, a warm presence against his leg. Together they watched the city's evening dance, finding comfort in shared silence. The cat's steady purr seemed to approve of these small steps toward change.

Tomorrow's schedule, and his daily visit to a particular flower shop, occupied his thoughts. The professional boundaries that once seemed so crucial now felt more like barriers to genuine connection.

Pulling his journal closer, Reggie began to write, acknowledging the day's growth with unaccustomed honesty. The words flowed easier now, less guarded, truer.

Chapter 6

Reggie arrived at the studio before sunrise, hidden in the pre-dawn shadows. His reflection in the glass doors revealed every wrinkle in his carefully chosen charcoal suit. He barely noticed the security guard's cheerful greeting as he trailed the producer's assistant through fluorescent hallways.

The green room's mirror revealed what he'd feared——a man trying too hard to look perfect. His hands automatically went to his burgundy silk tie, despite its being already perfectly adjusted.

"Dr. Fitzwilliam? We'll need to powder that forehead," the makeup artist swooped in, her brush attacking the slight shine of nervous perspiration. As time went on, Reggie's internal critic escalated while he remained passive under her care.

His father's voice echoed in his memory: "Excellence demands perfection, son. The camera sees everything." The familiar weight of expectations settled around his shoulders like a lead coat.

The buzz of his phone cut through his spiral. Pam's message appeared: *You've got this, Dr. F. Just be yourself.* Before he could respond, another notification lit up his screen from Penelope: *Everyone needs some sunshine——even on TV.*

Warmth bloomed in his chest, unexpected and welcome. His reflection looked different now, less rigid, more real.

The producer stormed in, brandishing his clipboard like a weapon. "Remember, Dr. Fitzwilliam, keep it light but professional. We're aiming for accessible expertise."

Reggie started to mutter a rehearsed line, then caught himself. Forget depth, he thought. People need something real. Authenticity connects more than perfection.

The bright lights of the studio shone brightly as Reggie took his seat. Looking out at the audience, he felt like a deer trapped in the headlights. The cameras in front went on red signalling they were live. His heart thundered against his ribs as the host's perfect smile turned his way. "Deep breaths," he reminded himself, drawing on years of therapeutic practice.

"So, Dr. Fitzwilliam," the host began, "what inspired you to become a relationship expert?"

Though prepared to give a practiced response, he recalled Penelope's words: everyone deserves sunshine. Instead of his usual polished response, he spoke from somewhere more genuine.

His voice steadier than he felt, Reggie said, "It began with watching people hide behind perfectly imperfect facades—including my own." His hand moved unconsciously to adjust his tie, then stopped mid-motion as he caught himself. "I wanted to understand why we build walls instead of bridges, why we choose safety over connection."

The studio lights felt less harsh as he continued, drawing from the well of truth he'd discovered through his own journey. "We're all searching for authentic connection, but we're terrified of being truly seen. I became a relationship expert not because

I had all the answers, but because I understood the questions we're all afraid to ask."

His gaze swept across the audience, seeing beyond the bright lights to the human stories waiting there. "Sometimes the greatest expertise comes from acknowledging our own struggles and by being honest with ourselves. I learned early that what people show on the surface often masks deeper truths," Reggie continued, his voice finding its natural rhythm. "I wanted to help people find authentic connection--the kind I wished I'd seen at home."

For the following half hour, every question elicited surprisingly honest answers. He spoke about the cost of maintaining perfect facades, about how true healing often starts with allowing ourselves to be seen--really seen--by others.

Captivated, the audience absorbed every word, feeling the intensity of his insights drawn from both professional skill and personal experience. When he talked about the courage it takes to be vulnerable, several people nodded in tearful recognition.

He stated that our greatest strength sometimes comes not from perfection, but from honest acknowledgement of our flaws. The truth of it resonated through him, warming his voice with authentic conviction.

Audience questions arose organically, answered with genuine insight instead of rote learning. He spoke about trust, about fear, about the courage it takes to love despite past wounds--working to showcase the honest truth behind his professional opinions.

The studio lights, once harsh, now felt warm, as if sunshine broke through clouds. His heart had steadied, finding rhythm in authenticity rather than performance.

Before he knew it, the red lights blinked off, signalling the end of his segment. Relief flooded through him as the host thanked him warmly, clearly impressed by his candour.

Sitting in his dressing room afterward, Reggie acknowledged something had shifted. The reflection showed a man who seemed less perfect, but more alive. Although, an unsettling query crept into his consciousness——had all this attention sparked genuine transformation, or was he merely performing for the masses? His phone kept buzzing with support, appreciation, connection. Each message both validated and terrified him. They had seen him——really seen him——and they hadn't turned away. But could he maintain this new vulnerability? Or would the old mask slip back into place, comfortable as a well-worn suit?

The morning's studio tension still weighed on Reggie's shoulders as he entered his office. His perfectly polished shoes barely made a sound on the Persian carpet, yet the space felt charged with unspoken pressure.

Rising from his small leather chair, Freud greeted him with a vibrant purr that oddly contrasted with Reggie's anxious reflection in the window. The cat's golden eyes tracked his movement as he sought refuge behind his mahogany desk.

"Dr. Fitzwilliam," Pam's voice crackled through the intercom, "*Good Morning Australia* wants a follow-up segment, and three magazines are requesting interviews."

His hand moved automatically to adjust his tie. "Not now, Pammy. Please."

The phone's insistent buzzing grew more demanding with each passing minute. A deluge of emails filled his inbox, their incessant notifications creating a stressful cacophony that not even his meticulously crafted office could silence.

"I said not now!" The words escaped sharper than intended as Pam entered with his morning tea. Her slight flinch made him wince. "I apologise, Pammy. That was uncalled for."

"You're allowed to be overwhelmed," she replied, placing the tea on his desk with practiced care. "The segment was quite...revealing."

Freud abandoned his post to wind between Reggie's legs, purring loudly enough to cut through the mounting tension. Although his mind revisited his nationally televised weaknesses, the cat's presence kept him steady.

'What were you thinking?' His inner critic demanded. *'My father will——'*

The phone's screen lit up with his father's name, as if summoned by his thoughts. Reggie's hand froze mid-reach for his tea, anxiety crawling up his spine like ice.

"Dr. Reginald Fitzwilliam," his father's voice cut through the speaker with surgical precision. "That was quite a performance this morning."

"It wasn't a performance, Father." The words emerged steadier than he felt. "It was honest..."

"Honest?" The scoff carried years of disapproval. "It was weak. Fitzwilliams don't display their...struggles publicly."

Old hurts resurfaced, as raw as new wounds. "Perhaps that's exactly why we should..."

"You've worked too hard to build this reputation to throw it away on some misguided attempt at...what did you call it? Authenticity?"

The perfectly arranged certificates and awards on the walls, previously seen as achievements, now felt like suffocating chains. Reggie looked out the window, longing for the escape offered by the distant city. Through the glass, he could just make out the cheerful awning of Penelope's shop.

He said, remembering those green eyes and their understanding, "Nothing is getting thrown out." I'm developing something genuine.

Drowned out by the thunder of his own pulse, his father's reply was lost as his controlled composure threatened to unravel. Unexpectedly, Penelope's quiet "Just be you" grounded him.

"You'll never grasp what authenticity really means," Reggie remarked, even surprising himself. "Father, I must go now; I have a busy day ahead. "Goodbye," ending the call suddenly.

Taking a deep breath, Reggie straightened his shoulders. He reviewed his appointments, viewing each as a chance to embody the authenticity over perfection he'd advocated that morning.

"Pam," he said into the intercom, "I'm ready to receive those messages now." Reggie's hand hovered over the intercom in readiness, his perfectly knotted tie suddenly feeling too tight. Freud's golden eyes tracked his movement from the miniature leather chair, sensing his human's discomfort.

His voice maintained its professional calm even as his stomach churned. The outside light caught the dust motes dancing in his office, making everything feel surreal.

Another announcement came over the intercom. "Dr. Fitzwilliam, *People Magazine* is on line two. They're asking about your childhood...."

Reggie's hand yanked at his tie before he caught himself. The perfectly organised schedule on his desk now seemed like a fortress against the chaos of public attention. His father's words, "Excellence demands its price, son," resonated in his mind again.

"Not now," he muttered, more to himself than to Pam through the intercom. Freud approached Reggie, abandoning his post to silently support him as his professional demeanour weakened.

The phone kept lighting up with notifications. Each one felt like another crack in his carefully constructed walls. *Good Morning Australia* wanted to discuss his "journey from crisis to triumph." *People Magazine* sought childhood photos. Three different publications requested exclusive rights to his "story of redemption".

Reggie stood abruptly, needing movement. His reflection in the office window showed a man caught between pride and panic. The city sprawled below, oblivious to his internal struggle.

"Dr. Fitzwilliam?" Pam's voice again, gentler this time. "Should I clear your afternoon schedule?"

His hand pressed against the cool glass of the window. The professional part of him knew this attention validated his work, his recovery, his message. But the private part--the part that still struggled with being seen--felt exposed, raw.

Freud's soft myrrh drew his attention. The cat's steady gaze seemed to ask: *Wasn't this what you wanted? Assisting others through authenticity?*

"No, Pam," he finally responded, voice steadier than he felt. "Keep the schedule. Just...prioritise the requests. Professional journals first."

But even as he said it, another magazine's call lit up his phone. His relationship status, personal life, and healing process were all of interest to them.

Reggie sank into his chair, the weight of public scrutiny pressing against his shoulders. Freud jumped onto his desk, deliberately knocking over his perfectly arranged pens--a familiar gesture of support through disruption.

The morning stretched ahead, filled with the promise of more calls, more requests, and more exposure. His meticulously organised life felt like a fishbowl, leaving Reggie unsure of how to navigate its transparency.

The morning's pressure finally proved too much. Reggie stared at his office walls, each framed achievement feeling more like an accusation than accomplishment. His father's words echoed in his head, mixing with the constant ping of messages and media requests until the space felt more prison than sanctuary.

Without conscious decision, he reached for his coat. "Pammy, I need..." the words trailed off as he straightened his tie one final time.

"Go on," she said simply, understanding in her eyes. "I'll handle things here."

The walk to Penelope's shop passed in a blur of autumn air and racing thoughts. Each step took him further from his carefully constructed world and closer to... something else. Something real.

The familiar bell chimed as he pushed open the door, its gentle sound cutting through his churning thoughts. Penelope stood among her roses, copper hair catching the morning light as she arranged deep red blooms. Upon his arrival, her hands fell still; her green eyes, instantly concerned, met his.

"Dr. Fitzwilliam?" The soft question showed understanding without judgment.

"Reggie," he corrected, his professional mask cracking. "I think... after this morning's television debacle, we can dispense with formalities."

His usual eloquence failed him, leaving him speechless. He stood among the flowers, tie suddenly too tight, hands seeking pockets that offered no refuge.

"I saw the segment," Penelope offered, moving closer. "It was brave."

He couldn't stop a bitter laugh from escaping. "My father called it weak. Apparently, Fitzwilliams don't discuss their...emotional challenges on national television."

His voice shook on the last words, sarcasm failing to hide the raw hurt beneath. Penelope's quiet presence drew truth from him like poison from a wound.

"Years of reputation building are being thrown away on a misguided attempt at authenticity," he blurted, dropping all professional pretence. "Twenty years of maintaining perfect control, and I destroy it in thirty minutes of morning television."

Penelope continued arranging roses, her movements creating space for his words to breathe. "Sometimes the strongest things we do look like destruction to those who taught us to build walls."

The simple wisdom hit harder than his father's criticism. Reggie found himself sinking onto a nearby stool, surrounded by the shop's peaceful scent.

"I don't know how to do this," he admitted. "Be real instead of right."

"That's what you're doing," Penelope stated, adding another rose to her arrangement. "Being here, being honest——that's real."

Their shared vulnerability forged a bond far exceeding professional titles as the moment intensified. The shop's bell chimed again as a customer entered, reality intruding gently into their shared space.

Though Penelope offered aid to the newcomer, her presence anchored him to the present, a moment of profound revelation. He watched her work, professional mask forgotten as she handled the interruption with natural grace.

"My mother used to garden," he found himself saying when she returned. "Before Father decided it wasn't suitable for a doctor's wife. She loved roses too."

"And now?"

"Now she maintains perfect flower arrangements that never grow or change." The parallel to his own life hung unspoken between them.

Reggie noticed Penelope's gentle movements among the flowers; her quiet skill reminded him of his mother gardening years ago. Before the carefully curated arrangements, before excellence demanded the sacrifice of joy.

"Sometimes I wonder," he found himself continuing, "if I've done the same thing. Created a perfect practice that never really grows."

He adjusted his tie again, a habitual gesture rather than a necessary one. The morning's television appearance felt like a lifetime ago, though barely hours had passed.

"Growth is messy," Penelope said, trimming a rose stem with practiced ease. "That's why most people avoid it."

The truth of her words settled around him like the shop's peaceful atmosphere. Here, among the living, growing things, his father's criticism felt less crushing. The constant ping of his phone faded to background noise.

Reggie, observing her floral arrangements, revealed a twenty-year dedication to refining his therapeutic techniques. "Writing books about emotional connection while maintaining perfect professional distance."

"And now?" Penelope asked the question without judgment, only genuine interest.

"Now I'm sitting in a flower shop having an emotional crisis," he said with a short laugh. "Rather ironic, isn't it?"

"I'd call it human." Penelope added another rose to her arrangement, the deep red petals catching light. "Which might be better than perfect."

That simple observation proved more impactful than any therapeutic insight. Reggie studied her profile, the way she handled each bloom with care but without preciousness. No fear of imperfection, just appreciation for what was.

"How do you do that?" The question escaped before he could analyse it.

"Do what?"

"Make it look so simple. Being real instead of right."

Penelope's hands stilled on the roses. "Maybe because I never learned to be anything else." She met his gaze directly. "Not everyone had a father who demanded perfection."

The gentle challenge in her words made him sit straighter. "No, I suppose not."

"Though some of us had mothers who tried," she added softly, returning to her work. We sometimes show kindness by disappointing others' hopes.

Reggie stood among the flowers, their quiet presence a balm to his frayed nerves. The morning's chaos felt distant here, muted by the shop's peaceful atmosphere and Penelope's steady presence.

"You know," Penelope said, moving toward the lavender display, "sometimes the strongest people are those who admit when they're not strong."

Reggie's nervous hand movements toward his tie ceased as her impactful words resonated with him. Observing her, he noted her careful selection of a lavender sprig; its delicate scent wafted across the shop to him.

"For peace," she explained, holding it out to him. The simple gesture carried more understanding than any therapeutic platitude he'd ever offered his clients.

As he took the lavender, his fingers grazed hers, the fleeting touch unexpectedly warming him. Before he could retreat behind his professional mask, Penelope turned to the roses.

"White ones," she murmured, more to herself than him. "Yes, that's right."

The morning light caught her copper hair as she worked, and Reggie found himself studying the way she handled each bloom - confident yet gentle, no trace of his own desperate need for perfection.

"A white rose," she said, selecting one with particular care. "For new beginnings."

Their eyes met as she offered the flower, and Reggie saw in her green gaze the same understanding he'd been trying to teach his clients for years——that sometimes strength comes not from being unbreakable, but from being brave enough to break and grow.

"Thank you," he mumbled, his usual polished speech replaced by heartfelt sincerity. "For...understanding."

Penelope's accepting smile showed no criticism, only quiet understanding of what hid beneath his well-crafted exterior. "Sometimes we need someone to see our cracks as opportunities rather than flaws."

The moment stretched between them, heavy with unspoken possibility. Through the shop window, morning light painted patterns on the floor, and somewhere in the distance, a church bell chimed the hour.

Their shared look lingered, carrying the weight of recognition——that perhaps here, in this moment of vulnerability, something stronger than perfection was taking root.

Back in his office, Reggie held the white rose and lavender sprig protectively. Their subtle fragrance followed him, a gentle reminder of the flower shop's peace. Freud lifted his head from his miniature leather chair, golden eyes studying the new additions.

Three texts, two missed calls, and an urgent email shattered the quiet moment as his phone buzzed. Tension crept back into his shoulders, the morning's media appearance spawning endless requests for comments, interviews, appearances.

His fingers tightened on the rose stem before he caught himself. *'Breathe. Just breathe.'*

Pam appeared in the doorway; her cautious approach showed his earlier sharp words had affected her. "Dr. Fitzwilliam? *Channel Ten* called again. And the Morning Herald wants——"

He felt the familiar annoyance, yet the calming aroma of lavender distracted him. Penelope's words echoed: Sometimes the strongest people are those who admit when they're not strong.

"Thank you, Pammy," he managed, his voice steadier than he felt. "Let's schedule responses for tomorrow. Today needs...space."

The surprise in her expression made him wince internally, but her quick smile suggested he'd made the right choice.

His brief peace fractured as Cassandra's name lit up his phone screen. "That was quite a performance this morning, Reginald," she purred, her voice dripping venom. So...emotional."

The old urge to snap back rose sharply, but the white rose caught his eye. New beginnings, Penelope had said.

"Thank you for your feedback, Cassandra," he replied, professional courtesy holding despite the strain. "I trust you'll understand if I keep this brief. Client waiting."

More messages arrived, each demanding his attention, skills, and composure, increasing the pressure on him. His hands moved toward his tie, the familiar gesture offering false comfort.

But Freud's steady presence and the flowers' gentle reminder helped ground him. Pam's quiet efficiency in screening calls, her understanding of his needs without judgment, reinforced that he wasn't facing this alone.

"We'll need a system," he told her as she brought his afternoon tea. "For handling the increased media interest. Something that maintains professional boundaries while..." he paused, finding the right words. "While allowing for authenticity."

Pam's knowing smile suggested she heard what he wasn't saying. The afternoon settled into a new rhythm, not perfect but perhaps better for being real. The flowers stood in their vase, a quiet testament to growth, while Freud maintained his watchful presence from his chair.

The waning sunlight stretched dark silhouettes across the hallway whilst Reggie turned his key in the lock, Freud striding out of his carrier with stately determination. "A brief visit only, dear chap. Something tells me Mrs. Crumble's awaiting my arrival."

Freud's knowing look suggested an understanding of human emotions exceeding expectations, even surpassing a cat's. With his companion's dinner and water taken care of, Reggie returned, feeling lighter despite a difficult day.

The familiar peace of Mrs. Crumble's garden, with its roses nodding in the evening breeze, greeted him. His tie, already loosened from the day's battles, slipped further as his shoulders dropped their rigid posture. Here, in this sanctuary of blooms and understanding, the perfect Dr. Fitzwilliam could simply be Reggie.

"Right on time," Mrs. Crumble called from her rose bushes, pruning shears moving with practiced precision. A tea tray waited on the wrought iron table, steam rising from his favourite cup. Her knowing smile was free of judgment, only the warm acceptance he'd known since childhood.

"The TV appearance was a success," he started, sinking into his usual chair. "Though Father had other opinions."

"He usually does." Putting down her shears, Mrs. Crumble observed his slightly trembling hands as he went for his tea.

"I was too emotional, apparently. Not dignified enough for a Fitzwilliam." The bitterness in his voice surprised him.

Mrs. Crumble gestured to her garden. "Notice how each flower blooms differently? Some bold, some subtle, but all exactly as they should be."

The scent of roses wrapped around him, reminding him suddenly, sharply, of Penelope's shop. "The smell of roses," he admitted quietly. "Reminds me of her flower shop. In there, I can only be myself. She... sees through the walls."

"And that frightens you?"

"Terrifies me." His professional mask slipped further. "I don't know how to be seen. Really seen."

"Like these roses," Mrs. Crumble touched a bloom gently, "we can't flourish behind walls. Growth requires openness."

Reggie studied his hands, the day's tensions written in every line. "My whole career is built on being the expert, having the answers. But with her...."

"You're allowed to be the student sometimes, dear. Even experts need to learn."

The evening air carried the mixed fragrance of roses and lavender, echoing the flowers sitting in his office. "I'm not sure I know how anymore. To just...be."

Mrs. Crumble's gentle laugh held years of wisdom. "That's precisely why you need to try."

The garden's peace settled around them as Reggie considered his path forward. Each breath felt easier here, where expectations fell away, and truth could surface.

"You've built quite a support system," Mrs. Crumble observed. "Pam, your clients who trust you, Penelope, even that magnificent cat of yours. Consider trusting yourself as much as others place their trust in you.

Gratitude welled up unexpectedly. Only this garden, wisdom, and acceptance remained constant amidst the change.

As evening deepened, the garden's tranquillity seeped into his bones. Tomorrow would bring new challenges, but here, in this moment, growth felt possible. The path ahead seemed clearer, not easier perhaps, but clearer.

The key turned in Reggie's door, and Freud greeted him with a dignified myrrh, golden eyes assessing his human's state after the evening's wisdom.

Darkness retreated as Reggie moved through his apartment, each light bringing warmth to the carefully ordered space. His tie, finally slipped free. The silk whispered as he hung it precisely with his jacket, muscle memory maintaining order even as his mind sought peace.

His shoes found their proper place, the routine grounding him after a day of emotional upheaval. The wooden floor felt solid beneath his feet, anchoring him in the present moment.

As Reggie made his evening tea, the quiet hum of the kettle filled his kitchen. He carefully topped up Freud's food bowl. The cat's appreciative purr provided a counterpoint to the muted television news.

Reggie sank into his leather armchair, relaxing after a tense day. The morning show replay caught his attention; there *he* was, speaking about perfection not being the goal. His own words echoed back: "The best expertise comes from being honest about our own journey."

The tremor in his hands, once his professional facade faltered, was instantly noted by his sharp eye. Yet instead of the usual self-recrimination, he found himself recognising something different——authenticity. Growth, perhaps.

His phone lit up with Penelope's message: *Caught your repeat showing. You were brave today.*

Reggie hesitated, composing and discarding professional replies. Finally:

Your flowers helped. Thank you for seeing past the perfect façade of Dr. Fitzwilliam.

She replied swiftly: "Perfect is overrated." Real is better.

As Reggie considered her words, steam rose from his teacup. Freud claimed his usual evening perch nearby, watching his human with knowing eyes. The cat's steady presence offered silent support as tomorrow's challenges waited beyond tonight's peace.

The familiar comfort of his evening routine wrapped around him——tea sipped slowly, Freud's gentle purring, the city lights twinkling beyond his windows. Here, in this private space, Dr. Fitzwilliam could simply be Reggie, still learning, still growing, still finding his way toward authenticity.

Chapter 7

R eggie woke just before his alarm, the first light tracing soft lines across his ceiling. At the window, Freud sat like a statue, tail curled in elegant contrast to the waking skyline. The cat's quiet presence anchored this liminal moment between night and day.

Reggie watched, still, as the shadows subtly shifted. Something felt different this morning––lighter perhaps, as if yesterday's authenticity had altered more than just his public persona. The weight of perpetual perfection seemed less crushing in the gentle dawn light.

Precisely and calmly, Reggie made his morning tea amidst the steam from the kettle. His fingers traced the hangers in his closet before selecting the navy suit, its familiar weight comfortable rather than armouring. The silk tie with its subtle pattern caught the morning light––chosen for preference rather than impression.

He straightened his collar, then checked his appearance in the mirror. The usual critical assessment softened, noting but not judging the slight shadows beneath his eyes, the hint of silver threading his temples. Progress, perhaps.

As the morning news played, Reggie silently reviewed yesterday's TV appearance feedback. "Refreshingly authentic," one critic noted. "Dr. Fitzwilliam brings warmth to expertise." His professional side would have once dismissed such observations. Today, he allowed himself to recognise their truth.

His social media was awash with posts and comments from colleagues. The familiar anxiety stirred but didn't overwhelm. He closed the apps before they could consume his morning peace.

The white rose on his desk caught his eye, its petals glowing softly in the early light. His phone still held yesterday's exchange with Penelope, words that had shifted something fundamental: "Perfect is overrated. Real is better." He began to smile.

Client files waited for review, their familiar organisation offering comfort rather than constraint. Today's schedule balanced therapy sessions with television follow-up meetings. The challenge of maintaining authenticity across both spheres loomed but felt possible.

His phone chimed softly––Penelope's message lighting the screen: *Hope the flowers brightened your morning.*

Reggie's fingers moved across the keys. *They remind me that growth needs both sunshine and courage. Thank you.*

Reggie arrived at his practice just as the first rays of sunlight touched the brass nameplate on the door. The familiar weight of his briefcase felt different—less like armour, more like a trusted tool of his trade. The morning air held a crisp promise that matched his tentatively optimistic mood.

The usual professional quiet of the practice's halls enveloped him as he went inside. Freud padded ahead, making his customary inspection of their shared domain before settling into his miniature leather chair. Reggie arranged his desk, the cat's golden eyes following his every move with a knowing assessment.

The practice itself seemed to hold its breath, as if sensing the subtle shift in its master's demeanour. Yesterday's television appearance had altered something in the carefully maintained atmosphere——not a crack in the professional veneer, but perhaps a softening around its edges.

Pam's arrival brought the gentle chime of China as she set his morning tea on the desk. Her smile carried warmth beyond her usual professional courtesy.

"They're rerunning your morning show segment," she said, smoothly adjusting the tea tray. "You've quite impressed everyone."

Reggie's hand moved to his tie, then stilled. "Thank you, Pammy." The words came easier than expected, without his usual deflection.

"We've had a lot of calls," she said, a hint of pride in her voice. "Seems authenticity suits you."

Uncharacteristically, he simply nodded, accepting her compliments without his usual deflecting behaviour. The tea's familiar comfort grounded him as he began reviewing the morning's messages.

The appointment list held its usual mix of regular clients and new consultations. Professional feedback had begun to arrive——colleagues noting the effective balance of expertise and approachability in his television manner. Each response required careful consideration, maintaining the delicate equilibrium between his evolving public presence and established therapeutic practice.

His colleagues arrived, their morning greetings subtly conveying their approval. Dr. Chen's quiet "Well done" held weight——the senior therapist's words always measured and sincere. Even Dr. Morris, usually reserved to the point of aloofness, offered a supportive nod.

Underlying the office's calm exterior, professional relationships subtly changed. Reggie responded with unexpected openness, his usual carefully maintained distance softening without compromising his authority.

As he organised the files for his first patient, Freud assumed his therapeutic position, tail curved elegantly around his paws. The white rose on the desk caught morning light, its petals a reminder of yesterday's courage. Reggie drew strength from its presence, a tangible link between his professional space and his emerging authentic self.

His phone buzzed and a message from Marilyn lit up his screen: *Watched the show. About time you let them see the real Reg. Proud of you, you stuffy old thing.*

He felt the support surrounding him, a comforting presence that highlighted his self-imposed professional isolation. Gratitude welled unexpectedly, for both the long-standing connections he'd maintained despite his walls and the new ones forming as those walls lowered.

Reggie settled into his leather chair as Sandra Brown entered. Freud maintained his usual therapeutic position. Sunlight illuminated Sandra's wedding ring; the very ring she almost took off during their first marriage counseling session.

"I saw you on television yesterday," Sandra offered, her smile genuine. "It was...different, seeing you speak so openly."

The familiar need to remain distant, to keep things professional, came over Reggie. Instead, he found himself nodding. Personal experiences often inform our professional perspectives.

The session flowed differently, Sandra's usual hesitation giving way to deeper sharing. Her words about marriage struggles carried new weight, meeting his carefully measured responses.

"It's like you said on TV––about perfection not being the goal," she ventured. "Chris and I...we're learning that too."

Aware of his own growth, Reggie leaned forward slightly to respond. "Understanding takes courage. Beyond what perfection can achieve."

The therapeutic space between them shifted, Sandra's tears coming freely now as she described a breakthrough with Chris. Freud moved closer, offering his silent support as she spoke of fear and hope in equal measure.

"How did you learn to be so...real about it?" she asked.

Reggie hesitated, torn between professionalism and genuine connection. "Through my own journey of understanding that walls, while protective, can also isolate."

Feeling lighter after Sandra's session, Reggie reviewed his notes. His usual clinical observations flowed differently, coloured by this new integration of professional expertise and personal growth.

Cassandra's sharp knock interrupted his reflection, her entrance carrying its usual calculated precision.

Inspecting her nails, she declared, "The Psychology Council is discussing your TV appearance." "Some feel it might blur therapeutic boundaries."

Reggie felt the familiar tension, but something was different. "Maintaining professional boundaries safeguards our clients, Cassandra. Authenticity serves them."

As Cassandra departed, her attempt at disruption falling flat, Reggie's phone lit with another message from Penelope: *Hope your morning's blooming well.*

The white rose caught his eye as he replied, its petals reminding him of her words about new beginnings.

Reggie approached his next client's file in a new way. His clinical observations remained sharp, but they carried a new depth.

Session showed marked progress. The client shows a positive response to authentic therapeutic techniques. He stopped writing, recalling Sandra Brown's tears—not of sadness, but happy realization.

Beside the schedule, the untouched sandwich was a poignant reminder of Pam's unspoken worry. The morning's changes settled around him like afternoon light.

He received a flood of professional feedback on the show via email. His long-time colleagues offered cautious support, speaking with thoughtful consideration.

"Appreciated your honest approach to therapeutic boundaries..."

"Refreshing perspective on professional authenticity..."

His publisher's message practically vibrated off the screen: "Ratings surpassed expectations!" Your vulnerability is resonating with the public. Book sales spiking!"

Automatically, Reggie adjusted his tie, then paused. Not everything needs perfecting.

Marilyn's arrival interrupted his thoughts.

"Thought you might forget to eat," she announced, clearing space on his desk. "Again."

"I have lunch," he protested, gesturing vaguely at the forgotten sandwich.

"That's not lunch, that's a prop for your workaholic tendencies." She disregarded his weak objection and sat down in the client chair. "So, television star, how are you really doing?"

Today, the familiar question felt heavier than usual. Reggie found himself considering it rather than deflecting.

"It's... unusual," he confessed. "Being noticed."

"Good different?" Marilyn's knowing glance suggested prior knowledge.

"Terrifying different." He paused, recalling green eyes and white roses. "But perhaps necessary different."

"That reminds me," Marilyn teased, smiling, "Pam was talking about a specific florist...?"

Despite his professional demeanour, Reggie felt himself blushing. "Penelope has been...kind."

"Kind enough to make you forget your perfectly adjusted tie?" Her gesture unscrewed a slightly loosened collar.

"Cassandra's not pleased about the show," he deflected, but without his usual sharpness.

"Cassandra's always dissatisfied," Marilyn replied. "But she's being particularly pointed about your television success."

The practice is undergoing a shift in dynamics.

"Good," Marilyn stated firmly. "Some things need to shift."

Reggie considered boosting his TV appearances, writing books, and changing how he works. His typical need for control was absent despite the future's uncertainty.

Reggie considered boosting his TV appearances, writing books, and refining his methods.t, at long last. Sometimes growth happened in these quiet moments, between friendship and food, trust and truth.

Okay, I've talked enough about myself. "Let's focus on you," Reggie urged, wanting to avoid making their friendship all about himself. With a warm smile, he encouraged, "Tell me, what's been happening in your world lately?" "Mine hasn't been as exciting as yours," Marilyn admitted, smiling broadly, "but I'll tell you, anyway."

Reggie found closing his client file effortless after a successful morning. Freud maintained his therapeutic position, golden eyes tracking his human's movements as afternoon light warmed the office.

Reggie's careful note organisation couldn't quite silence the client's lingering "Thank you for today, Dr. Fitzwilliam." The session's breakthrough felt different somehow - more authentic after yesterday's television appearance.

His next appointment's file lay ready, professional mask settling back into place when Cassandra's unexpected entrance disrupted his preparation.

"The TV producer called again," she announced, her perfectly timed statement as precise as always. "They mentioned considering other options for the relationship segment."

Reggie stopped abruptly, reviewing his notes while Freud bristled at being interrupted. "I wasn't aware you were handling my media correspondence, Cassandra."

"Oh, I'm not. They reached out directly." Her smile didn't reach her eyes. "Given our history, they thought I might have...insights into your past."

The old tension returned; However, things had changed since yesterday's broadcast.

Reggie softly stressed, "Our work history is simply that: History."

"Is it?" Cassandra's approach disrupted the office's calm with her scent. "Your father always thought we made an excellent team."

I no longer care what my father thinks of my career path. The strength in his voice surprised them both.

Cassandra's composure faltered slightly. The Psychology Council might scrutinise your recent emotional outbursts.

Reggie, calmed by Freud, said, "The Council prefers genuine therapeutic methods." As you well know."

Reginald, there are dangers in authenticity. Particularly given your...weaknesses.

His newfound clarity made the usual manipulative attempt useless. My so-called vulnerabilities make me a more effective therapist. Something you've never understood."

"The show needs someone stable, reliable——"

"The show," Reggie interrupted firmly, "needs someone real. Now, if you'll excuse me, I have clients waiting."

Cassandra's exit was less triumphant than normal; her strategic move proved ineffective. Unknowingly, Reggie let out a breath he'd been holding.

As Reggie tidied his desk, a contented purr from Freud filled the quiet office, a feeling of victory settling upon him. Purposefully, he opened his next client's file; the afternoon's challenge only strengthened his resolve.

With the day's last client gone, Reggie settled in at his desk, the fading light creating long shadows on his orderly files. Freud, in his small chair, kept his nightly watch, observing his human's usual routine performed with less precision than normal.

"Quite a day," Reggie murmured, adding last notes to his client files. Despite his recent fight with Cassandra, his pen smoothly recorded his professional notes.

Organising his desk changed the office; it was warmer, less like the sterile haven it once was. More real. Penelope's white rose caught the evening light, its petals a gentle reminder of possibilities.

His tie loosened slightly as he processed the day's events. Cassandra's manipulative actions, his surprising resilience, and his colleagues' growing support all pointed to a new pattern: change isn't always a threat.

From his window, Reggie saw Penelope's warmly lit shop beckoning in the early evening. His hand moved automatically to adjust his tie, then stopped. *Perfect isn't the point anymore*, he reminded himself.

The decision formed quietly, without the usual analysis that preceded his personal choices. Sometimes, he realised, the bravest thing was simply taking the next step.

"Hold my calls, Pam," he said, grabbing his coat. "I'm heading out early. I'm coming back later for you, Freud. "

Pam's knowing smile followed him as he left the practice, evening air cool against his face. Though the city buzzed with the energy of the day's end, he was fixated on the inviting light from Penelope's nearby shop.

His professional mask softened naturally as he walked, years of careful distance giving way to something more authentic. With every step closer to the florist's, Cassandra's threats, his father's disapproval, and his own perfectionism felt less heavy.

From his vantage point at the window, he watched Penelope organise late deliveries, her movements as graceful and calming as they had been when he'd panicked days earlier. Her genuine smile made his carefully prepared words unnecessary as she looked up, sensing him.

As he stepped inside, the shop bell chimed a welcome, its familiar floral scent and sense of possibility enveloping him.

"The famous Dr. Fitzwilliam returns," Penelope greeted warmly, setting aside her work. "Though something tells me this isn't about flowers."

Reggie, abandoning his usual professional demeanour for genuine hope, blurted, "Actually, I was wondering if you'd like to grab a bite."

The moment hung between them, fragile as a newly opened bloom, filled with the same delicate possibility he'd witnessed countless times in his therapy sessions but never quite experienced himself.

"Like a date?" Penelope enquired. Reggie dipped his chin in agreement, resisting the compulsion to fidget with his immaculately positioned necktie. He was surprisingly and terrifyingly lost, even though he'd guided countless clients through similar predicaments. Penelope easily agreed, her knowing emerald eyes bypassing his usual defences. The warmth in her expression appeared to acknowledge and embrace all his carefully constructed barriers, each anxiety he'd maintained. "I know a charming little place just down the street."

"Perfect," Reggie replied, then caught himself. "Well, perhaps not perfect...."

"But real," Penelope finished, flashing a knowing smile.

Chapter 8

Reggie paused at the restaurant entrance, his trained eye instinctively scanning the cozy interior. Warm lighting cast a gentle glow over wooden tables, while soft jazz provided comfortable cover for private conversations. His usual instinct to control every aspect of a situation wavered as Penelope's quiet presence beside him offered a different kind of security.

"There's a nice corner table," she suggested, seeming to understand his need for space to process. The familiar weight of his tie felt different as they made their way through the restaurant, less like armour and more like habit.

Though attempting to ignore his professional side, he noticed the table provided a clear view of both exits and the street. Penelope settled across from him, the evening light catching her auburn hair and making his carefully prepared conversation starters unnecessary.

"This mushroom risotto is delightful," she smoothly interjected, calming his anxiety. "Though their coffee really is terrible."

His genuine, not practiced, laugh surprised them both. "Then perhaps wine instead?" The words came naturally, without his usual careful consideration.

Their orders placed, Reggie navigated unfamiliar territory. While he typically used small talk professionally, her genuine curiosity about his television appearance altered their relationship.

"You were different on TV," she observed, her green eyes holding his gaze. "More real than the perfect Dr. Fitzwilliam standards you hold yourself to."

"Terrifying," he admitted, his usual defences falling away. "My father always said Fitzwilliams must always uphold dignity—no matter the cost."

"And what does Reggie say?"

The question hung between them as their wine arrived. He considered his response, feeling the weight of years of careful distance.

"Reggie is...learning that dignity and authenticity aren't mutually exclusive."

Penelope's smile encouraged more truth. "Though I'm rather awful at this part."

"Which part?"

"Being seen. Truly seen." He traced the wine glass stem, grounding himself in the rhythm of the motion. "In therapy, I know the rules, the boundaries. This is..." he sighed.

"Scarier?" she offered gently.

"Terrifyingly so."

As the restaurant filled, their conversation grew more intimate, forming a private space amidst the evening's activity. Reggie found himself sharing pieces of his story he usually kept carefully filed away——his father's relentless pursuit of excellence, his mother's distant presence, the safety he'd found in professional success.

Penelope listened with the same tender attentiveness she gave her flowers, offering gentle truths of her own—stories of small-town roots, dreams of owning a shop, and the peace she found in helping things grow.

"Sometimes the strongest blooms come from the most careful nurturing," she said, understanding flowing between them. "Not from forcing growth."

Reggie, normally very guarded, found himself affected by the honesty of her words. Their empty plates testified to time passed comfortably, wine glasses marking the gradual lowering of walls.

"Now, how about a cup of their terrible coffee?" The words surprised him as they left his mouth, more playful than his usual measured tone.

"OK," Penelope said, her green eyes dancing with mischief, "but I warn you when I said it's terrible, I mean, it's terrible."

"Surely, it couldn't be that bad?" Reggie's usual analytical nature and skepticism kicked in. He'd survived years of terrible coffee during his training, after all.

The waiter interrupted their conversation by efficiently placing two plain white cups in front of them. The coffee's aroma seemed promising enough, though Penelope's knowing look suggested otherwise.

Reggie lifted his cup with the same careful consideration he gave everything, noting the proper temperature, the decent crema on top. His first sip, however, shattered any illusion of acceptable coffee.

"That *is* terrible." He set the cup down with deliberate care, fighting the urge to check if his tie had somehow protected him from the assault on his taste buds. The bitter, burnt flavour lingered unpleasantly.

Penelope's warm, genuine laugh almost made up for the awful coffee. Almost.

"I did warn you," she stated, leaving her drink alone. "Some things you just have to experience for yourself."

"I'd like to do this again," he found himself saying, professional polish giving way to simple hope. "Perhaps without the terrible coffee next time."

Penelope's smile carried the same warmth that had first drawn him into her shop. "I'd like that too."

The weak grey light of dawn filtering through his curtains woke Reggie before his alarm. Perched upon the ledge, his cat's inquisitive meow hinted that the observant creature had sensed an unusual shift in his master's demeanour. The memory of last night's dinner conversation with Penelope lingered like a warm cup of tea, both comforting and energising.

This morning, his normally precise military routine felt gentler, less focused on flawlessness and more on the day's promise. Even Freud seemed to notice, watching with apparent approval as Reggie moved through his morning routine with unusual lightness.

Reggie made his morning tea, the kettle whistling as he moved through the kitchen without his usual tension. His hand reached for his favourite cup––the one Mrs. Crumble had given him years ago.

Reggie was surprised he chose his charcoal grey suit so easily––Pam had once complimented how it brought out his eyes. The tie selection, usually a careful deliberation, took mere seconds. He found himself tying it with deliberate looseness, the knot comfortable rather than constraining.

"Rather different this morning, aren't we?" he murmured to Freud, who responded with what seemed like approving purr.

At his desk, the morning schedule demanded attention. Though his next TV appearance was imminent, he surprisingly didn't feel his typical anxiety. Instead, he found himself considering how to balance this new public role with his private practice——and perhaps his private life.

His phone lit up with a message from Penelope. *Morning. Hope your tea's better than last night's coffee.*

Reggie's fingers moved across the keys without their usual careful consideration: *Much better. Though the company made even terrible coffee worthwhile.*

The smile that formed felt natural, unguarded. Freud, in a show of support for Reggie's newfound genuineness, left his spot and rubbed against his legs.

While reviewing patient files, he had a short return to reality. Professional boundaries would need careful navigation with these emerging personal feelings. Yet for once, the challenge felt less like a wall to maintain and more like a path to discover.

As Reggie collected his briefcase, he checked his reflection in the hallway mirror. The man looking back seemed different——still Dr. Fitzwilliam, but perhaps more Reggie too. His tie sat slightly looser, his smile came more easily, and his shoulders carried less of perfection's weight.

Reggie locked his apartment door. The morning energy felt new and right.

With a productive session completed, Reggie closed his leather notebook as his client prepared to leave. Her steps carried more confidence than when she'd arrived, a minor victory he allowed himself to appreciate.

"Same time next week, Dr. Fitzwilliam?" She adjusted her handbag strap.

"Of course. Pam will check the details. His professional tone remained steady, though his internal energy felt lighter somehow.

Reggie commenced his session notes as the door clicked shut, Freud observing from his miniature chair. The morning's peaceful rhythm broke as his phone lit up with the producer's name.

"Dr. Fitzwilliam speaking."

The audience reaction has been phenomenal. We'd like to discuss expanding your weekly segment."

Reggie's hand froze above his notes. "I maintain certain professional boundaries——"

"Of course, of course. But perhaps we could explore——"

"My practice takes priority. The segment must work around that." His tone carried quiet authority.

The producer's enthusiasm dampened slightly. "We'll make it work within your parameters." "Please liaise with Pam__" Cassandra's calculated entrance interrupted his response. She leaned against his doorframe with practiced casualness. "Thank you," Reggie quipped to the producer, "but we'll leave it there for now." Looking squarely at Cassandra as he hung up the phone.

"Reginald, another media interview?" How...demanding it must be."

"Don't worry, Cassandra; I've got this." His voice remained neutral, professional distance maintained.

"The Council has expressed concerns about the practice's..."

"Which remains exemplary." Reggie met her gaze steadily. "Was there something specific you needed?"

Cassandra's sharp reply was cut short by Pam's appearance with a flower delivery. A small arrangement of white roses and lavender sat in a crystal vase, Penelope's artistic touch evident in every detail.

"Special delivery, Dr. Fitzwilliam." Pam's knowing smile carried warmth.

A suspicious look crossed Cassandra's face as she eyed the flowers. "How...domestic."

Reggie simply nodded his thanks to Pam, maintaining his professional composure despite the warmth spreading through his chest at the sight of Penelope's card nestled among the blooms.

"If you'll excuse me, Cassandra. I'm expecting my next client any minute now.

She retreated with obvious reluctance, leaving Reggie to read Penelope's message in private: *Better than terrible coffee. I hope these make your morning better.*

Freud's knowing purr suggested the cat wasn't fooled, although Reggie maintained a subtle, professional smile. Reggie moved the vase on his desk so the morning light illuminated the petals beautifully.

The space felt his again, peaceful despite Cassandra's attempted intrusion. He reviewed his next client's file, professional focus returning naturally, though the flowers' gentle presence remained, much like the quiet joy they represented.

Freud settled more comfortably in his chair as Reggie prepared for his next session, both content in the moment's calm. They had met the morning's challenges with a new kind of strength—one that didn't require perfect control to maintain.

A hint of anticipation coloured Reggie's measured stride as he neared the café. The familiar weight of his leather briefcase offered little comfort against the unfamiliar flutter in his chest. His hand moved to adjust his tie, then stopped, remembering Penelope's words about seeing more of him without it.

From the café, he saw her sitting at a corner table, sunlight glinting off her auburn hair. His professional demeanour automatically as she looked up, her warm smile reaching her eyes in a way that made his carefully maintained walls waver.

"No terrible coffee this time," Penelope said to him, her gentle teasing lacking the sharp edges he usually encountered in professional exchanges.

"A brave promise." He settled into the chair opposite her, noticing how naturally the moment felt despite its newness.

The barista approached with practiced efficiency. Penelope ordered with easy familiarity, "The house blend, touch of milk," while Reggie found himself choosing based on her recommendation rather than his usual precise specifications.

"Trust me on this one," she said, eyes twinkling. "I wouldn't lead you astray after last night's disaster."

Her laugh at his mock sceptical expression surprised them both with its authenticity.

The coffee arrived, its rich aroma suggesting redemption for the previous evening's experience. Their conversation flowed with unexpected ease, professional personas giving way to something more genuine as they exchanged childhood stories. "Father was rather demanding when it came to excellence," Reggie discovered himself confiding, the sentiment spilling forth without his customary restraint. "Mum and Dad just wanted me to be content, not flawless," Penelope offered. "Being perfect is rather taxing, don't you think?" Her expression brightened with the observation.

"Now I'm learning that perhaps perfection isn't the point." His admission carried weight, truth offering itself without professional analysis.

His phone abruptly interrupted her reply. The producer's name flashed insistently.

"Sorry, I should——"

"Of course." Penelope smiled, accepting without judgment their worlds colliding.

He declined the call with practiced efficiency, choosing instead to remain in this moment of shared understanding.

"Same time tomorrow?" Penelope asked as they prepared to return to their respective professional spaces. "I know another café that might surprise you."

"I'd like that."

The morning's shared coffee lingered in Reggie's thoughts, subtly changing the usual dynamic of his therapy session with Michael Bennett. Michael's session had taken an unexpected turn, his usual rigid posture softening as he spoke about his father's recent attempt at reconciliation.

"He surprisingly asked about my feelings," Michael said, his voice laced with wonder. "First time in forty years."

Reggie felt the weight of his own morning's revelations about his father. "Sometimes the hardest walls to break are the ones we've maintained the longest."

"Like your TV segment. It must have been a terrifying experience to be so open and exposed before such a big audience. Michael's insight caught Reggie off-guard, professional distance wavering.

"Perhaps that's exactly why it mattered," Reggie found himself saying, the words carrying fresh truth.

The breakthrough came quietly, as they often did. As Michael recounted a childhood memory—his father's relentless drive for perfection and the resulting inadequacy—his shoulders slumped, releasing tension.

"I used to hide in our garden," Michael admitted. "Only place I could just...be."

Reggie's mind flashed to Mrs. Crumble's roses, understanding flowing between therapist and client in a new way.

Reggie's notes took an unusual form as Michael, looking relieved, departed. He found himself noting not just professional observations but personal parallels––the shared weight of paternal expectations, the gradual discovery that perfection's cost might be too high.

Mrs. Crumble stopped by unexpectedly, as she sometimes did, with perfect timing and gentle wisdom. While pruning her roses, she thought of Reggie, so she decided to stop in. She sat down in the client chair, still wearing her gardening apron, which was dusted with soil.

"The roses told me you might need a moment of peace," she said, placing a small cutting from her prized lavender plant on his desk.

"The roses seem quite chatty lately," Reggie responded, his professional mask softening automatically in her presence.

"They know when someone's ready to bloom." Her eyes held knowing warmth. "Like your young man who came through just now. Sometimes growth requires letting go of old patterns."

The afternoon sun highlighted the fresh lavender as a comfortable silence filled the space around them. Mrs. Crumble's presence offered its usual clarity, helping him see the path forward.

"You're finding your way," she observed quietly. A comparison of your learned persona and your developing identity.

The truth settled in his chest, along with the memory of morning coffee and genuine laughter. "It's rather terrifying."

"The best growth usually is." She stood, patting his shoulder gently. "But you're stronger than you think, dear boy. Always have been."

As the city's edges softened in the evening light, Reggie collected his things, feeling the day's weight settle unusually. His tie, already loosened, came off entirely as he locked his office door. Having secured Freud in his carrier, Reggie opted for the longer way home, which was through the park.

The familiar path beckoned, gravel crunching beneath his shoes as he chose a different direction than his usual direct route home. The park's trees filtered the fading sunlight, their shadows painting patterns that matched his shifting thoughts.

A pair of ducks waddled past, unconcerned with his presence. Their simple acceptance of the moment struck him as profound after a day of such complexity. He found his usual solace by the small pond, yet felt more aware than usual.

The warmth from his coffee lingered in his memories of lunch with Penelope. Her laughter had changed the café's atmosphere, making the space feel less like an escape and more like a destination. The professional victories of the day——a breakthrough with Michael, standing firm with Cassandra, even the TV producer's continued support——felt secondary to those shared moments of genuine connection.

He observed subtle yet important alterations within himself. The way he'd handled Michael's session, allowing personal understanding to deepen professional insight rather than fighting to maintain perfect distance. Mrs. Crumble's lavender still carried its gentle message: growth requires space to bloom.

The upcoming TV segment seemed less intimidating now. Authenticity had served him better than perfection. The possibility of balancing public presence with personal truth felt more achievable, like finding steady ground after long uncertainty.

His mind was filled with Penelope, inspiring feelings of both fear and anticipation. Their meetings had become anchoring points to his day, each shared conversation building something he hadn't known he was missing. The careful walls between professional expertise and personal experience seemed less necessary, more limiting.

His phone felt heavy in his hand as he composed a message: *Today's sessions reminded me that sometimes the bravest choice is simply being real. Thank you for the coffee and the courage.*

Though tomorrow's schedule already included their usual coffee time, it now felt less planned and more spontaneous. The park's evening peace wrapped around him as he stood, ready to head home.

The city lights began their evening dance as he left the park, the day's insights settling into quiet certainty.

Chapter 9

Reggie arrived at his practice before the city had fully shaken off the morning chill. His shoes clicked against the polished floor of the empty corridor, each step carrying purpose. Once a fortress of professional excellence, the practice now felt like a space for genuine healing.

The smell of leather and old books greeted him as he opened his office door. His hands moved through the morning routine with practiced ease——curtains opening, desk organising, Freud's miniature chair positioning.

The unexpected flash of colour caught his eye immediately——a bouquet of sunrise-hued roses resting in Pam's careful arrangement on his desk. His fingers found the small card nestled among the blooms:

"For someone learning to bloom. - P"

"They arrived just as I was opening up," Pam offered with a warm smile, her tone carefully neutral despite the obvious pleasure in her eyes.

Halting mid-adjustment, Reggie paused his hand from his tie. The roses demanded attention, their presence both challenge and invitation. His schedule book lay open, the morning's first appointment not until nine-thirty.

The decision became unexpectedly clear. His usual methodical planning gave way to something more spontaneous as he gathered his coat. "I'll be back before the first client," he told Pam, her raised eyebrow suggesting she knew exactly where he was headed.

His professional stride softened into something more natural as he walked the streets, which felt different. Each step toward Penelope's shop peeled back the layers of Dr. Fitzwilliam's practiced persona, revealing more of the man simply known as Reggie.

He paused at the shop window, watching Penelope as she worked. Her movements held the same grace he'd noticed that first panic-driven visit, but now he allowed himself to truly see it.

The familiar bell announced his entrance, but this time he didn't need its sanctuary. Penelope's smile held the warmth of shared understanding as she looked up from her flowers.

"The roses were perfect," he said simply, professional eloquence giving way to genuine appreciation.

"Like someone I'm getting to know," she replied, her green eyes holding his with gentle certainty.

Reggie watched, mesmerised, as Penelope meticulously cared for her gorgeous roses. Her hands moved with practiced grace, each motion precise yet gentle. She trimmed away dead leaves and positioned blooms with an expertise that reminded him of his own careful approach to therapy - though her work produced far more immediate beauty.

As she worked, the morning light illuminated her face, highlighting the delicate shifts in her expression. A small frown of concentration when she encountered a stubborn stem, a soft smile of satisfaction when a bloom settled perfectly into place.

Sunlight caught her auburn hair, casting a soft halo that made her seem almost ethereal among the blooms.

"Dr. Fitzwilliam," Penelope said, her gaze fixed on the roses, "you're studying me very intensely." "Professional curiosity?"

Reggie felt warmth rise in his cheeks, caught in his observation. "Your technique," he managed, professional mask slipping slightly. "It's rather like therapy - knowing exactly where to make the cuts, how to encourage growth."

Penelope paused, green eyes meeting his with unexpected understanding. "Except I don't have to maintain quite so many professional boundaries with my roses." Her smile held gentle teasing as she set aside her pruning shears.

As the time approached for him to return to his practice, Reggie realised he felt more centred than any morning meditation had ever achieved. The prospect of his nine-thirty appointment no longer loomed as a professional obligation but as an opportunity to bring this same authentic presence to his work.

"Thank you," he said as he stood to leave, the words carrying more weight than a simple appreciation for roses.

Penelope's smile suggested she understood exactly what he meant. "Roses aren't the only things that need proper nurturing to bloom," she replied, her green eyes holding his for a moment longer than strictly necessary.

Reggie sank into his leather chair, the morning's warmth from Penelope's lingering as his first client arrived. Sarah Mitchell's familiar presence carried a different energy today, her eyes catching on the sunrise roses before finding her usual seat.

"They're beautiful," she offered, gesturing to the flowers. "They remind me of hope."

Reggie felt his professional mask shift, not dropping but softening. "Sometimes beauty appears just when we need it," he replied.

As Sarah began sharing her week's struggles, Reggie listened differently. Though he remained clinically distant, a warmer feeling was present in their conversation.

"I took your advice," Sarah said, "about being vulnerable with John. It was terrifying."

Reggie observed, "But you still did it," his own recent vulnerability giving him deeper insight. "That takes remarkable courage."

The session flowed with unusual ease, their therapeutic connection deepening as Reggie allowed his own growing insights to inform his guidance without compromising professional boundaries.

"How did you learn to trust again?" Sarah asked, the question hitting closer to home than she knew.

Reflecting on recent coffee shop conversations, he replied, "The goal isn't perfect safety.""Growth requires risk."

The door opened without warning, Cassandra's calculated interruption carrying familiar intent. "Oh, I'm sorry, I thought––"

"We're in session, Doctor Linton," Reggie interrupted, his quiet, authoritative voice replacing his usual defensive tone. My schedule makes it obvious.

Cassandra's retreat was sooner than anticipated, possibly due to the unexpected, stronger resistance. Reggie, though interrupted, returned his therapeutic attention to Sarah.

"I apologise for the interruption. Now, where were we? Ah yes, discussing courage in vulnerability."

By session's end, Sarah's posture and confidence had improved. "Thank you, Dr. Fitzwilliam. Something's different today...in a good way."

Reggie allowed himself a small smile as he made his final notes, the roses catching morning light like a quiet victory.

Reggie closed his leather-bound notebook, Sarah Mitchell's successful session settling into a quiet satisfaction. In his small chair, Freud, with his golden eyes, watched Reggie relax briefly between patients.

His phone buzzed with the producer's familiar number. "Dr. Fitzwilliam," she began, enthusiasm clear, "the audience response has been incredible. We'd like to expand your segment."

"Following our previous conversation," Reggie cut in, his voice now calm and steady. "The focus remains on healing, not entertainment."

"Naturally," she conceded, maybe taken aback by his calm assurance. "Your authenticity is what connects with viewers."

Reggie smiled, reviewing his afternoon; therapy and TV prep were harmoniously scheduled. His calendar showed a careful balance now—–professional commitments alongside coffee shop possibilities.

The cafe's inviting interior was visible through its large front window, adding to its cozy charm. Reggie spotted Penelope already seated at a corner table, her presence as warm as the aroma of freshly brewed coffee that filled the air.

His usual calculated movements softened as he navigated between comfortable chairs and potted plants, the space feeling more like a garden sanctuary than a coffee shop.

Penelope looked up from her book, her green eyes crinkling with genuine warmth. "Found it alright then?"

"Hard to miss with your excellent directions," Reggie replied with a soft smile.

The cafe hummed quietly, a perfect backdrop for conversation as others were lost in their own thoughts. Penelope had already ordered his coffee; she'd been paying attention to his preferences.

"Black, two sugars," she said, pushing the cup toward him. "I took a chance."

"A successful hypothesis," he offered, surprising himself with the easy banter.

A comfortable, content silence settled between them, needing no words. Sunlight caught the edge of Penelope's auburn curls, and Reggie studied how they caught the light instead of analysing the moment.

With gentle curiosity, Penelope inquired about young Reggie. "Before the perfect suits and television appearances."

His vulnerability and defensiveness should have been apparent. Instead, the story of his first therapy client——a neighbour's cat with apparent anxiety——spilled out naturally, drawing genuine laughter from both.

"So, you've always had a way with troubled souls," Penelope observed, her insight warming rather than threatening.

Reggie concurred, explaining how this, despite the four legs, resulted in Freud's adoption. "He interviewed several therapists before choosing me."

Their chat turned professional but remained friendly. "The producer wants to expand the segment," he shared.

"And how do you feel about that?" Penelope asked, the question carrying no agenda beyond genuine interest.

"Surprisingly comfortable," Reggie admitted. This feels less like a performance and more like growth.

"Growth often does," she offered, understanding in her smile.

The cafe's clock moved too quickly, afternoon appointments looming. Still, they both lingered, relishing the remaining time together.

"Same time Friday?" Penelope suggested, hope and certainty mixing in her voice.

"Yes, please," Reggie said, his words flowing effortlessly. Hesitantly, they paused at the doorway, reluctant to end the magical moment. The afternoon light painted everything in gentle gold, making promises about possibilities neither was quite ready to name.

Reggie made his way back to his workspace, with the aroma of his midday brew still drifting through his consciousness. The familiar space felt different somehow, as if the walls had absorbed some of the warmth from his time with Penelope. Freud looked up from his therapy perch, golden eyes studying his human's relaxed demeanour with apparent approval.

Settling into his chair, he was embraced by the quiet as the late afternoon sun threw soft shadows across his desk. His usual need to restore professional order immediately felt less urgent, the transition from personal to professional space flowing more naturally.

"Quite an afternoon, old friend," he murmured to Freud, who responded with a knowing purr.

His hands moved automatically to organise the day's session notes, the familiar routine grounding him. The email from the producer concerning next week's segment remained in his inbox, its usual anxiety-inducing effect absent. His fingers traced the outline for the upcoming show——*Breaking Down Barriers: Why Emotional Walls Keep Us Apart*.

Reggie examined his schedule; next week's appointments and television commitments melded into a manageable whole instead of conflicting demands. The balance felt possible, less like a tightrope walk and more like a natural flow between different aspects of himself.

His mind wandered back to the café, remembering Penelope's authentic interest in Reggie's initial therapy client. The memory brought a smile to his face.

"I'm actually enjoying the uncertainty," he admitted to Freud, the revelation surprising them both.

The sound of Cassandra's heels in the hallway preceded her "casual" entrance. She leaned against his doorframe with less force than normal.

"Quite the extended lunch break," she observed, her tone probing for weakness.

Reggie continued organising his notes, his response measured but defensive.

"Time well spent, actually. The show's segment on breaking down barriers practically wrote itself."

Cassandra's subtle frown hinted that she'd hoped for a different reaction. The Psychology Council may raise doubts about——

"The Council," Reggie interrupted smoothly, "has already approved my schedule adjustments. Your professional concern has been noted.

The quiet confidence in his voice seemed to catch them both by surprise. Unlike her usual self, Cassandra quickly retreated, leaving Reggie to enjoy the calm that came from effortlessly and calmly setting boundaries.

His office felt more his own now, the space reflecting not just professional accomplishment but personal growth. Penelope's morning flowers, bathed in the late afternoon light, served as a reminder that some things only bloom naturally with time and space.

The evening air carried a gentle warmth as Reggie gathered his belongings, each movement unhurried. Contemplation replaced his normal brisk efficiency as he straightened his desk for the final time. Freud watched from his perch, whiskers twitching with apparent approval at his human's relaxed demeanour.

The practice halls echoed differently at this hour, his footsteps marking a steady rhythm as he made his way toward the exit. Pam's early departure and knowing smile implied a deeper understanding of his afternoon at the cafe than she let on.

Stepping out into the fading light with his feline companion secured in the travel cage, Reggie chose the winding path through the parklands to his apartment, his typical drive for efficiency surrendered.

The hours slipped by unnoticed as he processed the day's events. The morning's flowers, Cassandra's retreat, the producer's enthusiasm - each piece settling into place with unexpected ease. But it was the cafe moments that lingered most vividly: Penelope's genuine interest in his work, her quiet understanding of his careful steps toward authenticity.

The park's central fountain came into view, its steady sound matching his thoughtful pace. Personal growth gave new perspective to his professional successes. His successful handling of Cassandra felt less about maintaining control and more about simply standing in his truth.

His phone weighed in his pocket, Penelope's last message still unanswered. Comfortably seated on the bench, he composed his response, fingers pausing above the keys before typing: Today's coffee was perfect. *Tomorrow deserves an encore.*

Her reply came quickly: *Same time, same place, even better conversation?*

Looking forward to it, he sent back.

The path home beckoned as evening settled more firmly around him. Each step carried him forward with quiet certainty, the day's warmth still presents in memory and promise.

Chapter 10

Reggie arrived early at his practice, the air unusually heavy—an unease settling in his chest before he even opened the door. His footsteps echoed through the quiet halls as he made his way to his office, Freud's travel cage swaying gently in his grip.

An unusual quiet hung in the office, a stillness before the workday began. As he settled Freud into his usual spot, the cat's ears twitched with unusual alertness, golden eyes tracking something unseen. Reggie's hand moved automatically to straighten his tie, the familiar gesture offering little of its usual comfort.

Reggie sat at his desk, the hum of his computer filling the silence of the early morning. His inbox was already teeming with emails, but one subject line froze him mid-sip of his coffee: **"Notice of Investigation – Allegation of Serious Professional Misconduct."**

He clicked it open, his stomach knotting, dread spreading like ink with each line.

"Dear Dr. Fitzwilliam, The Psychology Council of NSW has received a formal complaint alleging serious professional

misconduct. The complaint, filed by Ms. Lily Thompson, includes accusations of inappropriate therapeutic boundaries and unethical conduct during your sessions. The allegations are under investigation and have been referred to the Heath Care Complaints Commission (HCCC). You are required to submit a formal response within 14 days.

*Failure to respond promptly may result in further disciplinary action, up to and including suspension of your registration pending the outcome of the investigation."**

Reggie's heart pounded as he opened the attached document. It was meticulous—Lily had accused him of making inappropriate personal remarks, breaching confidentiality, and acting in a manner that blurred the professional-client relationship. She claimed that these actions had caused her emotional harm and undermined her trust in therapy.

His eyes scanned the details:

- *"During one session, Dr. Fitzwilliam made a personal comment about my appearance that I found unsettling."*

- *"I later discovered that aspects of my case were referenced—albeit anonymously—on a public platform, which left me feeling exposed."*

- *"His behaviour created confusion about the boundaries of our professional relationship, leaving me feeling unsafe and unsupported."*

It felt as though the air had vanished from the room. These weren't just accusations about his practice—they struck at his character. His reputation, his clients, his livelihood—all of it was now at risk.

For closer examination, Reggie printed and reread the document multiple times.

A sharp knock at the door snapped him out of his spiralling thoughts. Pam stepped in, balancing a tray of tea. Her calm composure cracked the moment she saw his expression. "Reggie, what's wrong?"

He gave her the printed complaint. "Lily Thompson has filed a formal complaint with the Psychology Council. She's accusing me of serious misconduct."

Pam quickly read the document, her brow furrowing. "This... this doesn't even sound like you. 'Unsettling personal remarks'? 'Breaching confidentiality'? Reggie, you would never cross those lines."

"I know," Reggie said tightly, running a hand through his hair. "But she's painted a picture that will look damning to an investigator. If they decide there's enough merit to her complaint, they could suspend my registration."

Pam set the paper down and crossed her arms. "You need to call Deborah Matthews. This isn't something you can handle on your own."

Reggie nodded. "I already forwarded it to her. But if this gets out, it'll destroy everything I've built. Even if I'm cleared, the stain on my reputation—"He broke off, unable to finish the sentence.

Unbeknownst to them, Cassandra stood just outside the door, her hand frozen on the door frame. She had come to drop off some paperwork but stopped when she overheard Lily's name. A satisfied smirk played on her lips as she leaned closer, eavesdropping on their conversation.

Pam's voice lowered, but her frustration was evident. "I've worked with you for years, Reggie. I know your integrity. Someone's pulling strings to make this happen."

Cassandra stepped into the room; her expression carefully crafted to show concern. "Reggie, I couldn't help but overhear... a complaint. What's going on?"

Reggie maintained his position behind his desk, physical barrier matching his emotional ones. "Thank you for your concern, Dr. Linton. I have it well in hand."

Her attempt at sympathetic understanding fell flat against his professional shield.

The Psychology Council's investigations, particularly when the HCCC is involved, are known to be very detailed. If you need any support..."

"That won't be necessary," his voice carried quiet authority that left no room for further discussion.

His phone vibrated with Penelope's morning message, their coffee plans now complicated by this new development. His response took longer to craft than usual, professional distance creeping into personal connection as self-protection rose instinctively.

Once the morning routine began, Reggie purposefully took his usual spot. Client files arranged with extra precision, schedule reviewed with heightened attention. Each action built his professional shield higher, creating the distance from both threat and connection.

Freud, perched on his therapy spot, watched intently, his tail giving occasional twitches as his human performed these controlled movements. The morning light strengthened gradually, but the shadows seemed reluctant to fully retreat from the office corners.

Upon Rita Williams' arrival, Reggie observed the morning light had moved to its calming angle in his office. His hand moved automatically to adjust his tie, the gesture more shield than habit now. Freud maintained his professional position, though his tail twitched with unusual alertness.

"Good morning, Rita. Please, have a seat." Despite the morning's turmoil, his voice projected a practiced, warm professionalism.

Seated comfortably in the leather chair, Rita launched into her weekly report. Reggie nodded at intervals, his therapeutic training maintaining the session's rhythm despite the ethics complaint weighing heavily on his thoughts.

"Dr. Fitzwilliam?" Rita's voice cut through his momentary distraction. "You seem unlike yourself today."

Reggie shifted slightly, professional mask strengthening. Rita let's concentrate on how you're doing. You were discussing your workplace boundaries?"

His thoughts wandered to the complaint, Penelope's unanswered message, and Cassandra's satisfied smile. Each intrusive thought met firm professional resistance as he guided the session back to its therapeutic purpose.

Rita's tale of workplace conflict mirrored his own, causing him unease. "I felt like everything I'd built was under attack," she explained, unknowingly echoing his morning's revelation.

His phone vibrated silently––his lawyer's name appearing briefly before he turned it face down. Despite the outside crisis, professional ethics ensured the session's priority.

"And how did you maintain your boundaries?" he asked, the question serving both client and therapist.

As he saw his reflection in the window—perfect tie, perfect posture, perfect professional facade masking the morning's flaws—Rita's reply grew fainter. The ethics complaint seemed to sit on his desk like a physical presence, though it existed only in his email.

"That's a significant insight, Rita," he responded automatically, therapeutic training bridging his momentary distance.

The session concluded with appropriate therapeutic progress noted, his pen moving across the page with deliberate precision. Meticulous word choices and professional documentation ensured excellence, even amidst the brewing external storm.

As Rita's footsteps faded down the hallway, Reggie allowed himself one moment of truth. His hands were flat on his desk; his shoulders slumped under the weight of professional and personal burdens. The morning's bright promise had transformed into something heavier, demanding choices he wasn't ready to face.

The next client's arrival time approached on his perfectly synchronised clock. Reggie straightened his tie once more, professional armour settling back into place. Though an ethics complaint lingered in his inbox, he prioritised the need to provide the best possible therapy.

The lawyer's presence was formidable as Deborah Matthews, SC, stepped into Reggie's office, her tailored suit and efficient stride exuding authority. Her briefcase, carefully fastened, suggested the immense challenge that lay before her. Reggie stood to greet her, his tie perfectly aligned, every movement deliberate—a man determined to project control even as the ground beneath him threatened to crumble.

"Dr. Fitzwilliam," Deborah began, settling into the client chair opposite him. Her intense stare surveyed the room, changing the comfortable therapy space into a place of conflict. "We need to address the Thompson complaint immediately. This is no small matter."

Reggie's hands remained steady as he slid the printed complaint across the desk. "You've seen the allegations?"

"I have." She retrieved a pair of reading glasses from her briefcase and reviewed the document again, her expression unreadable. The allegations are serious - crossing boundaries, causing emotional harm, and breaking confidentiality. Each one carefully constructed to erode your credibility."

Reggie inhaled deeply, struggling to keep his voice measured. "It's completely unfounded. My conduct was professional; I did not breach confidentiality or make inappropriate remarks. But the way it's written..."

"...is designed to make you look guilty," Deborah finished, her tone clipped. This was expertly written to exploit the language of professional ethics. It's strategic and malicious."

He nodded, leaning forward. "It's the timing. It coincides with the announcement of my television appearances. Someone is attempting to exploit this to ruin my reputation."

Deborah set the complaint aside and fixed him with a steely gaze. "We need to treat this with the utmost seriousness, Reggie. A NSW Psychology Council complaint, forwarded to the Health Care Complaints Commission, could threaten your registration. If they decide to pursue an investigation, it won't just be about this one client—they'll dig into every part of your practice."

Reggie's stomach churned. "And the television show?"

Deborah exhaled sharply. "It's a vulnerability. Public exposure while under investigation could make you look unprofessional, even unethical. We may need to put your appearances on hold, at least for a while.

His phone vibrated on the desk—a call from the producer. It was the third time they'd tried to reach him that morning. Reggie silenced it, but Deborah's pointed glance made it clear she noticed.

"This isn't just about optics," she said. "It's about protecting your reputation, your practice, and your future. Going forward, all decisions must be made to protect your professional integrity.

Before he could respond, a soft knock interrupted them. Cassandra stepped inside; her expression carefully composed. "Oh, I'm sorry," she said with practiced concern."I didn't realise you were in the middle of a consultation."

Her eyes flicked to Deborah then back to Reggie. "I just wanted to say how sorry I am to hear about... all this. If there's anything I can do to help, please let me know."

Reggie's professional mask slipped into place as he gestured toward the door. "Thank you, Dr. Linton. I appreciate your concern, but we're managing the situation."

Cassandra lingered, her voice soft and sympathetic. "It's just such an awful thing to go through. You don't deserve this."

Reggie recognised the subtle manipulation in her words, the calculated sympathy designed to lull him into complacency. He met her gaze evenly, his tone steady. "Thank you for your support, Dr. Linton."

As Cassandra left, Deborah leaned back, her face hardening. "She's a sly one," she declared bluntly.

Reggie rubbed his temples, exhaustion settling over him. "I'll deal with her later. Our immediate priority is the response.

Deborah nodded, returning to the documents in front of her. "Tomorrow, I'll draft an initial reply to the Psychology Council, but you'll need to review it carefully. The stakes are high, Reggie. If they find cause to escalate this, you could face license suspension—or worse."

The words hung in the air, heavy and unyielding. The office, once a sanctuary, now felt like a cage. As Deborah outlined the steps ahead, Reggie felt the weight of every decision pressing down on him. Protecting his practice meant sacrifices—distance, control, and walls he couldn't afford to let crumble.

Each step forward felt heavier than the last, but Reggie knew there was no turning back.

In the quiet after Deborah left, Reggie allowed himself one moment of acknowledgment. The morning's bright possibilities now lay buried beneath professional necessity, personal joy becoming a liability in the face of crisis.

An unusual energy now filled his usually healing office. The walls that had glowed rose higher, stronger than necessary. Excellence demanded nothing less.

Reggie, surrounded by papers, meticulously reviewed Lily Thompson's file. Each session note stood as testament to professional boundaries maintained, therapeutic progress documented with precise care. With steady strokes, he charted their collaboration on the legal pad.

"Treatment goals met... appropriate termination... continued progress reported..." Reggie muttered, his voice barely audible as he constructed his defence. The familiar weight of excellence pressed against his shoulders while he gathered evidence of his professional standards.

He lingered over the final notes from the session. Something in Lily's last visit had shifted, though his documentation revealed nothing concrete. Professional instinct suggested manipulation he hadn't recognised then, too focused on celebrating her progress.

As he chronologically organised his records, the clock's steady ticking heightened his awareness of time. Each paper represented another brick in his professional wall, evidence of boundaries maintained, and ethics upheld. His fingers followed the outline of his hard-earned therapist registration, the weight of that accomplishment fresh in his mind.

With cruel precision, 2:50 PM approached. The usual anticipation of afternoon coffee twisted into something sharper as he maintained his chosen distance. Through his window, he caught glimpses of people entering the café across the street. The weight of his loss was compounded by the professional demands that prevented him from connecting with his emotions.

The cafe's afternoon crowd gathered below his window. His eyes caught on empty tables where possibilities had bloomed, now sacrificed to professional necessity. His position, while secure, felt limiting; excellence, as always, demanded its price.

His calendar lay open, future appointments stretching ahead in neat rows. Each slot represented another chance to maintain a perfect professional distance, to protect what he'd built through careful control and precise boundaries. As he rearranged his schedule, the cost sank deep, erasing pockets of personal happiness.

Reggie straightened his tie, the gesture automatic as he reviewed his position. The path forward narrowed to familiar territory––professional excellence above personal connection, walls rising higher with each careful choice.

Reggie's office grew dim as the grandfather clock ticked away the afternoon, its sound echoing in the quiet space. His shoulders carried the weight of the day's defensive manoeuvres, each careful response draining more energy than he cared to admit. His usual safe space felt like both a refuge and a prison, his control held only by his professional training.

Cassandra's entrance carried calculated timing, her knock perfunctory before claiming space in his office. Her carefully crafted concern didn't quite mask the predatory gleam in her eyes.

"Reginald, I thought we should discuss the situation." A false warmth laced her voice as she sat down in the client chair without invitation. "Given my past experience on the Psychology Council..."

Reggie maintained his seated position, professional mask firmly in place. "Indeed. Your experience appears especially pertinent to current events.

"Lily Thompson was quite distressed when she came to me." Cassandra's words carried precise weight. Her worries centre on your TV appearances and the boundary issues they presented.

"Interesting timing." Reggie's voice stayed calm as comprehension dawned on him. "Her complaint coinciding with your interest in the television segment."

Cassandra's smile tightened. "I merely provided a concerned former patient of yours with appropriate guidance."

"After approaching her specifically about my media presence?" The question hung between them, sharp with clarity.

The Psychology Council considers these issues to be extremely important. Her threat wrapped in professional concern. Reducing your public appearances might be a good idea.

Reggie straightened in his chair, professional authority settling around him like armour. Cassandra, I maintain impeccable therapeutic boundaries. As the council will confirm."

"The network might prefer less...complicated talent." Her words carried calculated weight.

My expertise led to my hiring by the network. His response held quiet strength. "Not my ability to be manipulated."

Cassandra's mask slipped, briefly showing her frustrated ambition. "You're risking everything for what? Television fame? A florist?"

"I'm protecting my practice from manufactured crisis." His boundary held firm. "Your concern is noted. And unnecessary."

Tense seconds ticked by on the grandfather clock as they were measured across his desk. Despite a high personal price, professional detachment ensured flawless control.

"You've always been so careful, Reginald." Cassandra rose, adjusting her jacket. That change would be a real shame.

"Indeed." His response carried quiet warning. "Professional ethics matter deeply to me. All aspects of them."

Her exit left disturbed air in its wake, reality settling heavily in the space she vacated. Reggie remained at his desk, strategy forming as he accepted the path ahead. The growing professional distance would shield what mattered most; it served a crucial purpose.

As he prepared for what was to come, the clock ticked on steadily. His office held different energy now, sanctuary becoming fortress as he accepted the cost of preservation.

With methodical care, Reggie secured each file, the familiar routine now laden with significance as evidence and defence were perfectly aligned. Lily Thompson's file took centre position, each documented interaction a testament to professional boundaries maintained. As he planned for tomorrow, the fading light outside mirrored his somber mood.

His phone held a string of missed calls and messages——the producer's concern, his lawyer's caution, and Penelope's silence all demanding different attention. The last thought caught unexpectedly, a personal cost he hadn't quite prepared for.

From his office window, Reggie clinically analysed the situation. Cassandra's manipulation revealed a simple strategy––the Psychology Council complaint timed perfectly with the television opportunity with Lily Thompson's distress weaponised for professional gain. Understanding settled like evening shadows. Some battles were timed strategically.

The walk home felt longer than usual, each step measuring the cost of his chosen path. His phone remained heavy in his pocket, Penelope's unanswered messages a tangible weight. Protection required distance, he reminded himself. Professional preservation demanded its price.

Tomorrow's strategy formed with each step. Deborah's meticulously documented defence of my case, detailing every interaction, would be submitted to the Psychology Council. The television show...that decision carried different implications now. To protect one's career, a temporary retreat may be necessary; strategic withdrawal offers strength, unlike public vulnerability.

Reality settled around him like his perfectly tailored suit. The path ahead held obvious purpose now, resolve strengthening with each step toward home. He would reclaim control through a perfect professional response, meeting each challenge with measured expertise.

The evening air, scented with flowers from a nearby garden, evoked memories of past expenses and decisions. Tomorrow would bring its own battles but tonight held clarity of purpose. Professional preservation had its own kind of peace, even as personal possibilities faded with the day's light.

His apartment building approached through gathering darkness, tomorrow's schedule already forming in his mind. Each step forward carried professional certainty, control reclaimed through careful planning, and perfect distance. The night claimed its territory as Reggie moved toward home, a path with grim resolve.

Chapter 11

The morning papers arrived with brutal precision, their screaming headlines tearing through Reggie's carefully composed breakfast ritual. "TV THERAPIST MISCONDUCT SCANDAL" blazed from the *Daily Post*, while *the Chronicle's* more measured "RELATIONSHIP EXPERT FACES SERIOUS ALLEGATIONS" carried equal weight. His tea grew cold as he scanned each article, professional reputation dissected in precise column inches.

Cassandra's strategic quotes, laced with "professional concern" for his patients, subtly revealed her careful manipulation. Lily Thompson's distress painted in emotional detail, while his own professional boundaries transformed into cold distance under media scrutiny.

His phone erupted with notifications--colleagues, producers, patients all demanding responses. His lawyer's call cut through the chaos with sharp clarity:

"Say nothing publicly. We'll issue a statement by noon. Every interaction must go through proper channels now."

Reggie tightened his grip on his tie, grounding himself in strategy. Their defence would need to be flawless. His professional mask settled into place with practiced ease, though the morning's headlines had shaken its foundations.

Entering the practice felt like running a gauntlet—cameras and reporters transforming his sanctuary into hostile ground. Questions flew like arrows.

"Dr. Fitzwilliam, how do you respond to the serious allegations?"

"What about your future television appearances?"

"Did you breach professional standards?"

His silence maintained professional dignity as he moved through their barrage, each step measured, every gesture controlled. The practice door closed behind him with blessed finality, though its usual protection felt temporary now.

With quiet efficiency, Pam waited, her computer displaying their altered schedule. Her calm presence offered familiar support as they managed the morning's crisis.

"I've moved your sensitive cases to Dr. Harrison," she reported. "The board wants your response by five, and your lawyer needs the notes on the Thompson file."

As Reggie reviewed each article under the fluorescent lights, the practice's quiet efficiency enveloped him, exposing the accusations within. Lily Thompson's complaints, carefully weaponised, carried strategic weight and distress. The truth revealed itself in careful reading——professional expertise transformed into calculated distance, therapeutic boundaries twisted into emotional abandonment.

To Reggie, the NSW Psychology Council's conference room resembled a courtroom, its polished oak and leather exuding professional gravity. His tie, knotted with surgical precision, felt more like armour than fabric as he stepped into the hearing room. The panel consisting of the Psychology Council of NSW and the Health Care Complaints Commission (HCCC) members' faces revealed nothing as he took his seat, their collective presence forming a wall of professional scrutiny.

With meticulous care, Board Chairman Dr. Eleanor Matthews readjusted her glasses. "Dr. Fitzwilliam, we're here to address serious allegations regarding your professional conduct."

Reggie stayed calm as serious charges of unethical behaviour, boundary crossing, and confidentiality breaches surfaced. Each accusation landed with calculated weight, Lily Thompson's complaints woven through with strategic precision. His lawyer's steady presence beside him offered silent support as they listened.

"Ms. Thompson alleges multiple instances of unethical conduct and inappropriate therapeutic boundaries, along with a breach of confidentiality," Dr. Matthews continued, her tone carrying careful neutrality.

Reggie responded calmly and deliberately, his evidence meticulously organised. Session notes revealed consistent boundaries, professional standards maintained with exacting care. Each interaction documented precisely, therapeutic progress tracked with careful attention.

"My actions clearly followed ethical guidelines," he said, his voice calm despite the pressure. The evidence mounted in careful order——correspondence, treatment plans, and professional boundaries maintained without deviation.

Cassandra's arrival carried a fake sense of concern, her testimony wrapped in professional courtesy that barely masked its true intent. Given my role as Ms. Thompson's current therapist, I felt compelled to alert the panel to her distress.

Reggie recognised the manipulation beneath her words. Years of professional rivalry crystallising into this moment. Her carefully crafted narrative transformed therapeutic boundaries into weapons of accusation, professional confidentiality into a tool for sabotage and her deliberate misinterpretation of the professional-client relationship into an attack on his integrity. Yet he maintained his calm, understanding that the reaction would only serve her purpose.

The weight of potential career consequences pressed down on him as he defended his reputation. This moment of judgment is the culmination of years of careful practice, professional expertise, and therapeutic success. Television opportunities, speaking engagements, his entire future hanging on the panel's decision.

His resolve strengthened with each passing moment, professional truth standing firm against calculated attack. The evidence spoke clearly for those willing to see——consistent care, maintained boundaries, therapeutic progress documented with precise attention.

Dr. Matthews' voice cut through his thoughts. "The board will require time to review all evidence presented. We'll have our decision by 2pm."

The weight of their imminent judgment bore down on Reggie as he gathered his materials, his every move measured against his professional reputation. His professional future rested solely on their decision, focusing entirely on this pivotal moment.

Reggie returned a few hours later for the verdict, each step carrying the weight of his entire career, and the Psychology Council of NSW conference room felt colder. His perfectly pressed suit offered little comfort against the chill of judgment. Through the window, he glimpsed gathering media, their presence a stark reminder of how public this private battle had become.

Dr. Matthews cleared her throat, the sound echoing in the oppressive silence. Panel members arranged their papers with deliberate care, their expressions carefully neutral. Reggie's heart hammered in his chest, but he stayed outwardly calm.

Dr. Matthews, her voice authoritative, addressed Dr. Reginald Fitzwilliam, stating that the NSW Psychology Council and Health Care Complaints Commission had reviewed all evidence concerning Ms. Lily Thompson's complaints.

His fingers pressed against the armrests, knuckles whitening beneath professional control. Each word fell like a gavel strike.

"We find substantial evidence supporting the allegations of unethical conduct and breach of therapeutic boundaries. However, we find no evidence in breach of confidentiality." The words sliced through his carefully maintained composure. Your recent public appearances have also raised concerns regarding your professional conduct.

As Dr. Matthews read Section 150 of the Health Practitioners Regulation National Law (NSW), she suspended Reggie's Psychologist's Registration for six months pending review, Reggie's world shrank to a pinpoint.

The carefully constructed walls of his professional life began to crumble. Television opportunities, speaking engagements, his practice——everything he'd built with such precise care, dissolving under the weight of calculated betrayal.

Exiting the back door to avoid the waiting media, Reggie maintained his dignified stride, each step toward his office a study in controlled devastation. His usual safe haven of work now felt like a monument to his failed professional ambitions.

Reggie walked slowly down the practice corridor, each step measured. The suspension letter in his hand felt far heavier than a single page should. With a blend of concern and respect, staff members watched him go, their hushed discussions ceasing as he walked by. He kept his head high, professional mask firmly in place, though his heart sat like lead in his chest.

Outside his office, Pam waited with red-rimmed eyes and a stack of appointment cards. Her usual efficiency warred with obvious emotion as she outlined the afternoon's tasks.

"I've started calling tomorrow morning appointments," she began, voice wavering. "But the afternoon clients——"

"Thank you, Pammy." Reggie's own voice threatened to break. "We'll need to arrange referrals."

Although tears welled in Pam's eyes, she held her posture straight. "I've prepared a list of colleagues who might take emergency cases. And Dr. Montgomery has offered to handle your crisis clients."

The familiar click of his office door opening immediately caught Freud's attention. Forgetting his usual composure, the cat anxiously circled Reggie's legs, his golden eyes showing worry. Now, the space felt less like a sanctuary and more a reminder of everything on pause.

Silence pressed against his ears as Reggie settled at his desk. Files waited in precise order——each client's journey carefully documented, each relationship now requiring careful transition. His hand trembled slightly as he reached for the first folder.

"Dr. Harrison has space for the Harris family," Pam offered quietly, tablet in hand. "And Dr. Chen can take Mr. Roberts."

Reggie nodded, throat tight. "Make sure you covey my sincere apologise."

Each referral felt like a small betrayal, necessary but painful. Years of trust carefully built, now requiring gentle transfer to capable colleagues. His pen moved steadily across recommendation letters, each word chosen to ensure continuity of care

Through his window, he could see Penelope's shop across the street, its warm light now unreachable. The thought of her learning about this through headlines, of her name being dragged into this mess if anyone discovered their coffee meetings, solidified his resolve.

His phone showed three missed calls from her, each one an accusation of trust he couldn't afford to maintain. Protection, he realised, sometimes meant ensuring others couldn't be hurt by association. With careful precision, he blocked her number, adding one more brick to walls that now seemed more necessary than ever.

Reggie approached Penelope's shop for the last time. Each step felt heavier than the last, his perfectly polished shoes carrying him toward a necessary devastation. The once welcoming shop, usually radiating warmth, now symbolised the things he had to protect by destroying it.

Gazing in the shop window, he barely recognised the impeccably dressed man staring back; his eyes burdened by difficult decisions. Through the glass, he could see Penelope arranging flowers, her movements carrying the grace that had first caught his attention. The sight made his chest ache.

The bell's cheerful chime felt like a betrayal as he pushed open the door. Penelope looked up, her smile blooming then fading as she caught his expression. The professional mask he'd perfected over years felt like lead on his face.

"Reggie?" She sounded worried, though he hadn't earned her concern. "I've been trying to reach you."

"I know." The words came out clipped, controlled. Perfect distance in two syllables.

She set down her flowers, moving toward him with the natural warmth he'd have to extinguish. "I saw the news. You don't have to handle this alone."

"Indeed, I do." His voice maintained its careful neutrality, each word chosen for maximum effect."That's why I'm here

Comprehension dawned in her eyes, their green fading like autumn leaves. "Don't do this."

"The board's decision is final." He kept his hands clasped behind his back, maintaining physical distance to match the emotional walls rising. "My practice is suspended for the next six months. My reputation is destroyed. I can't...I won't let anyone else suffer because of me.

"I don't care about——"

"But I do." The interruption came sharp, necessary. "Everything I touch turns to ashes right now. I won't let that include you."

Penelope stepped closer, her movement forcing him to take a step back. The hurt in her eyes cut deeper than any ethics board judgment.

"So, you're choosing to push everyone away? That's your solution?"

I'm safeguarding what's valuable to me. His voice remained steady even as his heart shattered. "Some distance is necessary."

"That's not protection, Reggie. That's fear."

The truth in her words threatened to crack his resolve. He straightened his spine, channelling every lesson in perfect control of his father had ever taught.

"Perhaps. But it's my choice to make."

She reached for him, but he moved back again, maintaining the growing chasm between them. Each inch felt like miles.

"Please don't do this," she whispered.

"It's already done." The words came out perfect, practiced, poisonous. "Goodbye, Penelope."

As he left, the cheerful bell mocked him, its sound a stark contrast to the warmth he'd finally come to trust. Though each step was agony, he held his posture, pace, and control perfectly.

He didn't look back. He couldn't. Some sacrifices demanded absolute commitment, even as they destroyed everything worth saving.

The brass nameplate on Dr. Anne Montgomery's door gleamed dully as Reggie stood before it, his usual professional composure hanging by threads. His trembling hand, clutching the suspension letter, reached for the therapy office door; entering felt different now.

Anne's warm office held none of his precise arrangements, its comfortable chaos a stark contrast to his carefully curated space. The leather chair creaked as he sank into it, his perfectly pressed suit feeling more like a straitjacket than armour.

"It's been a long time, Reggie." Anne's voice carried the weight of twenty years of counselling and professional respect.

His careful walls, already cracking, began to crumble under her gentle scrutiny. The tie that had felt like a noose all morning now hung loose around his neck, his usual perfect posture abandoning him as he leaned forward, elbows on knees.

His voice cracked, revealing an uncharacteristic vulnerability as he confessed his lack of knowledge. "I don't know how to be on this side."

The silence from Anne gave him the room his professional experience required. The afternoon light caught dust motes dancing between them, each moment of quiet drawing out more truth than he'd allowed himself in years.

"Everything I built..." his voice cracked. "Everything I am...."

His father's voice echoed in the silence, *"Excellence demands perfection, son. Anything less is failure."*

The weight of generational expectations pressed down, each carefully constructed achievement now lying in ruins around him. After placing the suspension letting forcefully on the table, his hands twisted together, professional composure finally shattering completely.

"Suspended... six months... the practice," he managed, each word carrying fresh pain. "My clients... Pam... Penelope...."

He felt something break loose inside him when he heard her name. The memory of her shop's warmth, her gentle understanding, the safety he'd walked away from——each remembrance cutting deeper than the last.

His admission, "I pushed her away," carried all the weight of his carefully constructed walls. "Thinking I was protecting her."

Anne's soft "Tell me about her" unleashed emotions he was unaware of.

"She saw me," his voice was barely audible. "Not Dr. Fitzwilliam. Not my father's son. Just...me. And I couldn't...I didn't know how to...."

The truth he'd been avoiding finally surfaced: "I don't know who I am without the practice. Except for the perfect reputation. Minus...."

"Without the walls?" Anne's gentle prompt carried years of professional understanding. Reggie, nodded slowly.

"Sometimes our greatest fear isn't failing others, but letting them see us fail," Anne shared gently.

The future loomed dark and uncertain, each carefully planned step now lost in shadow. Yet Anne's steady presence offered something he'd forgotten how to accept——support without expectation, understanding without judgment.

"Where do I even start?" The question carried all the weight of his shattered world.

"That's already happened," Anne stated softly, confidently. "You're here."

The key turned heavily in Reggie's apartment lock; each familiar motion now weighted with fresh meaning. Darkness greeted him, broken only by city lights filtering through windows he'd forgotten to shade that morning. In the silence, the sound of his dress shoes clicking on the hardwood floor felt strange and out of place.

Freud's quiet "myrrh" of welcome carried none of his usual judgment, the cat's golden eyes reflecting understanding beyond human capacity. His faithful companion padded closer, offering silent support as Reggie stood motionless in his own entryway, unable to fully step into this space that no longer felt like home.

The pile of unopened professional journals mocked him from the side table, their glossy covers reflecting city light. Each one probably contained an article he'd written, advice he'd given, expertise he'd shared. His practice keys sat heavy in his palm, the metal warm from being clutched throughout his therapy session with Anne.

Framed photos caught his eye--graduation, his practice opening, book launches. Each perfect moment captured and displayed, his father's proud smile never quite reaching his eyes. *"Excellence demands perfection, son."* The words echoed differently now, their poison finally clear.

The window drew him like a magnet, city lights blurring as he searched for one darkened shop. Penelope's shop was far in the distance, the space where warmth and possibility once lived now as dark as his future. His normally tidy desk held an abandoned coffee cup, a symbol of his life's increasing chaos.

Anne's words from their session replayed: "Sometimes our greatest fear isn't failing others, but letting them see us fail." The truth of it ached in his chest, each carefully constructed wall now revealing its true purpose——not keeping others out, but keeping his own fear contained.

Freud's warm weight pressed against his leg, offering comfort without demand. For the first time since the panel's verdict, since walking away from Penelope's shop, since watching his carefully constructed life crumble, Reggie allowed the tears to fall. His professional mask finally dropped completely, leaving only the man beneath; a man who was scared, uncertain, and devastatingly real.

Chapter 12

Newspapers thudded against Reggie's door, weighted with more than headlines. He stood frozen in his kitchen, the automatic coffee maker gurgling in mockery of his normal routine. Freud watched from his perch, golden eyes radiating the concern Reggie couldn't yet face.

Shaking, Reggie picked up the papers, their bold headlines accusing: "RESPECTED THERAPIST'S REGISTRATION SUSPENDED!" The words blurred before his eyes, but their impact remained crystal clear. His perfectly ordered morning, like his perfectly ordered life, lay in ruins at his feet.

With mechanical precision, the TV turned on; a habit he couldn't break. Cassandra's carefully composed face filled the screen, her words portraying concern. "As his colleague, I'm deeply concerned about the impact on our patients...." The remote slipped from his suddenly numb fingers, clattering against hardwood he'd had specially installed.

His laptop chimed with mechanical indifference. A formally worded email from the publisher arrived, stating my contract was under review in light of recent developments. The TV show cancellation followed moments later, each professional death arriving in his inbox with pristine formatting and hollow regret.

His phone incessantly buzzed with messages from colleagues; some worried, some inquisitive, all demanding replies he couldn't muster. The walls of his curated apartment pressed inward, every framed achievement now a cruel echo of excellence undone.

Marilyn's call broke through his spiral, her voice carrying decades of friendship: "I don't believe any of it, Reg. Not for a second."

Mrs. Crumble's message followed, offering sanctuary with her usual gentle wisdom: *My garden's always open, dear.*

A colleague's message arrived last, loyalty clear in every word: *We're all here for you, Dr. Fitzwilliam.*

He remembered his father's voice, each word—"Fitzwilliams don't fail"—resonating with renewed significance. The crushing weight of perfectionism, instilled through years of careful instruction, pressed against his chest. Every past triumph now felt hollow, every achievement tainted by present reality.

His hands moved without conscious thought, confirming his appointment with Anne. The small act of accepting help now felt monumental.

Dawn broke over the city as he stood at his window, the light offering no comfort but perhaps a path forward.

Freud's gentle head-butt said more than words could. In that small gesture lived a truth: some bonds endure, even through darkness.

That morning, Reggie's hand shook as he reached for Anne Montgomery's office door, the newspapers in his other hand looking like proof of his impending dismissal. His usually confident stride had abandoned him, leaving each step toward her waiting presence feeling like a march toward judgment.

The creamy and sage-toned office, a reflection of Anne's composure, surrounded him, a stark contrast to the turmoil hidden beneath his controlled exterior. The leather chair——so familiar from the other side——now felt like a confession booth.

"I assume you've seen these." His voice cracked as he thrust the newspapers toward her, their headlines screaming accusations he couldn't bear to read again. The paper landed between them like a gauntlet.

"RESPECTED THERAPIST'S LICENSE SUSPENDED" burned itself into his vision. Something snapped inside him, a dam breaking after decades of perfect control.

"Twenty years!" his voice rose, hands shaking as he paced back and forth. "Twenty years of perfect ethics, perfect boundaries, perfect everything!" The professional mask shattered completely, rage spilling out in jagged pieces. "And she ripped it out from under me. Used my own standards against me!"

Uncharacteristically, his fist slammed against the wall, the physical pain barely registering through his fury. "I followed every rule! Every protocol! Every bloody professional guideline!" The words tore from his throat, raw and primal. "And for what? To have it all destroyed by someone who——" his voice broke, the rage suddenly draining away like water.

Reggie collapsed into the chair, the fight leaving him as quickly as it had come. His perfectly pressed suit felt like a costume now, a remnant of someone he used to be. "I don't even know who I am without this," he whispered, the admission costing more than all his previous shouting. "Dr. Fitzwilliam, the expert. The author. The perfect bloody therapist." A bitter laugh escaped him. "What's left when all that's gone?"

Anne's silence held the space as he finally faced the question he'd been running from his entire career. "Maybe," he said slowly, the words feeling foreign in his mouth, "maybe I've been hiding behind the title all along. Using professional excellence to avoid...everything else. To avoid real life."

The truth settled around him like a heavy blanket. "I don't know how to do this," he admitted, voice barely audible. "I don't know how to be...just Reggie."

Anne leaned forward slightly, her presence steady. "Perhaps that's exactly where the actual work begins."

The path ahead looked impossibly long from where he sat, each step requiring a courage different from professional excellence. But for the first time since the accusations began, he could at least see it––a way forward through the darkness, if he could find the strength to take the first step.

The familiar crunch of gravel marked each step as Reggie made his way down Mrs. Crumble's garden path. His shoulders hunched against the threatening sky, the weight of the morning's therapy session still heavy in his bones. The garden welcomed him as it always had, roses nodding in the pre-storm breeze, their fragrance a memory of simpler times.

Mrs. Crumble appeared at her greenhouse door, a steaming cup of tea already waiting. "I thought you might swing by today." Her gentle certainty wrapped around him like a familiar blanket as the first fat drops of rain fell.

The greenhouse enveloped them in its warm, green-scented sanctuary. Reggie took the offered teacup, its warmth spreading through his cold fingers. Here, among the potted geraniums and climbing vines, he felt his professional armour finally crack completely.

"This is where I hid," he whispered, his gaze locked on the corner where a small boy used to hide behind terracotta pots. "After Father's...discussions about perfection." The memory surfaced with surprising clarity——the sound of his patent leather shoes on the greenhouse floor, the way his perfectly pressed school uniform had collected dirt from the pots, the relief of finding sanctuary from impossible expectations.

"You were such a serious little boy," Mrs. Crumble observed, her hands busy with a pot of lavender. "Always trying so hard to be perfect."

Rain drummed against the greenhouse glass, creating a cocoon of sound around them. "I thought if I was perfect enough, professional enough..." his voice trailed off as understanding bloomed like one of Mrs. Crumble's prized roses.

"Sometimes," Mrs. Crumble said, her eyes on the storm beyond the glass, "the strongest plants are those that bend with the wind rather than standing rigid." Her words carried the weight of decades of wisdom. "They survive what breaks their prouder neighbours."

As the rain subsided, sunlight streamed through the clouds, turning the greenhouse into a dazzling crystal palace. Each droplet on the glass caught the light, scattering rainbows across the earthen floor. Something tight in Reggie's chest began to loosen as he watched nature's display of destruction and renewal.

"Perhaps," he said slowly, finding strength in the simple truth, "it's time to learn how to bend."

Rising from his seat, Reggie felt different - not lighter exactly, but more grounded. The path ahead still looked daunting, but at least now he could see it through the clearing rain.

A heavy blanket of night descended upon Reggie's apartment; his grandfather's clock ticked away the moments of his restless energy. His perfectly polished shoes traced patterns across the hardwood floors as he paced, unable to find stillness in the gathering darkness. Freud watched from his perch on the windowsill, golden eyes tracking each turn with feline patience.

The walls of his carefully curated space seemed to press closer with each pass. Reggie's measured steps were a counterpoint to his rapidly beating heart. Even his precisely arranged bookshelf offered no comfort tonight, each spine a reminder of expertise now questioned.

As if by instinct, his trembling fingers located the concealed drawer, pulling out the old client files he'd saved. Not the official records, no, these were his personal notes——the genuine stories behind his professional success. Pages of breakthrough moments, of lives changed, of trust earned and healing witnessed.

The weight of the papers felt different now as he read through them. Each success story carried a bittersweet edge, each carefully documented victory a reminder of what he'd lost. His own handwriting tracked his journey from eager young therapist to respected expert, each page marking another brick in the walls he'd built so carefully.

Rain still lingered in the air as Reggie found himself on the streets below, drawn out by an energy he couldn't contain within four walls. His feet carried him down familiar paths, past shuttered shops and quiet cafes. Each step brought him closer to Penelope's shop, its darkened windows reflecting streetlight like tears.

His heart clenched at the sight of fresh flowers still visible through the glass, their beauty untouched by his absence. A single rose stood in the window, its petals catching the last light like a reminder of everything he'd pushed away.

The park bench welcomed him with familiar indifference as stars began emerging through breaking clouds. Away from his professional life and public persona, the truth revealed itself to him with surprising clarity. Each star appearing seemed to mirror a realisation about himself——the walls he'd built, the fear he'd hidden, the heart he'd protected too well.

Memories of his own therapeutic advice surfaced unbidden. How many times had he told clients to trust, to open up, to risk? His own words came back to him now, carrying extra weight: "Sometimes, it's not failure we fear, but having others witness it."

The irony didn't escape him as he sat there, professional expertise turned back on itself like a mirror showing every carefully hidden crack. In helping others find their truth, he'd somehow lost sight of his own.

His feet found their way home as understanding settled into his bones. Each step felt more grounded, more real than the careful performance of perfect Dr. Fitzwilliam had ever been. He formed a fresh idea—not a return to what was lost, but perhaps a path toward something more authentic.

Hope crept in cautiously as he climbed the stairs to his apartment, as tentative as the stars were now fully visible above the city. He didn't hope to restore what was lost, but to discover what might replace it.

The desk lamp cast a warm circle in Reggie's darkened study, its glow catching dust motes that danced like memories in the air. The blank page before him seemed to taunt his usually exact words, its void mirroring the emptiness in his soul. His Mont Blanc pen——a gift from his father upon earning his doctorate——felt heavier than usual in his grip.

From the corner of the desk, Freud, his golden eyes mirroring the lamplight, watched his human's unusual uncertainty. The cat's tail twitched occasionally, marking time with the grandfather clock's steady rhythm.

Words finally began flowing, hesitant at first then gaining momentum like a stream breaking through ice. His perfect penmanship wavered as truth found its way onto paper, each letter carrying weight beyond mere ink:

"Dear Father,

Excellence demanded perfection, you always said. But perhaps excellence isn't in being perfect. Perhaps it's in being real...."

Tears splashed onto the paper, blurring certain words but making others somehow clearer. His hand trembled but kept moving, decades of unspoken pain finally finding voice.

Your approval was never unconditional. Every achievement measured against an impossible standard. I built walls so high trying to prove myself worthy, I forgot how to live within them."

The following page held an unknown ache.

"Dearest Penelope,

I pushed you away, thinking I was protecting you. I was protecting myself. Your warmth terrified me because it made me want to be more than perfect; it made me want to be real."

His heart bled onto the paper as truth emerged without a filter.

"You saw through every careful wall, every precise word. Your kindness made me brave enough to consider being imperfect. I'm sorry I wasn't brave enough to let you stay."

The last letter addressed himself, words flowing with unexpected clarity.

"To the man behind the title:

You are more than your father's expectations. More than your professional reputation. More than the walls you built to protect yourself. You are human, flawed, and worthy of love not despite this but because of it."

As midnight approached, each letter found its envelope. His hands moved steadily now, addressing each with careful intention. As truth emerged, the night grew still; every sealed letter marked progress toward reality.

Freud's gentle purr broke the silence as Reggie's pen finally stilled. The cat moved closer, offering comfort as his human sat quietly in the lamp's warm circle, letters before him like bridges to a different dawn.

As dawn broke, Reggie lay awake in bed, gazing at the ceiling. Sleep had proven elusive after the night's confessions, his mind too full of newly acknowledged truths to find rest. Relaxed on his favourite spot, Freud, with his golden eyes, followed his human's restless pacing.

The city outside held its breath between night and day, that liminal space where anything felt possible. Reggie's running shoes——barely used since his carefully scheduled life imploded——waited by the door like an invitation.

He walked down deserted streets, his steps echoing the rhythm of his pulse. Each impact with the pavement seemed to jar loose another piece of carefully constructed armour, leaving him lighter with each block. The cool morning air filled his lungs, replacing the stuffiness of sleepless contemplation.

The park welcomed him with familiar paths, though everything looked different in this gentle hour. Birds began their morning chorus, their songs carrying no judgment, no expectations. The grass held traces of dew, each drop catching the growing light like tiny promises.

His body moved with increasing surety, muscles remembering a rhythm he'd forgotten he knew. Last night's letters echoed in his mind, but their weight felt different now, transformed by motion and morning light into something more like possibility than pain.

As the sun rose, it softly painted the sky, each color hinting that new beginnings needn't be perfect. The park's empty paths offered no demands, no need for careful words or precise gestures. Here, in this moment, he could simply be.

As light spilled over the horizon, Reggie found his stride matching his heartbeat, both steady and strong. The morning held no judgment, only the simple truth of breath and movement and growing light. Each step carried him further from the man he'd built himself to be and closer to the man he might become.

Dawn's gentle fingers and his own quiet epiphany touched the familiar path home. His apartment building rose before him, no longer a fortress of solitude but simply shelter, waiting to house whatever version of himself he chose to become.

Chapter 13

Reggie arrived at Anne's office in running gear, sweat cooling on his skin in the crisp morning air. His usual precisely pressed suit remained at home, along with the armour it represented. Each step up to her door felt steadier, grounded in a way that surprised him.

Anne's arrival with two steaming mugs of coffee made the familiar couch feel different today. Her raised eyebrow at his attire carried no judgment, only curiosity.

"You're early," she noted, settling into her chair.

"I ran here." The words came easily, without his usual careful consideration. "Actually, I've been running since dawn."

Anne's gentle silence invited more as she passed him a cup. The warmth seeped into his palms, grounding him in the moment.

I wrote letters last night," he said, voice steady. "To my father. To Penelope. To myself."

"Tell me about them."

The pain felt different now, acknowledged rather than buried. "I told my father I'm done trying to be perfect. Told Penelope the truth about why I pushed her away. Told myself it's time to find out who I am without the walls."

Anne inched forward. "That's significant progress, Reggie."

"It feels..." he searched for the right word, "terrifying. And somehow right."

They sat with that truth for a moment before Anne spoke again. "What's different this morning?"

"His voice––my father's––it's quieter now. Still there, but less...demanding." Reggie's hand moved to adjust a tie that wasn't there, then dropped back to his lap. "And Penelope...I miss her. That's new too, allowing myself to miss someone."

"And who are you discovering beneath those walls?"

"Someone who runs at dawn, apparently." A small smile formed. "Someone who might be ready to find out what's next."

Anne nodded, her professional attention sharp despite the early hour. "What steps are you considering?"

"Maybe... appeal to the board. "His voice carried quiet determination."And I need to stop hiding––from myself, from others, from the truth."

"That's a solid foundation to build on," Anne observed. "Same time next week?"

Reggie nodded, the morning light catching the honest sheen of sweat still on his skin. "Same time. Though perhaps next time I'll arrive in more professional attire."

"Wear what feels true," Anne suggested as he rose to leave. "That seems to work for you."

Reggie located his regular park bench, feeling renewed after his morning run. The familiar weight of his suit felt less like armour and more like a deliberate choice. A flash of blonde hair caught his attention as Marilyn approached, carrying two takeaway cups and wearing the determined expression he'd known since university.

"You look terrible," she announced, settling beside him and passing him coffee. "In a good way."

The bench had witnessed countless conversations over the years—exam stress, career leaps, quiet regrets. Today it held something new——raw honesty without professional veneer.

"I've been running," he offered, accepting the coffee.

"Since when do you run?"

"I started at dawn." He paused, sipping the perfectly made coffee; she'd known his order for years now. "Since the walls started coming down."

Marilyn's quiet presence invited more as memories surfaced: late-night study sessions, her unwavering support when he'd chosen therapy over "proper medicine", her steady friendship through every carefully constructed success.

"Remember our third-year ethics paper? You treated it like it was the Magna Carta."

"Rather ironic now."

"Or perfectly fitting." She turned to face him fully. "Tell me about Penelope."

The name caught in his throat, the soft ache of truth hitting him.

"I pushed her away," he admitted, words falling into the morning air. "Blocked her number and told her I couldn't see her anymore. To protect her, I told myself. But really...."

"It was to protect yourself," Marilyn finished gently.

"She saw through every wall. Every perfect suit, every careful word." His hands tightened around the coffee cup. "It terrified me."

"And now?"

"Now I miss her. Now I understand what I lost in trying to protect what I'd built."

Marilyn's hand found his shoulder, the touch grounding him. "You're allowed to be human, Reg. You're allowed to need people."

The tears came unexpectedly, but he let them fall. No tie to straighten, no professional distance to maintain. Just honest grief for walls that had protected and imprisoned him.

"I don't know how to do this," he confessed. "How to be...real."

"Yes, you do." Marilyn's voice carried decades of certainty. "You've always known. You just forgot while trying to be perfect."

As understanding dawned, the morning light illuminated his tears. Marilyn's presence held space for both his pain and his possibility, just as she had since their university days.

"She made me laugh," he whispered. "Genuine laughter, not polite chuckles. She gave me flowers for courage and terrible coffee just to see me smile."

"Sounds like someone worth fighting for."

"I'm not sure I deserve——"

"Stop." Gently but firmly, Marilyn interrupted. "That's your father talking. What does Reggie want?"

The question hung between them as joggers passed, the park holding its morning rhythm. Finally, truth emerged without professional filter.

"I want to be worthy of her flowers. Of terrible coffee. Of her way of seeing through walls to something real."

"Then be that," Marilyn said simply. "Not Dr. Fitzwilliam. Not your father's son. Just Reggie, who's finally brave enough to be seen."

As Reggie left the park, a message appeared on his phone. Dr. Fitzwilliam, I need to talk to you, can we please meet?"

A few days later, a coffee shop's afternoon quite wrapped around Reggie as he watched Lily Thompson approach his table. Her steps carried the weight of fear and something else––determination, perhaps. The familiar professional distance he might have maintained weeks ago dissolved in the face of shared pain.

Settling across from him, Lily's hands trembled. "Dr. Fitzwilliam, I––" her voice caught, eyes dropping to her twisted fingers.

"It's just Reggie now," he offered gently, his cup cooling between his palms. The words held no bitterness, just simple truth.

As Lily recounted her story in broken pieces, tears welled up. Cassandra's careful manipulation, the promised research position, the subtle pressure building week by week. Each revelation landed like stones in still water, ripples of understanding spreading between them.

A trembling Lily, quoting Cassandra, said, "Sharing my experience with you would be beneficial to the study." However, the questions took a different turn. The pressure...." She gazed directly at Reggie and declared, "she distorted the truth."

Reggie's therapist ear recognised the courage in his confession. "When did it start?"

"After your TV show announcement." The words tumbled faster now. "She said your methods were questionable, that speaking up would protect others. But it was all lies." Lily's tears finally fell. "I'm so sorry. I never meant––"

"I know," Reggie said softly, surprising himself with the truth of it. "It isn't your fault. You never should have been put in that position." The anger he'd expected to feel had transformed into something else——understanding, perhaps even compassion.

From his bag, he produced a clean sheet of paper. They spent the next thirty minutes crafting her statement, Lily's hands growing steadier as truth overcame fear. Each detail documented, each manipulation exposed, building a foundation for justice rather than vengeance.

"Will you help me make this right?" Lily asked, hope threading through her voice.

"We'll do it together," Reggie assured her, his own healing somehow strengthened by offering support. "Truth has its own power."

The afternoon light softened their shared pain as they planned next steps——the board's statements, evidence gathering, the careful process of rebuilding what manipulation had broken.

"I was so afraid to face you," Lily admitted as they finished their now-cold coffee.

"Sometimes the hardest truth takes the most courage," Reggie replied, understanding flowing both ways. "But it's always worth it."

A quiet determination marked the end of their meeting; both felt lighter afterward. Not an ending, but perhaps a beginning.

Reggie pushed open the familiar gate to Mrs. Crumble's Garden, his steps lighter now. Lily's confession had lifted a weight he hadn't realised he was carrying. The roses nodded in the gentle breeze, their fragrance wrapping around him like welcome.

Mrs. Crumble waited in her usual spot, two cups of tea already steeping. Her knowing smile suggested she'd sensed this visit coming, as she always did.

"Lily Thompson, the one who made the complaint, came to see me today," Reggie began, settling into the weathered garden chair. His voice held steady where once it might have shaken. "She told me everything about Cassandra's manipulation."

"And how did that feel?" Mrs. Crumble asked, passing him a cup of Earl Grey.

"Like pieces falling into place." Reggie watched the steam rise. "Not just about the complaint, but about myself too."

Mrs. Crumble's hands continued their gentle work with her roses as she listened. "The most beautiful flowers often grow after the most severe trimming," she noted, her gardening advice seeming more poignant now.

"I've been thinking about Penelope," Reggie admitted, the name carrying both ache and hope. "About how I pushed her away to protect her."

"Or to protect yourself?" Mrs. Crumble's question showed only understanding, no judgment.

"Both, I suppose." His fingers traced the teacup's rim. "I was so afraid of being seen as imperfect. I forgot that love sees past facades, anyway."

"Like these roses," Mrs. Crumble gestured to her prized blooms. "They don't hide their thorns, yet we love them all the more for their complete truth."

The evening stars began appearing one by one as Reggie finally voiced what his heart had known for weeks. "I...I love her, Nancy. And I'm terrified."

"Good," Mrs. Crumble smiled. "Fear means it matters. The question is: what will you do with that fear?"

Reggie watched the last rays of sunlight paint the garden in twilight hues. His path forward felt clearer somehow, illuminated not by perfect certainty but by honest purpose.

"I think," he said slowly, "it's time to be as brave as Lily was today. To speak truth, whatever the cost."

Mrs. Crumble's garden held its peaceful wisdom as night settled around them, the stars offering their quiet light to tomorrow's possibilities.

Reggie returned to the comforting embrace of his study, its familiar scent of leather and books enveloping him. Freud claimed his usual evening perch, golden eyes tracking his human's movements as Reggie approached the drawer where he'd hidden last night's letters.

His hands steadied as he lifted them out, the weight of unspoken truths settling in his palms. The city lights beyond his window cast gentle shadows across the pages as he settled into his leather chair.

The letters emerged one by one. Each word carried the raw honesty of midnight confessions, truths he'd been too afraid to face in daylight.

"These are quite different to read now, old friend," Reggie whispered to Freud, who responded with a sympathetic purr. The pain in the words felt different after Lily's confession, after Mrs. Crumble's garden wisdom. Less like wounds and more like stepping stones.

As he approached the window, the city spread out before him, its twinkling lights resembling countless possibilities. His path forward crystallised with unexpected clarity——not the perfect certainty he'd once demanded of himself, but something more real.

At his desk, fresh paper waited. His pen moved with quiet purpose as he began his statement to the board. Not a defence this time, but an offering of truth:

Given the new evidence, I'd like to respond to the accusations made against me. But more importantly, I wish to address the culture of silence that allowed such manipulation to flourish."

The words flowed naturally now, strength replacing perfectionism, truth replacing careful distance. Each paragraph built not a wall but a bridge——between who he'd been and who he might become.

He hesitated above Penelope's letter, his heart calm in spite of its fragile contents. The fear remained, but it felt different now——less like a warning and more like a sign of what mattered most.

Freud's gentle headbutt against his hand drew a smile. "Yes, I know," Reggie acknowledged. "Time to stop hiding."

As he planned for the next day, a tranquil night enveloped him. His reflection in the window showed someone different——not the perfect Dr. Fitzwilliam, but perhaps someone better.

The pre-dawn air nipped at Reggie's face as he laced his running shoes, Freud watching from his perch with sleepy approval. His feet found their rhythm on the empty streets, each step carrying him further from the man he'd been.

The city slept around him as his mind cleared with the steady motion. Professional distance gave way to simple forward movement, his usual careful analysis replaced by the pure act of running. His breath formed clouds in the cool morning air as he found his path through familiar streets.

His steps slowed as Penelope's shop came into view, its darkened windows reflecting the streetlights. The ache in his chest had nothing to do with running as he paused, remembering coffee conversations and honest laughter. The truth of what he'd lost - and what he might still find - settled over him like morning dew.

The park welcomed him with its usual quiet dignity. Bathed in the growing light, the bench waited. His breath steadied as he sat, legs grateful for the rest, mind clearer than it had been in weeks.

The future spread before him like the lightening sky. Understanding grew with the dawn as he watched the park slowly wake around him. The path ahead would require more than professional expertise or careful control. It would demand something he'd always feared—being truly seen.

His fingers traced the bench's familiar wood as the decision crystallised. Growth would require distance——not the walls he'd hidden behind, but the space to become someone new. Someone real. Someone worthy of trust, of forgiveness, of love. Just as he and Mrs. Crumble had discussed all those months ago when it came to her roses.

Strength built with each breath as he stood, muscles warm despite the morning chill. The journey home carried a new purpose, each step knowing rather than searching. Hope rode his shoulders like the rising sun as he faced the day ahead, no longer running from but running toward.

The city stirred around him as he approached his building, the weight of yesterday's letters and tomorrow's tasks balanced by the simple clarity of morning movement. His reflection in passing windows showed someone different——someone ready to face whatever came next.

Chapter 14

Reggie's footsteps echoed down the marble corridor of the NSW Psychology Council, each click a steady beat toward truth. The familiar weight of his briefcase held evidence of both his innocence and his journey——carefully organised notes, Lily's sworn statement, and proof of Cassandra's manipulation.

Reggie, in his pursuit of truth, was alone this time, without a lawyer.

The mahogany doors opened to reveal five stern faces behind the curved board table. Morning light filtered through tall windows, catching dust motes in its beam.

His chair resembled a witness stand, its polished surface reflecting a man ready to present the truth—not defend it. Each document found its place, arranged not for a perfect presentation but for honest telling. His hands moved with steady purpose, laying out the truth in manila folders and typed statements.

The panel's chairman's voice cut through the quiet. "Dr. Fitzwilliam, you may begin."

Reggie spoke clearly and steadily, devoid of his typical professional refinement. "Thank you for hearing from me today.

What I present isn't a defence but a truth: one that reveals not just individual actions but systemic vulnerabilities in our profession."

Like chapters in a book, each document revealed more of the overall story. His words carried neither plea nor pride, just simple facts laid bare under fluorescent lights and scrutiny.

The room's energy changed when Lily arrived. Her hands trembled as she took the seat beside him, but her spine stayed straight. Her voice wavered but held as she revealed Cassandra's manipulation——the promised research position, the carefully crafted complaint, the pressure applied during each appointment with surgical precision.

Lily's voice rang through the silent room, steadied by the truth in her written words. "Said it was my duty to protect future patients. But she was protecting her own ambitions."

Questions came like arrows from the panel.

"Why didn't you report this earlier?"

"Which evidence opposes the claims?"

"What are the claims against Dr. Linton?"

Every answer resulted from diligent preparation and sincere reflection. Reggie's responses carried neither defensive heat nor professional distance——just simple facts and documented truth.

Heavy silence filled the room as the panel deliberated. Their whispered conference seemed to stretch the time itself as Reggie sat, hands folded, dignity intact. The chairman's voice finally cut through the quiet: "In light of fresh evidence, the board temporarily upholds the suspension of Dr. Fitzwilliam's Psychologist Registration, pending the outcome of a full investigation of all parties involved."

Reggie nodded once, his posture remaining unchanged, accepting the decision. The upheld suspension didn't feel like defeat. It felt like the beginning of something larger—a reckoning, and perhaps, a chance for redemption.

For the first time in weeks, Reggie opened his office door, the usual click of the key sounding unfamiliar. Freud's carrier swung gently in his other hand - he'd missed his feline colleague's therapeutic presence during their forced sabbatical.

The morning light caught dust motes dancing through his practice rooms, everything exactly as he'd left it that dark day. His degrees still hung straight on the walls, though their significance felt altered now. Less like shields, more like milestones on a longer journey.

"Welcome back, old friend," he murmured, Freud exiting his carrier and at once, with great composure, taking possession of his miniature leather chair. Some things, at least, remained constant.

Pam's gentle, efficient knock was her usual style. "Tea, Dr. Fitzwilliam?"

"Thank you, Pammy." His voice held new warmth. "And... thank you for staying." She placed the cup on his desk with practiced care. "The practice needs both its doctors." Her smile included Freud in that assessment.

The morning's work began with methodical purpose - files to review, evidence to organise, a practice to rebuild. Each document folder represented not just a case but a truth to be examined, a story that might help prevent future manipulations.

His phone buzzed with messages of support:

From Marilyn: "About time they saw sense. Need help sorting files?"

From Mrs. Crumble: "The garden's calling you. Tea later?"

From Anne: "Proud of you for choosing truth over defence."

The investigation would take time, he knew. Cassandra's manipulations had far-reaching consequences, impacting more than just his professional life. But here, in this familiar space with Freud's steady presence and Pam's quiet support, the path ahead felt clearer.

A fresh page greeted him as he opened his notebook. At the top, he wrote: *"Systemic Vulnerabilities in Therapeutic Practice - Recommendations for Reform."* Below that: *"When protection becomes prison: Examining professional boundaries in modern therapy."*

As Reggie wrote, Freud's approving purr filled the silence, each word heavy with the wisdom he'd gained through hardship. Sometimes the greatest professional insights came not from success but from surviving failure with integrity intact.

As he worked, the morning light intensified, stretching long rectangles across his Persian rug. Each note, each observation, each carefully documented pattern might help prevent another therapist from facing similar manipulation. His suspension had revealed not just personal vulnerabilities but professional blind spots that needed addressing.

Over the intercom, Pam announced that the Heath Care Complaints Commission investigator wanted to schedule an interview. "Of course." His response carried neither anxiety nor defence - just readiness to contribute to necessary change.

His office felt different now - less a fortress of professional perfection, more a space for honest work and genuine healing. The next few months ahead held possibility rather than punishment, a chance to examine and improve the systems they'd all taken for granted.

Messages of support continuously buzzed on his phone. Dr. Chen's carefully worded email spoke of unwavering professional confidence. Dr. Harrison's handwritten note carried decades of collegial trust. Even Dr. Montgomery, usually so reserved, had sent a brief but powerful message: "We stand with you."

His inbox overflowed with letters from colleagues, former students, and even clients eager to vouch for him. Each message added another thread to the tapestry of support being woven around him. Reggie felt their strength flowing into him, bolstering his resolve.

A clear strategy for vindication was presented by his lawyer. The Psychology Council of NSW and the HCCC investigation would take time, but truth had a way of emerging when properly documented. Each piece of evidence would build their case, showing not just his innocence but the systematic manipulation that had led to this crisis.

The path ahead looked clearer now. A temporary suspension will give time for a full investigation to uncover the truth and ensure justice prevails. His calendar, usually filled with client appointments, now held different meetings——legal consultations, panel hearings, preparation sessions.

Reggie stopped what he was doing, the burden of his career interruption weighing heavily on him. Twenty years of practice now suspended; hundreds of therapeutic relationships interrupted. The cost felt enormous, yet somehow worth bearing for truth's sake.

He performed administrative tasks mechanically. Each mundane action carried its own kind of comfort, a reminder that some patterns remained even in crisis.

As Reggie meticulously documented his progress, the afternoon sun changed position. Evidence organised, strategy outlined, support documented. Minor victories in a larger battle, but victories. Freud's approving purr suggested his feline supervisor found the day's work satisfactorily.

Tomorrow would bring its own challenges, but today's careful preparation had laid proper groundwork. The suspension letter sat on his desk, no longer a weight but a temporary reality to face professional dignity and personal courage.

Evening settled over Mrs. Crumble's garden, painting her roses in soft twilight hues. Reggie followed the familiar stone path, his footsteps carrying less weight than they had in weeks. The scent of lavender and fresh earth wrapped around him like an old friend's embrace.

Mrs. Crumble waited by her wrought iron table, tea already steeping in her mother's China pot. Her silver hair caught the last rays of sunlight as she gestured to his usual chair.

"You're looking more yourself," she observed, pouring tea with practiced grace. "Less like Atlas carrying the world."

Reggie accepted the cup, letting its warmth seep into his hands. "Three months to clear my name. It feels... manageable now."

"Tell me about the hearing," Mrs. Crumble prompted, settling back in her chair. Her roses nodded in the gentle breeze, their petals catching the evening light.

Reggie's steady voice explained that the board had seen through Cassandra's manipulation. "Lily's testimony made the difference. She showed remarkable courage."

Decades of wisdom shone in Mrs. Crumble's knowing smile. "Sometimes the strongest growth comes from the deepest wounds."

"The investigation will take time," Reggie continued, watching a butterfly dance between blooms. "But for the first time since this began, I feel... hopeful."

"Your parents called," Mrs. Crumble said quietly, watching his response. "Your dad seems concerned." "Did he?" Reggie's laugh carried no bitterness. "That's new. Though I suppose public scandal finally got his attention."

"He asked about you. Not your practice - you." Reggie's hands stilled around his teacup. "I'm learning to separate my worth from my work. It's... challenging."

"Growth usually is," Mrs. Crumble agreed, reaching to deadhead a nearby rose. "Like these blooms - sometimes we need pruning to flourish."

"I've now been temporarily suspended by the board," Reggie said, her eyes on her careful gardening. "Time to examine not just my case, but the systemic issues it revealed."

"And what do you hope to find?"

"Ways to prevent this happening to others. Stronger safeguards. Clearer boundaries." Reggie paused, considering. "Perhaps some walls need examining, not just reinforcing."

Mrs. Crumble's hands moved with gentle purpose among her plants. "Like this garden - the strongest growth comes from proper balance. Too many walls, nothing blooms. Too few, everything tangles."

Reggie continued, his voice gentler now, "I've begun keeping a record of everything.""Each pattern, each vulnerability in our current system. The suspension might actually help create meaningful change."

"And your own patterns?" Mrs. Crumble's question carried gentle challenge. "Are you examining those too?"

"Anne's helping with that part," Reggie admitted, a small smile forming. "It seems I have some walls of my own that need assessment."

As twilight deepened, the garden grew quiet around them, only the crickets chirping. Mrs. Crumble's roses stood like silent witnesses to countless conversations, their perfume mixing with cooling tea and evening air.

"The next few months," Reggie mused, watching stars emerge. "Time enough to rebuild properly this time. Not just my practice, but..." He gestured vaguely, encompassing more than just professional concerns.

Mrs. Crumble, using her typical gardening analogies, wisely noted that some foundations require testing to ensure growth. "You're doing the work properly this time."

Reggie admitted he had support, remembering Pam's steadfastness, Marilyn's loyalty, and Anne's kind direction. "I'm learning that's not weakness."

Reggie sat in his home study, spreading the case files across his mahogany desk. Years of meticulous work, including session notes, correspondence, and professional reviews, were in each manila folder. Freud claimed his usual spot on the windowsill, golden eyes tracking his human's movements with careful attention.

A crackle from the speakerphone carried the lawyer's voice as she detailed the NSW Psychology Council and Health Care Complaints Commission's in-depth investigation of Dr. Linton. Lily Thompson's testimony carries significant weight."

Reggie's fingers traced the edge of his oldest case files. "We need to establish the pattern."

"Exactly. Your documentation habits are working in our favour."

Reggie was left to review two decades of professional history after the call concluded. He saw familiar names—successful cases, lives improved, and trust built and preserved. Each file told its own story of ethical practice and careful boundaries.

Between case notes, colleague emails arrived steadily.

"Twenty years of watching you help people, Reg. We're behind you."

"Your ethics have always been impeccable."

"The truth will show itself."

Former clients offered their own support:

"Dr. Fitzwilliam saved my marriage."

"His boundaries were always clear and professional."

"We'll testify if needed."

The testimonials gathered momentum as Reggie created a detailed timeline. Every date, interaction, and professional choice contributed to my vindication. His pen moved steadily across legal paper, mapping the path to truth.

Cassandra's manipulative tactics were now obvious: her strategic positioning, calculated pressure on vulnerable clients, and veiled professional jealousy. The pattern revealed itself through documentation and testimony.

The professional cost settled heavily as Reggie reviewed his career trajectory. Television appearances are on hold, book deals are being reconsidered, and my practice is temporarily shut down. Yet somehow the price felt worth paying——truth demanding its tribute in temporary losses.

His perfectly organised desk calendar showed empty weeks ahead. The cost was real, but the worth of truth felt greater.

Freud's quiet presence offered steady comfort as Reggie organised tomorrow's tasks. All files and evidence were strategically positioned. The night settled into focused purpose as he built his defence, one documented truth at a time.

The last case file clicked shut with quiet finality as Reggie straightened his desk. Freud watched from his cushion as the study lights dimmed, leaving only the desk lamp's warm pool. His body felt the day's weight, muscles protesting hours of focused work, yet his mind refused to quiet.

At the window, city lights painted familiar patterns across the darkened street. His office building stood silent, its windows dark where they should have been lit for evening sessions. The sight sent an ache through his chest.

Reggie pressed his forehead against the cool glass, cataloguing the cost. TV opportunities vanished, book contracts were put on hold, and my practice closed for the foreseeable future. His father's voice echoed from childhood: "Excellence demands sacrifice, son." For once, the memory brought neither shame nor defiance——just quiet understanding. This sacrifice served truth rather than perfection.

The Psychology Council of NSW suspension letter lay on his desk, its official letterhead catching lamplight. Each professional loss carried its own weight yet somehow felt lighter than the cost of silence would have been. Lily Thompson's courage deserved no less than his own.

"What do you think, old friend?" Reggie murmured as Freud padded over, offering his steady presence. "Rather, a price for truth."

The cat's gentle head-butt against his ankle brought a small smile. His father's voice surfaced again, but tonight the words held no power. Fear of imperfection had built his walls; perhaps courage would dismantle them.

Steam rose from his evening tea, its familiar scent grounding him as Freud settled nearby. His breathing found its natural rhythm, matching his companion's quiet purr. Hope felt tentative but present, like stars emerging through breaking clouds.

Exhaustion finally made itself known as Reggie gathered his tea things, tomorrow's challenges demanding rest. Freud proudly marched toward the bedroom, his tail held high.

Reggie's key turned in the practice storage room lock, the familiar scent of paper and filing cabinets wrapping around him. Freud, insistent on accompanying him, remained dignified atop a pile of old journals. The early morning light filtered through dusty windows, catching motes that danced in the quiet air.

His fingers traced file labels with practiced precision, years of professional documentation organised with characteristic care. His career's history, spanning two decades, was archived in each drawer: session notes, correspondence, and administrative records.

The search had started with a hunch, born from Lily's tearful confession. If Cassandra had manipulated one vulnerable client, perhaps there were others. With steady hands, he methodically sorted through the files, creating a timeline of her involvement with his practice.

A pattern emerged slowly, hidden in the careful documentation of inter-office communications. At the outset, there were slight inconsistencies—in client transfers, suggested referrals, and the subtle undermining of therapeutic relationships. His heart quickened as connections formed, each piece fitting into a larger picture of calculated manipulation.

Then his hands froze on a particular file. Three years ago, another complaint had been filed, then suddenly withdrawn. The client's signature appeared shaky and uncertain. Notes indicated Cassandra's involvement in the resolution. More files revealed similar patterns——threats disguised as concern, pressure applied through professional channels.

His hands trembled slightly as he spread the evidence across the storage room's small desk. Freud abandoned his perch to press against Reggie's leg, offering steady support as the truth emerged in black and white.

Multiple complaints had been filed, all following the same pattern. Vulnerable clients approached during periods of crisis. Professional openings were offered as enticement. Pressure applied with careful precision. Each incident documented in Cassandra's meticulous notes, her confidence in her methods evident in every word.

Anger rose hot and sharp as Reggie compared dates and details. Years of calculated manipulation, using his own clients' vulnerabilities against them. His good name became a weapon; his trustworthiness, a tool for manipulation.

His fingers were steady now as he reached for his phone, dialling Pam's number. Her quick intake of breath told him she understood the significance of his discoveries.

"I need you to make copies," he whispered. "Every file, every note. We need a complete record."

They worked quickly, efficiently, building their case with each documented incident. A clear pattern of years-long professional misconduct steadily emerged from the evidence.

His lawyer's number was next, the call brief but decisive. The ethics board would need to see everything, every piece of evidence carefully preserved and presented. The path to justice lay clear before him, built on truth rather than revenge.

Freud watched from his new vantage point as Reggie organized the files for transport, his quiet presence a reminder that some battles required steady patience rather than dramatic confrontation.

Chapter 15

As Reggie stepped into the familiar chamber of the NSW Psychology Council, the usual weight settled on his shoulders. His evidence was, as ever, meticulously organised. Years of professional documentation filled his briefcase, each file a piece of the truth he'd uncovered. His heart beat steadily; purpose had replaced the anxiety he'd felt last time.

The panel, which consisting again of the Psychology Council of NSW and the Health Care Complaints Commission, watched with measured interest as he took his place at the podium, their expressions carefully neutral. Cassandra's absence felt deliberate, as if she sensed the shifting tide.

"Dr. Fitzwilliam," the panel's Chair began, "you've requested this hearing to present your evidence on Dr. Linton and the case made against you?"

Distributing the first set of files, Reggie's hands moved steadily, ensuring each panel member received their carefully prepared dossier. "What you have before you documents a pattern of professional misconduct spanning several years."

His clear, strong voice projected as he presented the evidence. "Three years ago, a client filed a complaint similar to Ms. Thompson's. That complaint was withdrawn under circumstances that, upon investigation, reveal concerning similarities."

As he presented more files, each incident bolstering his case, the panel grew more attentive. "Further investigation has uncovered multiple instances of client manipulation, all following the same pattern."

Panel members consistently questioned points, seeking clarification and confirmation. Reggie's responses flowed with professional precision, every detail supported by careful documentation.

"And these notes?" One panellist was shown a particular page.

Reggie explained, "Dr. Linton documented her interactions with these clients herself." "Her methods remained consistent throughout each encounter."

Colleagues corroborated the pattern he'd found, their testimony bolstering his case. Dr. Matthews spoke particularly compellingly about similar experiences within her own practice.

The chamber fell silent as the prosecution revealed the final file—an unflinching account of years of manipulation. Panel members exchanged significant looks as they reviewed the documentation, the weight of truth settling heavily in the formal space.

Reggie remained composed at the podium while the panel commenced deliberations. He presented his case, revealing his truth. Now came the waiting.

Back in his office, Reggie was gazing out the window at the street when he felt Cassandra arrive. She appeared in the glass reflection, her usual composure showing the first faint cracks.

"I suppose congratulations are in order," she said, her voice carrying a brittle edge. "You didn't think you could keep me in the dark, did you? I have my ways, Reggie. A little birdie told me all about your dazzling performance at the Psychology Council."

Reggie turned slowly, noting how she positioned herself near the door——ready for flight or fight. The afternoon light caught the slight tremor in her hands, a detail that would have escaped him before all this began.

"It wasn't a performance, Cassandra. Just truth finally having its day."

Her laugh held no humour. "Truth? You've always been so certain of your truth, haven't you, Reginald? The perfect Dr. Fitzwilliam, never a step out of place."

"This isn't about perfection." He moved to his desk, where the evidence lay in careful order. Years of manipulation are at the heart of this. Patterns don't stay hidden forever."

Her mask cracked slightly. "Hidden? Like you hide behind your perfect suits and careful words? Behind your bestsellers and TV appearances?"

"We both know what this was really about." Reggie kept his voice steady as he began laying out the files. "Every complaint, every threatened career, every manipulated client, they all lead back to you."

"I was protecting our profession!" The words burst from her with unexpected force. "You're using therapy as entertainment, for yourself and your audience——"

"No." Reggie's quiet certainty cut through her rising voice. "This was about jealousy. About control. About wanting what someone else had built. This started years before the TV show was even a thought."

The truth of it hit her visibly. "You never saw me, did you? All these years, right here, while you built your perfect little empire."

Understanding dawned as pieces clicked into place. "Cassandra..." his voice softened with realisation. "Was there more to this than just professional rivalry?"

Her laugh turned bitter. "The great Dr. Fitzwilliam, expert on relationships, couldn't see what was right in front of him. Or chose not to."

"You tried to destroy my career because of unrequited feelings?"

"I tried to show you what real connection looks like!" Her control finally shattered. Forget professional detachment and rigid boundaries; let's embrace raw, messy, authentic emotions!

Reggie maintained his steady calm as her words echoed in the office. "By manipulating vulnerable clients? By threatening careers? By fabricating ethical violations?"

"It worked, didn't it?" Her smile held no warmth. "Finally got you to see me."

"I see you now, Cassandra. The Psychology Council sees you too. Each pattern, manipulation, and calculated move is documented.

Her posture shifted subtly, defeat creeping in at the edges. "So, this is your victory then? Your perfect professional revenge?"

"This isn't about victory," Reggie's voice held firm. "It's about protecting our clients, our profession, and the trust people place in us."

Emotion overwhelmed Cassandra, leaving her speechless and unable to articulate her feelings. Her silence spoke more than words.

"Goodbye, Cassandra." There was no triumph or malice in his voice. "I hope you find whatever peace you're looking for."

As Reggie gave his tie one last adjustment, the NSW Psychology Council chamber was bathed in the morning light filtering through its tall windows. His reflection in the polished door showed a man changed by struggle, yet stronger for it. Deborah, his lawyer, Anne, Pam, Dr. Harrison and Dr. Wilson flanked him like sentries, their quiet presence steadying his steps.

Inside, the chamber's familiar weight settled differently now. Months of investigation, meticulous evidence gathering, and careful truth-uncovering were etched onto each board member's face. Reggie took his seat with practiced grace, years of professional poise serving him well in this moment of reckoning.

The panel chairman's voice filled the space: "Dr. Reginald Fitzwilliam, we have reviewed all evidence thoroughly." Reggie opened his leather portfolio with a steady hand, prepared for anything.

Colleagues and peers from other practices filled the observer seats. Their presence powerfully demonstrated professional unity and resistance to manipulation and abuse.

"In light of the extensive evidence presented," the chairman continued, "this panel finds all allegations against Dr. Fitzwilliam to be without merit." The words felt like sunlight breaking through the clouds. "As a result of our findings... your Psychologist Registration is hereby fully restored... effective immediately."

Relief flowed through the chamber as the chairman turned his attention to Cassandra. Years of manipulation, documented pressure, and systematic abuse of position caused her usually calm exterior to crumble as they revealed their findings.

"Dr. Linton, in accordance with Section 150 of the Health Practitioners Regulation National Law (NSW) due to the serious misconduct presented... your registration is hereby suspended indefinitely."

Reggie caught a glimpse of raw pain beneath Cassandra's professional mask as she received her sentence. Despite everything, he felt some pity for her. Power and control had imprisoned her as surely as fear had once imprisoned him.

Colleagues surrounded him afterward, handshakes and congratulations flowing freely. Dr. Harrison's firm grip carried years of friendship, while Pam's eyes shone with unshed tears of joy. Reggie received a big hug from Anne. Each gesture reinforced the strength of professional community, of standing together against injustice.

"The practice will be stronger for this," Dr. Wilson assured him, his weathered face creasing with genuine warmth. With nods of agreement, others started strategising to rebuild trust and strengthen ethics.

Reggie stood in the chamber's centre, feeling the weight of his restored position settle properly on his shoulders. This practice requires improvements: increased transparency, enhanced support, and better protection against manipulation. His mind already mapped out improvements, ways to create something better from these months of challenge.

The morning light caught his practice keys as Pam returned them, their familiar weight promising tomorrow's possibilities. Not just restoration, but renewal. We're not just coming back; we're creating something better, wiser, and more useful.

Reggie made his way to the familiar bench. The garden's tranquillity soothed his frayed nerves from the morning's board hearing and exoneration. Freud's insistence on accompanying him highlighted the cat's unwavering loyalty. Mrs. Crumble's roses nodded gently in the breeze, their familiar scent grounding him in the present moment.

"Deep breaths, dear," Mrs. Crumble said softly, appearing with her usual perfect timing.

Reggie let his shoulders drop, professional armour finally loosening. "It's over, Nancy. Really over. And... as for Cassandra... she's been suspended indefinitely."

"And how does victory feel?" Beside him, she settled; her gardening apron smelled refreshingly of soil and new life.

"Not like victory," he admitted, watching a butterfly dance between blooms. "More like... truth finally having its moment."

Mrs. Crumble poured tea from her ever-present thermos, the familiar ritual bringing its own comfort. "Sometimes truth costs more than lies," she observed. "But it grows stronger roots."

"Like your roses?" A ghost of a smile touched his lips.

"Exactly like my roses." She gestured to a vibrant bush. "See how they reach for light after pruning? Sometimes we need cutting back to grow properly."

The tea warmed his hands as understanding settled. His practice would need rebuilding, trust carefully restored. But perhaps, like Mrs. Crumble's garden, it would grow back stronger for the pruning.

"The practice will recover," he said quietly, more to himself than her. "Different maybe, but...."

"Better," she finished. "More authentic. Like someone else I know."

His heart caught unexpectedly as movement from the street caught his eye––a flash of auburn hair that wasn't Penelope but could have been. The ache bloomed fresh in his chest.

"I miss her," he admitted, the words carrying weeks of carefully contained pain.

"Of course you do." Mrs. Crumble's voice held a gentle understanding. "Some flowers need proper seasons for blooming."

"And some need better gardeners," he added softly, remembering how quickly he'd pulled away when things got difficult.

"Some need patience," she corrected, "and faith in the growing season."

The garden's peace wrapped around them like a gentle blanket as the sun continued its slow descent. Somewhere in the distance, a church bell chimed the hour, its deep tones mixing with birdsong and the quiet rustle of leaves.

"One day at a time," Mrs. Crumble said, refilling his cup. "That's how gardens grow."

Reggie felt his breathing finally settle into the garden's rhythm. Professional victories and personal losses finding their proper perspective in this sanctuary of growing things. Tomorrow's challenges could wait; today, the beauty of the roses and quiet wisdom sufficed.

The familiar turn of Reggie's key in the lock echoed through his quiet apartment. Setting down his carrier, Freud made his way to his favourite windowsill, the cat's eyes heavy from a long and tiring day. As he loosened his tie, the gentle evening light cast soft shadows across his meticulously organised surroundings, easing the day's burdens from his shoulders.

His breath released slowly, carrying weeks of tension with it. The suspension lifted, his reputation restored, yet somehow those victories felt less important than the quiet peace settling around him.

The phone's buzz startled them both. His mother's name appeared, prompting Reggie's immediate reply.

"Reginald," her voice carried unusual warmth. "Your father and I just heard from Nancy."

"About Cassandra?" His hand automatically moved to straighten his already-perfect tie, old habits dying hard.

"About everything, dear." A pause, then: "Your father would like to speak with you."

Reggie's breath caught, but his father's voice emerged softer than he'd ever heard it.

"Son," the usual sharp edges missing. I have to admit I was wrong. About...many things."

"Dad?" His usually formal 'Father' forgotten in surprise.

"Excellence isn't about perfection," his father continued, voice rough with emotion. "It's about integrity. What you did today, standing up for truth, protecting others...that's real excellence."

Tears pricked unexpectedly at Reggie's eyes as decades of seeking approval suddenly met understanding. He softly confessed, "I picked that up from you." "About standing up for what's right."

His mother's gentle sobs in the background broke something loose in his chest. "Oh, darling," she came back on the line. Although we haven't always shown it, we've been very proud of you.

"Mum..." The childhood name slipped out, carrying years of longing for this connection.

"We love you, Reginald," she said simply. "Not for your success or your title. Just you, my dear boy."

The truth of it settled into his bones as they talked, years of family distance dissolving in simple honesty. His father's gruff affection, his mother's gentle understanding - gifts he'd stopped hoping for decades ago.

The conversation flowed naturally now, pain releasing with each shared memory, each quiet acknowledgment. A love long suppressed by professional obligations finally revealed itself.

When they finally said goodnight, the apartment felt different somehow. Freud padded over to claim his lap, purring contentedly as Reggie sat in the growing darkness, letting peace replace old hurts.

Tomorrow waited with its own challenges, but tonight held the quiet miracle of family healing, of walls lowering to let love in. His mother's last words were a soft, "Sleep well, darling." We're here now."

The soft glow of Reggie's desk lamp created a pool of warmth as he opened his leather-bound journal, its pages waiting for the day's truth. Freud claimed his usual evening perch, golden eyes watching as Reggie's pen found paper.

"Today brought endings and beginnings," he wrote, the words flowing easier now. "Cassandra's manipulation exposed, but her pain visible beneath. Perhaps that's the hardest truth——seeing humanity even in those who hurt us."

His hand moved steadily across the page, professional distance giving way to honest reflection. "Father's words changed everything. It wasn't about winning or proving a point; it was about acceptance. Love without conditions. Truth without masks."

The stack of support letters caught the lamplight. Every message empowered him, creating a strong foundation. Dr. Chen's steady loyalty, Pam's unwavering faith, Mrs. Crumble's gentle wisdom—a community standing with him through the storm.

Reggie's thoughts turned to his practice, seeing it with fresh eyes. To add warmth to the formal office, fresh flowers might help. His pen paused, heart catching. Not yet. Some healing needed perfect timing.

The city lights drew his gaze to the window, to the very distant shape of Penelope's shop. Dark now, but he could picture her morning routine—arranging fresh deliveries, creating beauty from simple blooms. His chest ached with familiar longing, but tonight it carried something new. Not desperation, but patience. Recognising that some gardens require time to flourish.

Looking at his reflection in the darkened glass, Reggie saw changes in himself. The perfect suit remained, but it felt less like armour now. Professional excellence still mattered, but it had found balance with human connection. His worth no longer measured in degrees and accolades, but in simple truth and genuine care.

Peace settled around him like a familiar blanket as he closed his journal. Tomorrow would bring its own challenges, but tonight held quiet certainty. Not in perfect answers or flawless performance, but in the strength to face whatever came with an open heart.

Freud's gentle purr accompanied Reggie's evening routine—teeth brushed, tie carefully hung, bed turned down with usual precision. Some habits remained, but they felt like choices now rather than chains.

The night wrapped around him as he settled into bed, Freud claiming his usual spot nearby. His mind held tomorrow's possibilities—practice reopening, relationships rebuilding, trust growing slowly but surely. Not with desperate need, but with steady patience and quiet strength.

Chapter 16

Confidently, Reggie opened the door to his practice. Freud padded beside him, a dignified shadow offering silent reassurance with every step. The morning light caught dust motes dancing in the reception area, making even the ordinary seem somehow significant.

His fingers followed the engraved nameplate, its letters now significant following months of doubt. Inside, his office waited exactly as he'd left it, yet somehow it felt different.

Pam's unexpected hug broke through their usual professional reserve, surprising them both. "Welcome home, Dr. Fitzwilliam," she managed, voice thick with emotion. Other staff members gathered, their presence filling the space with warmth and purpose.

The therapeutic team followed Dr. Harrison into the doorway. Their faces carried both support and expectation as Reggie settled behind his desk, Freud claiming his miniature chair with familiar dignity.

Reggie announced, his tone unwavering, "I've given this some thought." "About changes we need to make." He outlined his vision, including stronger ethical frameworks, regular peer supervision, transparent reporting systems. Each suggestion met with thoughtful nods and contributed ideas.

The phones began ringing almost immediately. Pam's calm voice managed returning clients with practiced grace—each booking a quiet affirmation of restored trust. "Mr. Bennett would like his regular Thursday slot," she announced, the simple normalcy of it striking Reggie's heart.

He moved through his office with purpose, adjusting items that had shifted in his absence. Fresh flowers appeared on his desk——Pam's kind welcome gift. Their bright presence caught the morning light. The space felt both known and newly discovered—like opening a favourite book and noticing lines you'd never truly seen before.

The morning's schedule took shape under Pam's careful attention. Team members' visits, filled with questions and suggestions, highlighted their strong professional community. Freud maintained his watchful presence as Reggie settled into the rhythm of practice life, his quiet purr a constant reminder of continuity through change.

Every restored appointment, team discussion, and small decision added to the foundation they were rebuilding together. Not just returning to what was, but creating something stronger, more resilient, more genuinely helpful than before.

Settling into the well-worn armchair, Reggie inhaled the delicate aroma of floral essence whilst melodic tunes drifted through the room. His practiced hands routinely organised the neat stack of paperwork, a ritual honed from countless repetitions. Freud padded silently to his miniature chair, assuming his therapeutic position with characteristic dignity.

Through the window, city sounds filtered in distantly, creating the familiar backdrop of their professional sanctuary. Reggie adjusted his tie, then deliberately lowered his hand. Some old habits needed changing, even as others provided comfort.

The gentle knock announced Michael Bennett's return. As Michael, his first returning client, walked in, Reggie felt his anxiety ease; their history of trust was evident in Michael's relaxed posture and sincere smile.

"Welcome back," Reggie offered, his professional tone carrying extra warmth. "To both of us, it seems."

Michael settled into the client chair, his eyes taking in the familiar space. "The room feels different somehow."

"Perhaps we both do," Reggie acknowledged, surprising himself with the candour. Freud's approving purr suggested he'd made the right choice.

Their session flowed differently than before. Reggie thoughtfully responded to Michael's comments on workplace pressures by relating his own experiences.

"Sometimes," he offered, "our greatest growth comes through our hardest trials." The words carried the weight of lived experience now, not just professional wisdom.

Michael leaned forward, responding to this new authenticity. "You've changed," he observed. "It's like...you're more present somehow."

Reggie nodded in acknowledgement of the truth. "We teach best what we most need to learn," he admitted. Freud's golden eyes watched this exchange with apparent approval.

Their conversation deepened naturally, professional boundaries still clear but somehow more human. Michael's confession about fearing vulnerability prompted a response from Reggie based on both his expertise and experience.

"Fear of being seen," he reflected, "often keeps us from our greatest possibilities." His journey resonated in the words, amplifying their impact through mutual understanding.

As their session progressed, Michael revealed his own breakthrough: a decision to trust despite uncertainty. Reggie found an unexpected parallel to his own journey in the sincerity of the other man's words.

"It's terrifying," Michael admitted, "but somehow...necessary."

"Growth usually is," Reggie agreed, their shared understanding creating deeper therapeutic connection.

They concluded their session with a quiet acknowledgment of progress made and challenges still ahead. Now, Michael's thankfulness felt less like a professional courtesy and more like a connection between people.

As Michael prepared to leave, Freud moved to the door in his usual ritual, but with what seemed like extra approval today. Dust motes, illuminated by the afternoon sun, swirled in the air, symbolizing my professional growth and personal fulfillment.

Reggie sat at his desk, finishing his session notes, a sense of satisfaction warming his chest. His return to work surpassed all expectations; every client interaction was enhanced by the profound insights gained from his recent professional struggles.

Freud stretched lazily in his miniature chair, golden eyes half-closed in contentment. Although the usual energy filled the practice, he felt a more genuine atmosphere.

Reggie adjusted his tie, more from habit than necessity now, and allowed himself a moment to appreciate how far they'd come. His impeccably organised desk showed his professionalism, contrasting with the fresh flowers hinting at personal growth.

The peaceful moment shattered as Pam burst through his door, her usual composed demeanour replaced by barely contained excitement.

"Dr. Fitzwilliam," she began, clutching a folder to her chest. "You need to see this immediately."

Reggie straightened, noting Freud's sudden alertness. "What is it, Pammy?"

"James and Veronica Sterling," she said, placing the folder before him. Their request was specifically for you. They're waiting in the front office."

Instantly, I recognised the names: James Sterling, a tech mogul, and his wife, Veronica, a social media influencer. Tabloids had been reporting on their relationship problems for weeks.

"They've been to three other therapists," Pam continued. "All very prestigious. But they want you."

Absorbing the implications, Reggie's hand automatically went to his tie. Every public appearance by the Sterling's would be dissected by the media to gauge their therapy's success or failure. His recent exoneration would further pique public interest.

"They saw your television appearance," Pam added softly. "Before everything happened. They said you seemed...real."

Reggie skimmed the couple's intake forms, noticing their pain despite their careful wording. He saw in their struggles a shared burden: the crushing weight of public expectation and the price of flawless appearances.

Freud padded across to examine the folder himself, his quiet presence helping Reggie focus. The stakes were clear: taking this case would thrust him back into the spotlight just as he'd found his footing again.

Yet something about their situation called to him. Perhaps it was the echo of his own journey in their need to appear perfect while falling apart. Perhaps it was the chance to apply his well-earned wisdom on authenticity and growth.

"Tell them I'll see them," Reggie decided, surprising himself with how right it felt. "We'll start tomorrow."

Pam nodded, understanding the significance of this choice. Turning to leave, Reggie saw his reflection: not the flawless Dr. Fitzwilliam, but a stronger, more genuine self.

Freud returned to his chair with what seemed like approval as Reggie began reviewing the Sterling's file. This case would test his ability to reconcile professional excellence and personal authenticity.

The afternoon light caught his university degrees on the wall, reminding him how far he'd come. Yet somehow, this felt like the real beginning of something important.

As Dr Fitzwilliam clicked the latch, comforting shadows from the enveloping darkness embraced his flat. The cat, his companion, stretched and padded to its beloved sleeping spot, its amber eyes droopy from a day of office lounging.

Reggie moved through his evening routine with practiced ease, kettle filling, tie finally loosening. Earl Grey's familiar aroma filled the kitchen as he gathered his thoughts, the weight of the Sterling's case settling on his shoulders.

The couple's file lay spread across his desk in his home office, looking like a complicated puzzle. Headlines screamed from his tablet: "Tech Power Couple's Marriage on Rocks", "Sterling Success Story Turning Sour", "Vernonia Sterling

Spotted Without Ring". A similar undercurrent ran through all the stories—a public appetite for failure and spectacle.

His pen moved steadily across fresh paper, professional observations mixing with personal insight. Sterling's public struggles mirrored his personal battles, the necessity of projecting an image while internally struggling resonated deeply with him.

"Different perspective now, isn't it, old friend?" Reggie murmured to Freud, who had claimed his usual spot atop the filing cabinet. The cat's tail twitched in what seemed like agreement.

Through his window, the city lights twinkled like stars. Penelope's shop, dark and distant, was hardly discernible. The familiar ache in his chest surprised him with its intensity, even after all this time.

With growing clarity, his notes read: "Public pressure is fracturing private lives." Need for authentic connection beneath perfect image. Fear of vulnerability amplified by constant scrutiny."

The parallels between his own journey and the Sterling's situation crystallised with sudden clarity. His recent experience with public judgment and private truth could offer unique insight into their struggles. Maybe his journey from crisis to authenticity can guide them.

Strategy formed with professional precision: "Create safe space for real connection. Address public pressure without letting it dominate. Use media scrutiny as tool for growth rather than barrier."

Reggie sat back, letting the pieces fall into place. He learned true strength wasn't about perfection, but authenticity and courage. This understanding could serve the Sterling's in ways his previous professional expertise alone never could.

Challenges and opportunities appeared as the path ahead became clear. Tomorrow's first session would set the tone for everything that followed. His experience, both professional and personal, had prepared him for exactly this moment.

Instinctively, Reggie walked from his apartment to Mrs. Crumble's garden. The weight of the Sterling files in his briefcase mirrored the heaviness in his chest—not unpleasant, but insistent, demanding his focus. Streetlights cast pools of warmth on the quiet pavement as he walked, each step bringing him closer to the wisdom he sought. Reviewing the case details, he saw parallels between their plight and his own experiences.

The garden gate creaked its familiar welcome as Mrs. Crumble appeared, silver hair catching moonlight, a knowing smile gracing her features. She'd clearly expected him.

"Tea's just ready," she said, leading him to their usual spot among the night-blooming jasmine. "I thought you might come tonight."

With grateful hands, Reggie sat on the worn bench and accepted the steaming cup. "A high-profile couple came to see me today," he began, the words finding their way naturally in this sacred space. "Their story...it's rather close to home."

Mrs. Crumble's quiet presence encouraged him to continue as he outlined the case——the public pressure, the cracking facades, the desperate need to maintain perfect appearances while drowning beneath them.

"They're losing themselves," he explained, tea cooling forgotten in his hands. "And each other. Under the weight of everyone watching, waiting for them to fail."

"Rather like someone else we know?" Mrs. Crumble's gentle observation landed softly.

"Yes," Reggie admitted, heart opening to the truth of it. "Their struggle with public scrutiny, the need to appear perfect...I understand it differently now."

"Look at these night flowers," Mrs. Crumble gestured to the moonflowers unfurling in the darkness. "They bloom when most aren't watching. Some truths need quiet spaces to emerge."

Understanding settled over Reggie like dew on petals. "I need to create a sanctuary for them," he murmured, seeing the path ahead more clearly. "A space away from the world's eyes, where they can remember who they are beneath the headlines."

"Just as this garden has always been for you," Mrs. Crumble agreed, her wisdom flowing as naturally as the evening breeze through her beloved plants.

The night held them in gentle silence as Reggie's thoughts crystallised into tomorrow's plan. This couple needed more than traditional therapy; they needed someone who understood their journey from the inside out.

"You're ready for this," Mrs. Crumble said simply, reading his unspoken concerns. "Your own path has prepared you."

Peace settled over him as the garden worked its familiar magic. Tomorrow's session took shape in his mind with growing clarity—not just professional expertise, but hard-won understanding guiding the way.

Chapter 17

Gentle morning light filtered through the stained glass of the Victorian Terrace, casting soft patterns across the thoughtfully arranged therapy room. Reggie adjusted the last cushion on the antique sofa, his movements deliberate and measured. This converted parlour, with its high ceilings and period details, offered a different sanctuary than his usual office. While he is seeing the Sterling's, this will serve as his temporary practice once a week.

Freud settled into his velvet wingback chair, his grey presence lending warmth to the carefully curated space. The cat's golden eyes tracked Reggie's movements as he made final adjustments - positioning fresh flowers just so, ensuring the subtle lavender diffuser provided calm without overwhelming.

"What do you think, old friend?" Reggie murmured, surveying their work. "Peaceful enough?"

He was drawn to the window by the faint sound of car doors slamming shut in the distance. Veronica Sterling's elegant figure emerged first, her media-perfect posture already showing signs of strain. James followed, his hand hovering near but never touching her back—a silent distance that spoke volumes to Reggie's trained eye.

Pam had planned their entrance via the private garden gate, thus evading the paparazzi who typically pursued them. Reggie met them at the door himself, noting how Veronica's shoulders dropped slightly as she crossed the threshold into the quiet space.

"Welcome," he said simply, leading them into the parlour. "I thought we might appreciate some distance away from the usual business of offices."

James, tech mogul, sat down first, his confidence faltering in the intimate setting. Veronica perched beside him, maintaining careful inches between them. Freud's quiet presence drew her attention, a small smile cracking her perfect facade.

"He's part of the team," Reggie explained, settling into his chair. "Sometimes the best therapy comes with a side of fur."

The joke, gentle as it was, seemed to release something in the room. Veronica's perfectly manicured hands twisted in her lap as she began speaking.

"The pressure's relentless," she murmured, her usual public persona gone. "Every charity event, every product launch...they're all watching for cracks."

James shifted, instinct warring with habit as he fought the urge to maintain their perfect image. "We used to be able to just be us," he added, his own walls beginning to lower. "Now everything's a performance, even when out of sight."Reggie leaned forward, the shared understanding settling quietly between them. "The weight of public expectations," he offered. "It becomes heavier than any real burden."

Veronica gasped as they shared a look of understanding. "You know," she said softly. "You've been there."

"Yes," Reggie acknowledged, his own experience lending weight to the simple word. "And I learned that sometimes our greatest strength lies in letting the perfect facade crack just enough to let real healing begin."

At last, James's hand met Veronica's, their fingers interlacing, and the room's atmosphere changed. Freud chose this moment to pad over, offering silent comfort as he settled between them.

"How do we start?" Veronica asked, her free hand automatically stroking the cat's soft fur.

"By remembering who you are beneath the headlines," Reggie replied, watching hope begin to grow in their eyes. "And by trusting that some spaces are safe enough to be real in."

Reggie observed subtle shifts in posture as the session concluded—a turning toward one another, shoulders relaxing, the earlier defensiveness gone. Small steps, but significant ones.

"Same time next week?" Still holding Veronica's hand, James asked as they stood.

"Same private location," Reggie confirmed, walking them to the garden gate. "This space is yours now. A sanctuary from the world's eyes."

He watched them leave, noting how they walked closer together than when they'd arrived. First steps on a long path, but steps taken together.

Reggie sat in the leather chair, meticulously documenting the Sterling's session notes while protecting their privacy. His pen moved steadily across the page: "Initial session shows promising signs of reconnection. Both parties demonstrating willingness to lower public facades in safe space." Freud maintained his watchful presence from the windowsill, occasionally offering quiet approval.

The phone's buzz interrupted his flow.

"Dr. Fitzwilliam," Pam's voice carried its usual efficiency. "Three media outlets are requesting comment on the Sterling's. They're checking if you're their new therapist.

"Standard response, Pammy," he replied, adjusting his tie unconsciously. "No comment on any client matters."

"Completed," she confirmed. "Though they're getting creative with their attempts."

He reread his notes, professionalism battling with empathy. Sterling's public pressure struggles mirrored his own recent journey, creating a strong sense of connection.

"Rather familiar, isn't it, old friend?" he murmured to Freud. The cat's knowing look suggested agreement.

Marilyn's arrival brought coffee and her usual direct approach. She placed a steaming cup on his desk, claiming the visitor's chair with familiar ease.

"The Sterling's," she began, noticing their file on Reggie's desk.

"Client confidentiality, Marilyn," he reminded her as he secured their file from prying eyes, though his smile softened the words.

"I'm not asking for details," she countered. "Just checking on you. High-profile cases bring their own pressure."

Their conversation shifted to safer ground——general therapy approaches, professional ethics, the balance of public interest and private healing. Marilyn's presence offered its usual comfort, her understanding of his journey adding depth to their discussion.

"You seem different with clients now," she observed. "More...real."

"Experience tends to do that," he acknowledged, his recent struggles lending weight to the words.

"It suits you," she replied simply. "This new version of Dr. Fitzwilliam."

Their professional discussion continued, touching on therapeutic approaches and the evolution of practice.

The Victorian Terrace's study hummed with quiet activity as Reggie reviewed the morning's messages. Reporters relentlessly bombarded his phone, each more determined than the previous to invade the Sterlings' privacy.

"Another one from *The Daily Mail*," Pam reported.

"Standard response," Reggie replied, adjusting his tie as he studied the growing list of inquiries. "No comment on any client matters, no exceptions."

From his vantage point, Freud observed Reggie meticulously planning the week's schedule. Seclusion was guaranteed at the Victorian Terrace, which boasted a private entrance, secure grounds, and, crucially, privacy. Each session carefully timed to avoid any overlap, any chance of exposure.

His clinical supervisor, Dr. Ellen Benner, arrived precisely on time, her presence bringing familiar comfort to the wood-panelled room.

"Your high-profile couple," she began, settling into the leather chair. "These types of cases bring unique challenges."

"They need space to be real," Reggie shared, careful to maintain client confidentiality even in supervision. "The public pressure——"

"Something you understand firsthand," Ellen observed gently.

"Yes," he said in agreement. "Though that experience might be exactly what they need."

Their discussion flowed naturally through therapeutic approaches and professional boundaries, each point strengthened by Reggie's recent journey. His own growth lending depth to his clinical understanding.

"Your practice has evolved," Ellen noted. "There's a different kind of strength in your approach now."

The morning's final hour brought focused planning as Reggie coordinated with his team. Enhanced security and privacy protocols safeguard their carefully constructed sanctuary.

"The back gate needs checking," he reminded Pam. "And the privacy screens for the garden——"

"Already handled," she assured him. "The grounds are secure."

Each preparation felt like building another layer of protection, creating space where healing could begin without the world's watching eyes. He meticulously planned the next steps, creating session structures that offered support within strict ethical guidelines.

Freud's quiet presence offered steady approval as Reggie reviewed his plans, the cat's golden eyes reflecting understanding of the delicate balance being struck between professional duty and human compassion.

Reggie moved through his end-of-day routine with practiced ease, the quiet stillness of his apartment offering a welcome reprieve from the day's demands. The chamomile tea he'd carefully made steamed, its delicate aroma blending with the musty smells of aged books and leather.

Freud padded alongside him to the balcony, their nightly ritual unchanged yet somehow different. The leather-bound journal opened easily to today's page as he documented his professional development. He wrote of client relationships strengthening via shared humanity, the words now flowing easily. *"Professional distance maintaining while authentic presence growing."* Each entry marked another step in his evolution from perfect expert to fellow traveller on the healing path. The leather portfolio closed with a satisfying finality, tomorrow's blank pages waiting for new progress.

The evening's contemplation gave way to quiet resolve as Reggie prepared for bed. His nightly routine felt different somehow, each action carrying the weight of tomorrow's decision. From his bathroom counter perch, Freud observed Reggie's methodical suit-hanging and tie-straightening; these orderly habits now soothed rather than confined him.

His reflection caught his eye as he brushed his teeth, showing him a man changed by recent months. The perfect facade had softened into something more real, more human. Professional success had taught him expertise; failure had taught him authenticity. Both lessons seemed necessary now.

In his bedroom, he sat on the edge of his bed, fingers absently stroking Freud's fur as the cat settled beside him. "Tomorrow morning," he said quietly, more to himself than his feline companion, "I'm going to see her. Tell her everything. How sorry I am. How wrong I was."

The words he'd need started forming in his mind, not the careful script of a relationship expert but the truth of a man who'd learned the hard way about walls and worth and what really mattered. Believing he was shielding her, he'd distanced himself, only to discover he'd been safeguarding himself from vulnerability and deep connection.

Freud's gentle purr offered its usual comfort as Reggie lay back; mind full of tomorrow's possibilities. The city lights painted patterns on his ceiling, each one seeming to spell out Penelope's name. He'd rehearsed perfect speeches in this same bed during sleepless nights, but now he knew - only the truth would do. Simple, unvarnished, real.

"I was wrong," he practiced softly to the darkness. "I thought I was protecting you, but I was really hiding. I'm sorry." The words felt right - not perfect, but authentic. Like the man he'd become.

Sleep approached slowly as he planned his morning. He'd go early, before her first deliveries arrived. Bring coffee perhaps - a peace offering and reminder of shared moments. But mostly bring himself, walls down, heart open, ready to risk being seen rather than being perfect.

Freud settled into his usual spot at the foot of the bed, golden eyes reflecting both wisdom and approval. Tomorrow would change everything - either healing what he'd broken or confirming its end. But for the first time, Reggie felt ready to face either outcome with authenticity rather than armour.

His last conscious thoughts were of Penelope's shop, of flowers and forgiveness and the courage to try again. Tomorrow morning couldn't come soon enough.

Chapter 18

The bell above Penelope's shop shattered the morning stillness—its cheerful chime clashing with Reggie's thundering heart. Sunlight painted the flower-filled space in warm hues, catching dust motes that danced like tiny stars in the charged air. The coffee tray trembled slightly in his grip as he stepped inside.

Penelope stopped arranging her morning flowers, her hands hovering over the lilies. The physical impact of seeing her again knocked the carefully prepared words from Reggie's mind, leaving only raw emotion in their wake. He felt her slight but definite recoil as a physical blow. Her hands gripped the counter's edge, knuckles whitening as she steadied herself. The distance between them felt both infinite and suffocating.

"Penelope..." Reggie began, his voice faint across the space. The coffee suddenly felt heavy in his hands, the fresh coffee aroma a mockery of his hope.

"D-don't," her voice cracked on the single syllable. "Please don't."

But the words came anyway, spilling out like water through broken glass. "I love you, Penelope. I think I always have, even when I was too afraid to admit it."

She flinched, as though the words struck her. "Love isn't enough, Reggie. Not when there's no trust."

"I've changed," he started, taking an instinctive step forward, only to halt when she matched it with a step back.

"Have you?" Tears filled her eyes, but didn't fall. "Or have you just gotten better at convincing yourself you have?"

The truth burst between them—raw, uncontainable. "You pushed me away," Penelope continued, her voice rising slightly. "When I would have stood beside you through everything, you decided I wasn't worth the risk."

"I was trying to protect you," Reggie's voice broke on the words.

"No." Her laugh held no humour. "You were protecting yourself. Like you always do."

"I loved you," she added, the past tense landing like a physical blow. "More than I've ever loved anyone. But I can't trust you with my heart again."

The morning light caught Penelope's tears as they finally fell, turning them to amber diamonds on her cheeks.

"I understand," he managed, though the words felt like glass in his throat. "I'm sorry" seemed inadequate, but he offered it anyway, backing toward the door.

The bell's final chime marked his exit—a cheerful note turned elegy for what might have been.

With no destination, Reggie's feet moved, the city a blur, each step a beat of his inner hollowness. Professional masks lay shattered, leaving only raw humanity in their wake. Tears threatened but didn't fall as his body moved on autopilot through familiar streets, turned strange by grief.

Mrs. Crumble's garden gate appeared like a beacon in the morning light, its familiar creak welcoming him home. Reggie's legs gave way as he reached the weathered bench, his hands trembling as they gripped the worn wood.

"She was right," his voice cracked on the words. "I pushed her away. I broke her heart."

Mrs. Crumble silently approached, producing tea unceremoniously. The warmth seeped into his stiff fingers as the first tears finally fell.

"I told myself I was protecting her," pain erupted from somewhere deep inside. "But I was protecting myself. I'm always protecting myself."

The crisp air carried the scent of roses as Mrs. Crumble settled beside him. "Sometimes," she offered gently, "we must feel the full weight of our choices before we can truly change."

As Penelope's words, "Love isn't enough when there's no trust," resonated, his understanding blossomed. His tears flowed freely now, each one carrying years of carefully contained emotion.

"I thought being strong meant never being vulnerable." Reggie's voice barely carried above the gentle breeze. "But I was wrong about that, too."

As he took deep breaths, the faint chirping of birds interrupted the tranquil silence. In this serene moment, he could feel a raw truth washing over him, bringing a sense of clarity and peace. Mrs. Crumble's wisdom, gentle and calming, settled around him like a soft blanket, while the comforting warmth of the tea spread through his chest, offering soothing relief.

"The heart," she said softly, "has its own time for healing. Like these roses——some bloom again after the hardest frost."

As they sat together, the weight of unspoken truths dissolved, replaced by a comforting clarity. No professional distance remained, no careful walls, just a man learning to feel the full depth of love's cost and finding unexpected strength in finally letting go.

As Reggie later returned to his apartment, the key turned heavily in the lock, burdening him with the weight of rejection that settled around him like a physical presence. Freud's meow greeted him, golden eyes studying his human's defeated posture with feline understanding.

Reggie's fingers moved automatically to his tie, loosening the silk that suddenly felt like a noose. His shoes followed, each movement deliberate as he shed the last remnants of his professional armour. The apartment's familiar comfort offered no solace tonight.

At his desk, the leather journal opened with practiced ease, though his hand trembled slightly as he uncapped his pen. The blank page waited, patient as truth itself:

"Tonight, I learned the true cost of walls built too high. Professional expertise means nothing when we can't apply it to our own hearts. Penelope showed me that love without trust is just another form of fear...."

The words flowed faster now, pain finding voice through ink:

"How many times have I told clients that vulnerability isn't weakness? That trust requires risk. Tonight, I understood those words anew, watching love die in the evening light because I wasn't brave enough to live what I taught."

Client voices echoed through memory——their struggles, their breakthroughs, their courage in facing fear. Each session took on new meaning through the lens of his own pain.

We may learn more from our professional setbacks than our achievements. From understanding that expertise without experience is hollow wisdom."

Captivated by the city lights, he saw each window as a symbol of countless hearts experiencing love and loss. His reflection ghosted against the glass, showing him, a man stripped of pretence, finally facing his truth.

"We heal not by avoiding pain but by walking through it. Tonight taught me that lesson more deeply than any textbook ever could.

Our wounds, when acknowledged, become bridges of understanding. Our failures, when accepted, transform into wisdom. Perhaps this is the real meaning of being a healer——not by holding perfect knowledge, but a perfect willingness to grow through our own heart's breaking."

Freud's soft purr and the scratching of his pen soothed Reggie as he processed tonight's difficult lessons, preparing for tomorrow's healing. The journal's pages filled with hard-won understanding, each word a step toward something authentic and new.

As the night deepened, his professional detachment yielded to genuine human connection, his suffering forging the wisdom born of lived experience. Tomorrow waited with its own challenges, but tonight had taught him that sometimes our deepest healing comes through facing the very fears we've spent a lifetime avoiding.

As the sun rose over the city, Reggie sat on his bedroom floor, carefully tying his running shoes. Freud perched on the windowsill, his golden eyes tracking each deliberate movement as his human prepared for this morning's necessary ritual.

The city slept as Reggie's feet found their rhythm on empty streets. Yesterday's pain lingered with every step, each breath a reminder of Penelope's words. The steady pounding of feet against pavement offered its own kind of therapy——motion as medicine, movement as meditation.

His breath found its pattern as buildings blurred past. A professional insight: exercise acts as emotional release, letting the body handle what the mind can't yet. The distance grew between him and last night's devastation with each measured stride.

Sweat began to bead as his feet carried him toward familiar territory. As we neared the park entrance, the paths were still quiet in the early morning light. The bench where he'd shared so many conversations with Marilyn passed in his peripheral vision.

Dawn painted the sky in gentle colours as he rounded the park's final curve. Ahead loomed the practice building, its windows dark yet inviting. His steps slowed naturally as professional purpose began to overlay personal pain. Each stride now carried him not away from yesterday but toward today's responsibilities.

The key turned smoothly in the lock as Reggie claimed his professional space. Morning light streamed in through open windows, the office's familiar aroma anchoring him to his usual routine and duties. His desk waited, patient as always, ready for the day's work to begin.

Files spread across polished wood as Reggie reviewed his schedule. The Sterling's' file was compelling, his personal experiences adding new significance to their story. Professional strength flowed not despite personal pain but through it——each heartbeat adding authenticity to his understanding of human struggle.

Reggie's chair became his sanctuary as the morning sun grew brighter, yesterday's pain replaced by today's knowledge. His clients would find him changed——not weakened by vulnerability but strengthened by it, his professional expertise now tempered by lived experience of love's cost and courage's price.

Welcoming Jane Dean into his office, Reggie's professional demeanour displayed a newfound depth of personal understanding. Freud claimed his therapeutic position, golden eyes watchful as always.

Jane, settling onto the leather couch, remarked that Dr. Fitzwilliam seemed different today. Her fingers twisted the tissue she'd brought, though her eyes held more curiosity than distress.

Reggie adjusted his position slightly, allowing a small smile to surface. "I think I understand certain things better now," he conceded, his professional skills enriched by his own life experiences.

Jane's story emerged slowly, her words carrying the weight of recent heartbreak. "He just...walked away. Said he needed space, needed time..." her voice caught. "I thought love was supposed to be enough."

The pain in her voice echoed his own from last night, but rather than distancing himself professionally, Reggie leaned into the resonance. "Love isn't always the issue," he softly suggested.

"Sometimes it's about trust, and fear, and the courage to stay when everything feels uncertain."

Understanding deepened between them as Jane looked up, catching something new in his tone. "You sound like you know exactly what I mean," she ventured.

"I'm learning," Reggie acknowledged, professional boundaries holding while allowing authentic connection, "that loving someone takes more courage than we sometimes think we have."

The breakthrough emerged naturally as Jane's shoulders relaxed, responding to this new authenticity. "I've been so angry," she admitted. I blame him, and I blame myself for failing to keep him.

"Perhaps," Reggie suggested, his own recent pain lending weight to his words, "it's not about being enough. Sometimes people leave not because we're lacking, but because they're not ready to face their own fears."

Jane's breath caught as truth landed. "Have you ever felt that kind of pain?" she asked softly, her vulnerability mirrored in her voice.

Instead of deflecting professionally, Reggie allowed a moment of genuine connection. "Yes," he acknowledged. It turns out that our most profound pain can be a catalyst for remarkable personal development.

Tears fell freely now as Jane nodded, understanding flowing between them. "So how do we survive it?"

"One breath at a time," Reggie offered, his professional wisdom now grounded in personal truth. "We honour the pain by learning from it, by allowing it to teach us about ourselves and about love."

The session moved toward its close as morning light strengthened, both therapist and client changed by this shared understanding. "Thank you," Jane said quietly, standing. "For being real with me today."

Reggie nodded, professional boundaries maintained even as authentic connection held. "Sometimes healing comes not from having all the answers, but from knowing the questions together."

<h1 style="text-align:center">Chapter 19</h1>

The crisp morning air hinted at autumn as Reggie's running shoes tapped into their familiar rhythm on the city streets. His route, calculated weeks ago, passed Penelope's shop at exactly 7 a.m.—early enough to respect boundaries, late enough to let his heart remember.

The shop's windows remained dark as he passed, his pace steady despite the slight catch in his chest. Professional discipline kept his feet moving when his heart wanted to linger. Before he left, Freud had given him that knowing feline look—cats, after all, understood the heart better than most humans.

Penelope's 7:15 a.m. arrival altered the morning's energy. Through careful peripheral vision, Reggie observed her morning routine——keys turning, lights warming the space, flowers being positioned with her usual grace. He maintained his distance across the street, hidden by early commuters and delivery trucks, respecting the boundaries she'd set with painful clarity weeks ago.

His own schedule had subtly adjusted over the days. 7.30 a.m. now found him timing his cool-down stretches to coincide with her first arrangements of the day. The morning light caught her hair as she worked, her hands moving with familiar certainty among the blooms. Sometimes, when the timing aligned perfectly, their eyes would meet briefly through the window——no longer sharp with pain, but not yet soft with forgiveness.

By 7.45 a.m, their morning pattern had established itself. Professional nods replaced averted gazes. The space between them held less tension, more quiet acknowledgment of shared history and separate paths. He kept his distance, showing through action rather than words his respect for her boundaries.

At 8am, their delicate dance subtly changed. The sharp edge of heartbreak had softened into something more contemplative. Understanding seemed to grow in the quiet moments between his passes of the shop, her arrangements becoming less defensive barriers and more artistic expressions again.

As 8:15 neared, Reggie's morning routine adapted to its new pattern. His morning run no longer felt like penance—it had become patience, each step a quiet vote for trust to grow again. The day could begin properly now, his heart steadier for having witnessed her morning ritual, hope maintained in small moments of shared space and respected boundaries.

The morning light strengthened as he turned toward home, carrying with him the quiet certainty that some paths, though longer than expected, were worth the careful journey they demanded.

Reggie arrived at the office and began his pre-session routine, his client notes arranged before him. Sandra Brown's file revealed familiar patterns, but his perspective had shifted since their last meeting. The recent lessons of his own heart lent a deeper understanding to her struggles. Freud maintained his professional post in his miniature chair, golden eyes watching as Reggie's pen moved across the page, adding fresh insights to established observations. The theoretical framework that had served him for years now felt enriched by lived experience.

He wrote, "Resistance to vulnerability...," paused, recalling his own defences, adding, "...often hides a deeper fear of loss, not just a lack of trust." His hand moved steadily now, professional expertise finally married to personal understanding.

Reviewing past sessions with a new perspective, the quiet scratching of his pen marked a new beginning. Sandra's journey reflected aspects of his own - the careful walls, the professional facade, the fear masked as control. His notes took on new depth, clinical observations now warmed by genuine comprehension.

Every page brought a deeper understanding. Where once he'd seen textbook resistance patterns, he now recognised the courage it took to even consider lowering one's guards. His own recent vulnerability with Penelope had taught him the true weight of such choices.

The therapy room had a different feel, as though his personal development had altered its atmosphere. The carefully curated professional space now held something more authentic——permission for real humanity alongside expertise. Freud's approving purr suggested the cat had noticed this change too.

His method had naturally developed throughout these weeks. Clinical distance had softened into something more balanced. Theory and experience merged into more nuanced understanding, each informing the other.

The peaceful morning gave him time for quiet reflection before Sarah's session. His notes showed the progression clearly--from general observations to genuinely empathetic insights.

With renewed purpose, Reggie finalised his preparations, his pen moving swiftly. Each note reflected both his years of expertise and his recent growth through personal pain. The combination felt right--professional wisdom enriched by lived understanding, clinical knowledge deepened by real experience.

He completed his preparations as the clock steadily marked the passage of time. His final notes carried both professional authority and personal truth, a bridge built between textbook knowledge and heart's wisdom. Freud's steady presence witnessed this integration of head and heart, of theory and life, of professional excellence and human understanding.

Pam entered the office, head poking in, her expression apologetic. "Sarah just called—she's cancelling last minute. Something about an emergency. "Reggie frowned, hoping everything was alright, but nodded. "Thanks, Pam." He glanced at his schedule and decided to use the unexpected break to relax and prepare for his next client, Michael.

Stepping into Reggie's office, Michael Bennett felt more relaxed than before, the familiar routine grounding him. The months of work between them had carved out a quiet trust, an unspoken understanding that filled the space.

With a small nod toward the chair, Reggie prepared his pen to record their next step. Michael's usual tension seemed lighter today as he took his seat, something in his bearing suggesting readiness for deeper work. The city hummed quietly beyond the windows, creating their usual sanctuary from the world's demands.

Michael, his voice curious, commented on Dr. Fitzwilliam's newfound energy. "More...grounded, maybe."

Reggie considered the observation, feeling the truth of it settle in his chest. Personal experiences reshaped his approach, blending theory with practical understanding.

He mused that genuine presence may outweigh perfectly crafted responses, mentioning the effortless flow of truth now. Freud's approving purr suggested the cat had noticed this evolution too.

Michael leaned forward slightly, encouraged by this shift. "It's easier somehow, knowing you understand rather than just know."

Dust motes danced in the afternoon light between them, the silence heavy with unspoken meaning. Sensing the session's growing importance, Freud approached.

"I used to think strength meant never showing weakness," Michael continued, his own defences lowering in response to Reggie's authentic presence. "But watching you these past months...."

Reggie replied, "True strength comes from embracing our shared humanity," his professional insights now deeper due to personal experience. The leather chairs creaked softly as both men settled into deeper understanding.

Michael's exhaustion finally showed through his careful facade. "I'm tired of maintaining perfect walls."

Reggie suggested it might be time to distinguish protective walls from imprisoning ones, his experience giving his words impact. Freud's steady presence seemed to support this shared moment of truth.

The office held their silence, afternoon warmth wrapping around them as this new understanding took root. Professional skill and personal development combined to create authentic healing through shared humanity.

"How do we start?" Michael asked, voice carrying both fear and hope.

"By accepting that growth isn't about being perfect," Reggie responded, feeling the truth of his own transformation in the words. "It's about being real."

As the evening light shone through the rose arbour, the familiar sound of Mrs. Crumble's garden gate creaking welcomed Reggie. His earlier session with Michael still lingered in his thoughts, a testament to how much his practice had evolved. The roses nodded gently in the cooling air, their fragrance mixing with the promise of freshly brewed tea.

Mrs. Crumble stood by her weathered garden table, kettle already steaming. Her knowing smile suggested she'd been expecting him, as she so often did these days.

"Your timing's perfect, dear. The Earl Grey's just ready," she said, gesturing to his usual spot on the wooden bench.

Reggie settled into the familiar seat, feeling the day's tension begin to ease. Usual peace filled the garden as Mrs. Crumble poured tea, the birds singing their evening songs. Steam rose in the golden light, carrying comfort with its familiar aroma.

"Tell me about your day," she prompted, settling beside him with the ease of long friendship.

Reggie wrapped his hands around the warm cup, considering. "Something's different now. The connections feel...deeper somehow."

"Similar to these roses," Mrs. Crumble noted, indicating the flowers around them. "They grow stronger when they're properly tended."

"Michael noticed it too," Reggie continued, watching the evening light play through the rose petals. "Said I seemed more real."

Mrs. Crumble's quiet understanding encouraged him to elaborate. "I used to think professional distance meant perfect walls. Now I realise it's a matter of discerning which defences to drop.

"Ah," she smiled, pouring more tea. "Like a garden needs both structure and space to grow."

The cooling air carried the mingled scents of roses and evening as they sat in comfortable silence. A gentle breeze stirred the flowers, their movement catching the last rays of sunlight.

"You've found your balance," Mrs. Crumble noted, her eyes taking in both the physical changes in his bearing and the deeper shift in his presence. "Balancing work and life."

Reggie nodded, feeling the truth of her words. "The practice feels different now. More authentic in a way."

"Because you're finally allowing yourself to be authentic," she replied, wisdom carried in her gentle tone. "Your clients feel that truth."

A soft creak echoed from the wooden bench as Reggie moved, pondering what to say next. "I'm thinking of expanding the practice. Creating more spaces for real healing."

Mrs. Crumble's smile deepened as she gestured to her garden. "Like this space? A sanctuary for growth?"

"Yes," Reggie agreed, understanding flowing between them. "Somewhere people can feel safe enough to be real."

The evening light softened further as they discussed his vision, tea warming their hands as wisdom flowed as naturally as the breeze through the roses.

Reggie entered his study, the familiar space welcoming him with its leather-bound comfort. Silently, Freud took his usual spot on the window ledge as Reggie turned on the desk lamp. Its warm glow created an island of light perfect for reflection.

The weight of the day's sessions sat comfortably in his mind as he opened his journal, its pages ready to capture new understanding. Autumn's breath, mingling with the aroma of old books, drifted in through his slightly open window.

Reggie began reviewing his session notes, paying particular attention to Michael's breakthrough. His pen moved steadily across the page:

"Today marked a significant shift in therapeutic approach. Michael's reaction to genuine closeness versus ideal separation shows how combining experiences is key to healing.

His pen scratching rhythmically against the paper as he documented professional insights. Each note reflected the evolution of his practice, the way personal growth had deepened his ability to connect with clients.

His writing effortlessly transitioned into personal reflection.

"Mrs. Crumble's garden wisdom proves true again——healing grows stronger where experience has cut deepest. My own journey through loss and recovery has transformed my understanding of therapeutic connection."

As Reggie assessed his therapeutic approach, Freud's calm demeanour offered unspoken encouragement. The professional distance he'd once prized had evolved into something more nuanced: a careful balance of boundaries and authentic presence.

He noted the strength that had emerged from vulnerability, the way acknowledging his own healing journey had created deeper connections with clients. The wooden desk felt solid beneath his arms as he leaned forward, capturing these insights in careful script.

Organised with his usual precision, tomorrow's client files, holding new potential, waited nearby. Each session would benefit from this evolved understanding, this integration of professional expertise and personal truth.

The city settled into night beyond his windows as Reggie finished his notes, the familiar routine carrying fresh meaning. His evening tea cooled beside him, its comfort a constant through change.

Chapter 20

Reggie stood before the publisher's gleaming glass tower—a changed man, as his reflection quietly confirmed. The morning sun caught his perfectly knotted tie. He took a steadying breath, then entered through the revolving doors, his professional confidence enfolding him like a comfortable coat.

The elevator's smooth ride allowed him to compose himself. This meeting wasn't about proving himself—it was about offering something real. His new approach to therapy impressed the publisher, particularly following glowing client testimonials.

Cheryl Penn's corner office offered stunning city vistas. She greeted him with the practiced warmth of someone who saw manuscripts as potential profit margins.

"Reggie," she began, sliding a polished report across the desk, "your sales are consistently excellent." "Even through the...recent difficulties."

He meticulously reviewed the sales data, noting the consistent market performance of his previous works. The scent of fresh coffee permeated the space as Cheryl's assistant brought in a carefully arranged tray.

"The market's changing," Cheryl announced, tapping a market report with her perfectly manicured nails. "Readers want authenticity. Real stories. Real growth." She paused, letting the implication settle. "Your recent journey has created quite an interesting narrative."

Reggie took a thoughtful sip of the excellent coffee. "You're suggesting a new book?"

Cheryl leaned in, clearly excited, saying, "Let's combine your professional skills and personal experiences." "Your evolved approach—blending personal growth with clinical depth—is exactly what readers are craving and it's exactly what the market needs."

The leather chair creaked softly as Reggie considered her words. "It's not just about theory anymore," he offered, "but truth lived and learned."

"Exactly!" Cheryl's eyes lit up. We're thinking of calling it "Healing Together: A Therapist's Evolution from Ideal to Now". Your professional wisdom enriched by personal experience."

The contract's terms were the subject of discussion. This wouldn't be another expert's manual, but a bridge between professional knowledge and human experience.

"We'll want the manuscript in six months," Cheryl said, pushing the contract forward. "Your voice has evolved, Reggie. It's time to share that growth with the world."

The morning sun caught the pen as Reggie lifted it, purpose clear. Unlike clinical manuals, this book would weave together expertise and experience—a story of healing shared, not just taught.

Reggie entered his practice, the familiar scent of leather and lavender welcoming him back. His impeccably tidy desk was adorned with patterns of morning light, diffused through the delicate drapes. Freud emerged from his therapy perch, greeting his human with a dignified meow that seemed to acknowledge the morning's significance.

Setting his briefcase down, Reggie settled into his chair, the leather creaking softly beneath him. He had a publisher's contract in his bag, but before looking at it, he wanted to review his practice's evolution. His client notes spread before him, evidence of evolution in every carefully documented session.

"Look at this, old friend," he murmured to Freud, who had claimed his usual observation post. "See how the sessions have changed?" His finger traced the progression through recent weeks - less clinical distance, more authentic connection. Where once he'd maintained perfect professional barriers, now he found strength in shared understanding.

Pulling his previous session notes closer, Reggie noticed the subtle shifts in his therapeutic approach. His answers changed from textbook-perfect to authentic and lifelike. Each breakthrough now carried the weight of personal experience, theory transformed by truth.

"We're not just teaching anymore, are we?" he reflected, Freud's knowing purr agreeing. The sun highlighted his previously published books, achievements that now seemed incomplete. This new opportunity felt different, like aligning professional purpose with personal growth.

The practice's quiet buzz of morning activity filtered through his door as his colleagues arrived. Pam's gentle knock preceded her entrance with fresh tea.

"This afternoon's team meeting is scheduled," she said, placing his cup on the table. "Everyone's curious about the publisher's meeting."

Reggie touched the contract in his briefcase, nodding. "We're evolving, Pammy. The practice, our approach——everything's shifting toward something more authentic."

"It's about time," she smiled, her long-standing familiarity with him evident. "The team will support this, you know. They've seen the changes in your sessions, in the clients' responses."

The morning light strengthened as Reggie reviewed his schedule, each upcoming session now holding new possibility. His therapy style had already evolved organically; the book would document this, helping others find authentic connections in their healing practices.

Reggie stood in the Victorian Terrace's entrance, the stained-glass windows casting colourful patterns across polished wooden floors. He felt at home in the familiar space, its quiet dignity mirroring his renewed professional purpose. Freud padded silently beside him, golden eyes alert as they prepared for the afternoon's sessions.

The leather chairs and subtle lavender scent created the perfect therapeutic environment. Reggie adjusted his tie, not from anxiety but from practiced care. The afternoon appointments included the Sterling's and some other regulars.

Reggie sat ready, closing his eyes and focused on his breathing to get in the zone when Pam's gentle knock interrupted. "Dr. Fitzwilliam? The Sterling's are here."

The Sterling's arrived precisely on time, their entrance through the private gate ensuring absolute discretion. Veronica Sterling's carefully constructed public image revealed slight flaws, which indicated improvement instead of failing. James' hand rested protectively at the small of her back, a gesture that had been absent in their earlier sessions.

"The reporters are getting more persistent," Veronica noted, settling into her usual chair. The leather creaked softly beneath her as she adjusted her position. James sat beside her, close enough for their shoulders to touch, a welcome development.

"But they haven't managed to follow us here," James added, his tech-entrepreneur confidence carrying a new note of genuine relief. His fingers laced through Veronica's; this was nothing like their initial, staged show of affection.

Freud observed this exchange with his usual therapeutic insight, his tail curling with what appeared to be approval. The cat had shown excellent judgment of authentic versus performed intimacy throughout their sessions.

As Reggie sat down, the afternoon sun grew stronger, its warmth embracing the room's rich wood. Though his notes were open, he hadn't written anything; he valued real connection over detailed records.

Reggie observed the subtle shifts in the Sterling's body language - signs that would have been invisible to most but spoke volumes to his trained eye. Veronica appeared relaxed, while James' protective gesture seemed genuinely concerned, not for show.

"Shall we begin?" Reggie asked, his voice carrying the quiet authority that had drawn the Sterling's to his practice. "The media pressure," his voice was gentle but firm. "Tell me how you're managing it together."

Veronica's fingers tightened almost imperceptibly around James'. "It's different now," she said, her carefully modulated public voice softening. "We're facing it as a team rather than..."

Instead of reacting to each other, James concluded, his rapid speech slowing to match his wife's.

Freud's ears twitched with interest, his golden eyes tracking this exchange. The cat had proven remarkably adept at detecting authentic moments of connection, and his current posture suggested approval.

Reggie proceeded, recalling last session's discussion on building private areas amidst public scrutiny, noting Sterling's composure regarding their vulnerability. "How has that been working?"

James leaned forward slightly, his usual boardroom posture relaxing. "We've been having breakfast together. No phones, no tablets, no assistants. Just..."

"Only us," Veronica added, a real smile warming her face. "Like before all this." She gestured vaguely, encompassing their public life, their empire, their carefully curated image.

Reggie felt the weight of his own experience inform his response. "Sometimes the smallest moments of authenticity become our strongest foundations."

Warm patterns from the afternoon sun, shining through stained glass, danced across the therapy room. Veronica followed these patterns with her eyes, seeming to gather her thoughts.

With a barely audible whisper, she confessed, "I was scared." "Not of the media, not really. But of losing ourselves in what everyone expected us to be."

James' hand moved to cover hers, no cameras present to capture this gesture. "We were both afraid," he acknowledged. "But we never told each other."

Freud chose this moment to pad silently across to Veronica's chair, offering his brand of therapeutic support. The cat's presence often helped clients maintain their connection to vulnerable moments.

"Fear often speaks loudest in silence," Reggie observed, his own journey lending depth to these words. "But naming it together can transform it from a wall into a bridge."

A glance between the Sterling's spoke volumes of their past and present. The room held their silence, allowing this moment to breathe and settle.

"How do we maintain this?" James asked, his entrepreneur's instinct for practical solutions emerging. "When the pressure returns - because it will..."

"We remember this feeling," Veronica said softly, surprising both men with her insight. "This moment is real. We choose it again, every day. "Reggie nodded, recognising the echoes of his own learning in her words. "Authenticity is not a destination," he stated. "It's a daily choice, especially under pressure."

Reggie eyed the antique mantel clock; its soft ticking announced the session's close. The Sterling's had made remarkable progress, their connection now carrying the weight of authenticity rather than performance.

"Perhaps we should begin wrapping up for today," he suggested, noting how neither Sterling stiffened at the prospect of returning to their public lives. What did you get out of this session?

Veronica's hand remained comfortably entwined with James', her media-perfect posture softened by genuine ease. "The importance of these private moments," she said, her voice carrying new confidence. "Of choosing each other over expectations."

"And the courage to be real," James added, his tech mogul efficiency tempered by emotional awareness. "Even when it feels vulnerable."

Freud remained seated near Veronica, his approving gaze reflecting their progress. The cat had shown remarkable insight throughout their journey, often responding to authentic connection with subtle signs of encouragement.

While the Sterling couple collected their belongings, Reggie noted the spontaneous harmony of their actions, a stark contrast to their meticulously planned public performances. Now they moved as partners, not performers.

"Remember," Reggie offered as they prepared to leave, "authenticity isn't about perfect moments. It's about perfect presence in imperfect ones."

With a soft click, the massive oak door shut, leaving Reggie isolated with his thoughts and Freud's insightful stare. He settled at his desk, reviewing his notes while the afternoon light painted warm patterns through the stained glass.

The Sterling's' progress reflected something deeper about his own journey. Their battles with public image and private self-mirrored his journey from detached professionalism to authentic therapeutic intimacy.

Freud jumped onto the desk, deliberately placing himself between Reggie and the notes. His purr suggested approval of this moment of reflection.

"Yes, old friend," Reggie murmured, scratching behind the cat's ears. "We've each discovered something about authentic connection, right?"

The clock chimed softly, reminding him of his next appointment. He straightened his notes, adjusted his tie more from habit than necessity now, and prepared to welcome his next client. The steady afternoon light gently warmed the therapy room.

Seated at his desk, Reggie methodically reviewed his notes, his measured movements concealing the depth of his contemplation.

The quiet of his office wrapped around him like a comfortable embrace, the space feeling more like a sanctuary than a fortress these days.

The producer's call pierced the peaceful routine, her name lighting up his phone screen. Reggie's hand hesitated for just a moment, memories of his previous reluctance surfacing briefly before he answered.

"Dr. Fitzwilliam," her voice carried enthusiasm, "we'd like to revisit our previous discussion about the show."

Reggie settled into his chair, awareness of his professional growth lending new confidence to his response. "I've been considering that myself," he admitted, fingers absently straightening his tie. "Though my approach has evolved significantly."

"That's precisely why we're interested in you," she responded. "Your recent experiences, your take on authentic healing...."

Reggie reviewed his therapeutic approach, envisioning how it might translate to a broader audience. "If we proceed," he began carefully, "there would need to be clear ethical boundaries. Let's avoid sensationalism and exploiting vulnerabilities.

"Of course," she agreed readily.

"The focus must be on authentic healing," he continued, warming to the possibility. "Real understanding of human struggles, not just quick fixes or perfect solutions."

Reggie noted details of their discussion to shape content blending therapeutic wisdom and personal insight. His own journey would inform but not overshadow the professional guidance.

"We could start with a series on authentic growth through challenge," he suggested, professional pride evident in his voice as the plan took shape.

Freud's contented purring underscored the schedule's creation, his catlike stillness a persistent symbol of authenticity's value. As they finalised details, Reggie felt the comfortable weight of professional evolution settling around him.

As he reviewed their points of agreement, the late afternoon sun cast a warm glow across his office. Fresh tea steamed beside him, its aroma mixing with the familiar scent of leather and paper - the tools and textures of his practice. His pen moved confidently across the page, mapping out this new chapter with clear purpose and ethical foundation.

As Reggie settled into his familiar leather chair, the evening enveloped his study softly. Freud already claiming his usual perch near the window. The warm glow of his desk lamp created a circle of comfort as Reggie reached for his journal, its leather binding smooth beneath his fingers.

The day's quiet descended, bringing with it a sense of peace that still felt new - earned rather than assumed. His pen had just touched paper when the email notification chimed softly.

The invitation to be the keynote speaker at the International Association of Therapeutic Practice's upcoming conference was significant. Recognition dawned slowly as Reggie absorbed the implications.

Leaning back in his chair, Reggie let the possibility settle. His fingers traced the edge of his journal, mind already shaping the message he could share. Not just professional expertise, but authentic understanding of healing's true path.

"What do you think, old friend?" he murmured to Freud, who responded with his usual knowing purr. "A chance to share what we've learned about real healing."

As he wrote about authentic growth through challenge, integrating personal truth with professional wisdom and the power of vulnerability, the outline emerged organically. Every point reflected lived experience.

His pen moved steadily across fresh paper, excitement building as the vision took shape. This wouldn't be just another academic presentation - this could be something transformative. A way to help other therapists embrace authentic healing alongside professional excellence.

Reaching for his schedule, Reggie began clearing the dates. Tomorrow, he must tell Pam and organize client coverage. Already he could sense his team's support, their shared enthusiasm for this evolution of their practice.

The city lights twinkled beyond his window as he closed his journal, the night settling around him with comfortable certainty. Freud's steady presence offered silent approval as Reggie sat back, allowing himself to feel the quiet satisfaction of this new opportunity.

Chapter 21

Reggie stirred as dawn bathed his room in soft gold—consciousness returning with ease. No alarm needed anymore——his body had found its natural rhythm. Freud shifted at the foot of the bed, golden eyes already awake and watchful.

Beside his bed, Reggie picked up his journal, its pages a mix of professional notes and personal entries. The morning quiet held a different quality now, peaceful rather than demanding. His thoughts settled naturally, no longer racing with the day's requirements before it began.

As Reggie prepared his healthy breakfast of fruit and grains, the morning sun illuminated his gleaming kitchen—a stark contrast to the meals he'd forgone in his earlier, demanding career. His hands moved with quiet purpose, preparing food while his mind reviewed the day ahead. The International Association's conference preparations sparked genuine excitement rather than anxiety.

Freud was already making his way to his carrier as Reggie prepared to leave, golden eyes holding approval for this evolved morning routine. The apartment hummed with peace—a sanctuary, not a fortress. Each morning step felt purposeful, grounded in genuine determination rather than driven perfectionism.

With his briefcase in one hand and Freud's carrier in the other, Reggie prepared to leave, feeling their familiar weight. Morning light caught the city beyond his windows, promising another day of integrated growth, both personal and professional.

Reggie's office maintained its typical serene atmosphere, the polished Persian rug grounding the space as he began his workday. The soft strains of music mingled with the fragrant aroma of lavender, creating a soothing atmosphere as Reggie sat down. Freud, ever the professional, settled into his tiny leather chair.

The phones hadn't stopped ringing since the practice opened that morning. Pam's efficient micromanagement handled the increasing volume of appointment requests, her pride evident in each scheduling confirmation. Client testimonials filled his inbox, each message affirming the impact of his evolved approach to therapy.

"Dr. Fitzwilliam?" her voice came through the intercom. "Cheryl Penn from the publishing house is here."

The room was filled with Cheryl's enthusiasm as she scattered the contract papers on his desk. "The market's ready for your message, Reggie. Authentic healing through shared experience, it's exactly what people need."

As Reggie pored over the terms, his vision for the book sharpened. "We maintain the focus on real connection," he stated, pen hovering over the signature line. "No quick fixes or perfect solutions."

"Precisely," Cheryl concurred, her anticipation growing. "Your personal journey has given you something unique to offer. The way you've integrated professional expertise with authentic understanding."

Signing the contract felt less like a milestone, more like the next honest step. Freud's approving purr punctuated the moment, his golden eyes watching the proceedings with typical feline wisdom.

Michael Bennett's appearance signalled the start of his late morning session. The junior executive's transformation over recent months mirrored aspects of Reggie's own journey.

"I used to think strength meant never showing weakness," Michael shared, his posture relaxed in the familiar leather chair. "But what you've taught me about authentic connection...."

Reggie's lean forward subtly merged his professional expertise with his personal understanding. "Sometimes our greatest strength lies in acknowledging our human struggles."

Michael's breakthrough came organically, his insights stemming from self-discovery, not therapy. Freud maintained his watchful presence, his quiet support part of the healing atmosphere.

Following Michael's session, Reggie briefly enjoyed a moment of professional satisfaction. His notes flowed easily, capturing both the technical aspects and the human connection that had deepened his practice.

Freud padded over, offering his customary mid-morning companionship. Reggie's hand found the cat's soft fur as he reviewed his afternoon schedule. The conference preparation notes waited alongside client files, each element of his professional life now infused with authentic purpose.

From his window, he could clearly see the street, including the well-known path that went by Penelope's shop. The sight no longer carried sharp pain, though the quiet ache remained. Professional momentum had provided its own kind of healing, even as personal wounds continued their slower mending.

Reggie unlocked his apartment door, entering the quiet space, his briefcase full of the day's work successes. Freud immediately make his way to his favourite windowsill, the cat's golden eyes holding their usual knowing look.

The familiar comfort of home settled around him as Reggie shed his suit jacket and tie. His leather journal waited on the desk for him, its pages ready to hold the day's reflections.

Lamp light created a warm circle as Reggie settled into his chair, pen hovering over blank pages. Freud settled into his usual evening spot nearby, his quiet purring a soothing backdrop to his thoughts.

Memory flowed easily tonight:

"Today marked another milestone - the book contract signed, the conference keynote confirmed. But these professional wins feel different now...

"They're not walls to hide behind, but bridges to authentic connection."

"The practice has evolved as I have. Each client session now carries the weight of shared humanity rather than perfect expertise..."

"My own wounds, when acknowledged, have become my greatest tools for understanding others."

The city lights drew his gaze to the window, where Penelope's shop glowed softly in the evening darkness. The familiar sight of her silhouette among the flowers brought a bittersweet ache.

"I see her every day, yet the distance grows no easier. Perhaps that's the price of growth - carrying the weight of choices we can't undo.... The irony of helping others heal while my own heart remains broken isn't lost on me."

He breathed, recognising the authentic truth about healing.
"We don't just counsel pain, we walk through it together."
The book's potential impact emerged clearly:
"I don't want to write another perfect guide to relationships, but an honest exploration of growth through vulnerability.... Theory becomes truth only when tested by fire."

Freud's gentle head-butt reminded Reggie of dinner's necessity. He rose from his thoughts and went to the kitchen, the cat watching him intently. Simple meal preparations grounded him in the present moment, while gratitude settled quietly.

"For growth, even though pain....
"For companions who stay....
"For the chance to begin again...."

As dusk settled over Reggie's apartment, it's comforting embrace invited him inside after a long day furthering his knowledge of psychology. The moment he slid his key into the entrance, Freud's reassuring figure greeted him as reliably as ever.

Reggie shed his suit jacket with practiced care, loosening his tie as he moved through his evening routine. The peaceful solitude wrapped around him as he selected a book from his extensive collection, settling into his favourite armchair. Freud maintained his watchful presence nearby, his steady purr adding to the reflective mood.

The unexpected chime of his doorbell shattered the quiet, causing both man and cat to start. Reggie's brow furrowed in confusion——he rarely received visitors, especially at this hour. Rising cautiously, he approached the door, Freud padding silently behind him.

Opening the door revealed Mrs. Crumble's familiar figure, her gentle smile carrying decades of understanding. "Good evening, my dear," she announced, displaying the tin holding her celebrated lavender shortbread. "I thought you might need some company tonight."

Warmth flooded Reggie's chest as he welcomed her inside, memories of countless evenings spent in her garden washing over him. "Shall I make some tea?" he suggested, resuming their familiar pattern. Freud's approving gaze followed them to the kitchen, where Reggie busied himself preparing tea.

As they settled with steaming mugs, Mrs. Crumble's wisdom flowed naturally. "You've been carrying quite a weight lately, dear." Her words, gentle but direct, invited honesty.

"My thoughts keep returning to Father," he confessed, his fingers tracing his mug's rim. "About patterns I'm still trying to break."

"Patterns have their purpose," Mrs. Crumble observed, "but so does forgiveness."

Their conversation deepened as evening shadows lengthened, touching on years of parental expectations and the courage needed to forge one's own path. Because Mrs. Crumble provided a secure environment, Reggie felt comfortable expressing his usually hidden fears.

"You know," she said thoughtfully, "some of the strongest roses in my garden came from damaged roots. They just needed someone to believe they could bloom."

Understanding settled in Reggie's chest as they shared the shortbread, its familiar sweetness carrying comfort. Freud moved between them, offering his own form of support through gentle head-butts and contented purrs.

As the clock approached nine-twenty, Mrs. Crumble gathered her things, leaving Reggie with both physical warmth from the tea and emotional warmth from their connection. Their goodbye carried the weight of shared understanding, her gentle hug offering strength for tomorrow's challenges.

The apartment quieted after her departure, but the silence was now filled with possibility rather than weight

Reggie settled into his office chair, the familiar leather creaking beneath him as he surveyed his meticulously organised workspace. With practiced ease and dignified purpose, Freud padded across the room to claim his miniature therapy chair. The morning light filtered through the windows, casting a warm glow over the conference materials spread across his mahogany desk.

His fingers traced the edges of his keynote speech draft, each word carefully chosen to reflect both professional expertise and personal truth. His personal journey's therapeutic insights infused every page, converting theoretical knowledge into practical experience.

Opening his laptop, the smooth surface met Reggie's fingertips as he began refining his presentation slides. Each one needed to strike the perfect balance between professional insight and authentic vulnerability. He was engrossed in his work, the untouched coffee filling the room with its fragrance.

"Some of these needs more personal connection," he murmured to Freud, who responded with a knowing purr. Reggie adjusted his tie, a habit now carrying less anxiety and more purposeful preparation.

Marilyn's arrival opened the office door, her presence bringing a fresh perspective. "Ready for some brutal honesty?" she asked, settling into the client chair with the comfort of long friendship.

"Always," Reggie responded, giving her the newest draft. He watched her face as she read, noting each subtle reaction. Her thoughtful comments helped refine his message, suggesting places where his natural voice could shine through more clearly.

"You've come so far, Reg," Marilyn observed, looking up from the pages. "This isn't just professional expertise anymore, it's real wisdom."

Pride swelled in his chest as he considered the journey that had brought him here. His therapeutic mission, previously a shield, evolved into genuine purpose. With each of Marilyn's suggestions incorporated, Reggie's presentation grew more truthful, a fact reflected in Freud's steady, approving look.

Checking his schedule, Reggie began clearing the afternoon for final travel preparations. Through his office window, he caught a glimpse of Penelope's shop in the distance, the sight no longer bringing sharp pain but quiet acknowledgment. His steps remained resolute as he focused on tomorrow's conference, the promise of sharing his message filling him with quiet anticipation.

The keyboard's soft tapping filled the room as he made final adjustments, the leather chair's familiar comfort grounding him in the present moment. Professional confidence and personal truth infused each word, creating a message resonant with those on similar journeys.

Reggie's apartment exuded its usual stillness, the muted hum of the city beyond his windows a steady backdrop. His steps were deliberate as he spread the conference materials across his desk, the space around him alive with quiet focus. From his favourite spot, Freud, with his golden eyes, carefully watched Reggie arrange the conference papers on his desk.

The leather portfolio containing tomorrow's keynote speech lay open, its pages filled with carefully chosen words that bridged professional expertise and personal truth. Even with his experience, Reggie felt nervous, his fingers fidgeting with his notes.

"This is different, isn't it, old friend?" Reggie murmured to Freud, who responded with a knowing purr. This speech wasn't just about sharing therapeutic wisdom: it represented the integration of his professional knowledge and personal growth.

Rising from his desk, Reggie began pacing the familiar path between his study and living room. As he mentally reviewed his key points, self-doubt started to surface. Would his colleagues understand this new approach? Would they accept vulnerability as strength?

Freud jumped down from his perch, padding over to weave between Reggie's legs, effectively halting his anxious movement. The cat's steady presence grounded him, reminding him of all they'd weathered together.

"You're right," Reggie acknowledged, scratching behind Freud's ears. "We've earned these truths." Returning to his desk, he reread his speech, his resolve renewed.

Each slide in his presentation had been refined to perfection, balancing professional insight with authentic experience. His personal journey's therapeutic insights now shaped his approach, bridging theory and lived experience.

Reggie adjusted his notes, integrating personal stories that would resonate with his audience. His speech delivery had changed, moving from a purely professional tone to something more authentic.

Standing at his window, he felt professional pride swelling in his chest. Tomorrow's presentation offered the chance to share his message of authentic healing with colleagues who might benefit from his journey.

As he went to the kitchen to prepare a light dinner, Freud seemed to approve. The familiar routine helped settle his nerves as evening deepened into night. Tomorrow's challenges loomed, yet tonight offered a peaceful opportunity for preparation and resolve.

The city hummed softly beyond his windows as Reggie reviewed his morning schedule one last time. His resolute steps carried him through his nighttime routine, while Freud maintained his faithful vigil. Sleep waited with restorative promise, ready to prepare him for tomorrow's opportunity to share his transformed understanding of healing.

Chapter 22

As Reggie entered, a quiet energy filled the conference venue; his leather portfolio was held tightly under his arm. The familiar scent of coffee mingled with the sharp tang of freshly pressed suits and polished shoes. Attendees gathered in small groups, their excited chatter a gentle hum of anticipation filling the large hall.

Reggie scanned the room—seasoned professionals moved with ease, while newcomers fidgeted with name tags and nerves. He adjusted his tie and allowed himself a brief smile. Today was different. Today, the walls he'd long used to shield himself were lowered, and for the first time in years, he felt ready to step into this moment fully.

Backstage, the green room carried an air of focused calm. Assistants moved efficiently, ensuring that microphones were clipped, and schedules were adhered to. Reggie stood before a large mirror framed by warm, diffused lights. The man in the mirror was both familiar and changed—still polished, still poised, but softened by hard-won authenticity. He tugged at his tie again, the faintest tremor in his hands betraying the weight of what he was about to share.

The chairman's steady, clear voice began the introduction, echoing throughout the auditorium. "Our keynote speaker needs little introduction. Dr. Reginald Fitzwilliam...."

Reggie drew in a deep breath, gripping the leather-bound folder that held his notes. The audience's applause reached him before he even stepped onto the stage. When he finally emerged, the lights momentarily blinded him, but the solid feel of the podium beneath his hands was reassuring. As his eyes adjusted, he took in the sea of expectant faces, each gaze carrying a mix of curiosity and hope.

He started, his voice calm yet emotional, "For years, I've been your expert—a relationship guru, best-selling author, and therapist guiding others through the labyrinth of love." But the truth is, I've spent much of my own life running from the very thing I've dedicated myself to helping others find—the courage to be vulnerable."

The audience stilled, drawn into the raw honesty of his words. He could sense every subtle shift in the crowd, the collective hush amplifying each syllable he spoke. The spotlight glared, isolating him on the stage, but he pressed on—determined to share the truths he had spent so long avoiding.

"You see," he continued, his voice firm yet gentle, "I know the pain of rejection all too well. I've tasted the bitterness of trust betrayed, the sting of not being enough. And for so long, I allowed those wounds to shape me, to define me, until I had built walls so high that even I could barely see over them."

He paused, allowing the weight of his words to settle. In the stillness, he felt his own heartbeat pounding in his ears. The moment was terrifying and freeing—what he had long evaded now lay exposed before hundreds.

"However, things altered," Reggie stated, his tone becoming emotional. "Perhaps it was the quiet wisdom of a dear friend, the persistent kindness of a gentle soul, or simply the gradual realisation that the only thing I was truly protecting was my own fear."

For the next half hour, he continued to weave stories from his personal life—some humorous, others laced with heartbreak. He spoke of clients who had taught him invaluable lessons, of friends who had mirrored his own fears and triumphs, of moments when he'd nearly given up. He even peppered his talk with gentle jokes, eliciting warm laughter from time to time. Yet through it all, his candour and vulnerability remained the central thread, drawing the audience deeper into his world.

By the time he reached the forty-minute mark, you could hear a pin drop in the auditorium. People hardly shifted in their seats, so engrossed were they in his every word. It felt as though he had just started speaking, but the clock testified to his steady, heartfelt cadence.

Today, I address you not as an expert, but as a fellow traveller on this path. I've known the darkness of self-doubt, the paralysis of fear, the loneliness of the path less travelled. But I've also tasted the sweetness of forgiveness, the liberation of self-acceptance, and the life-giving power of authentic connection."

Pausing on those words, he then moved to his keynote's conclusion. The clarity in his voice and the unwavering sincerity in his gaze held the crowd spellbound.

"I challenge you to be brave," he said, his voice resonating through the large auditorium. "Be messy. Be unapologetically, beautifully human. Because it is in that sacred space—where we shed our armour and stand bare before one another—that we discover the most profound healing."

At last, after nearly an hour of opening his heart, Reggie bowed his head in gratitude. The audience erupted into applause, the sound washing over him like a wave. He drew in a shaky breath, offering a small, grateful smile as he stepped away from the podium. Though he felt an overwhelming sense of relief and pride, he was still oddly restless, as though waiting for something—or someone—he wasn't sure would come.

Though his presentation was emotionally heavy, Reggie descended, feeling joyful and light-hearted. The thunderous applause still echoed in his ears as he made his way backstage, Freud padding faithfully beside him. His professional mask, once so carefully maintained, had given way to something more authentic—a gentle smile that reached his eyes.

Colleagues rushed to congratulate him, their handshakes and praise washing over him like a warm wave. "Brilliant presentation, Dr. Fitzwilliam," and "Incredibly moving," they said. Reggie acknowledged them with a polite smile, though his thoughts were still caught in the emotional momentum of his speech. He was on the verge of slipping away, hoping to find a quiet corner to steady himself, when—out of the corner of his eye—he saw her."

He froze. Penelope stood at the edge of the gathering, her green eyes bright with unshed tears. He could hardly believe she had come, especially given her expression of pain and betrayal at their previous encounter. Time seemed to slow as their gazes locked, the hum of conversation fading into white noise.

"I'm proud of you," she said softly. "What you did up there...-showing your truth like that...-it took incredible courage."

Reggie's hands trembled slightly. "I learned it from you. You always saw through my walls, even when I was too afraid to let them down."

Tears spilled onto Penelope's cheeks. "I never stopped loving you," she confessed. "Even when it hurt too much to stay. Even when you pushed me away. I just...-I couldn't watch you hide anymore."

The admission struck Reggie like a physical blow, stealing his breath. Without thinking, he reached for her, and she stepped into his embrace. Her body fit against his just as he remembered, her warmth seeping through his carefully pressed suit. His own tears threatening to fall.

"I'm not hiding anymore," he promised, his voice rough with emotion. "No more walls. No more running. If you'll give me another chance...."

Penelope pulled back just enough to meet his gaze, her hands steady on his arms. "We'll take it slowly," she said. "One day at a time. But yes...-yes to another chance."

As Reggie hesitated at the entrance to Penelope's Flower Shop, its inviting exterior appeared before him, his heart pounding wildly. Beyond the glass, he observed her orchestrating a presentation of brilliant yellow blooms, her actions flowing with that unmistakable elegance from his memories. His feline companion accompanying him, voicing a supportive feline call from his carrier.

The shop's bell announced their arrival with a gentle chime. Penelope turned, her green eyes brightening as they found his. A symphony of familiar scents surrounded them; roses, lilies, fresh greenery, and rich earth intertwined.

"You came," Penelope said softly, setting down her pruning shears. Her smile, though cautious, reached his eyes. Looking back, Reggie gave an adoring smile.

He bent down and unlatched the door of Freud's carrier, gently coaxing him out. With practiced grace, the cat moved forward, his golden eyes taking in the strange environment.

Penelope tilted her head, curiosity lighting up her expression. "And who's this dashing visitor?" "This is Freud," Reggie said with a soft chuckle. My assistant, who's also my shadow therapist.

Freud wandered between the displays, pausing to inspect a row of delicate flowers. Penelope crouched slightly, extending her hand. Pausing briefly, Freud brushed her fingers, causing her to softly laugh.

"Well, Freud," she said, glancing up at Reggie, "you certainly know how to charm." Near Penelope's feet, Freud's calm presence eased the tension. Quiet laughter followed, the moment finding a natural rhythm as understanding passed silently between the three.

"Oh, I needed to say something properly. Without an audience or prepared speeches."

Penelope nodded slowly, prepared to hear what he had to say.

"Penelope," Reggie started, his voice thick with emotion. "What I did—pushing you away, building those walls—I was wrong. Terribly wrong."

She moved closer, her hands clasped before her. "You were scared."

"That's no excuse. I hurt you because I couldn't face my own fears." His words carried the weight of months of therapy and self-reflection. "You deserved better."

"We both did," Penelope replied, her voice gentle but firm. "You needed to find your own way to healing."

The silence between them held understanding rather than accusation. Sunlight caught the tears in Penelope's eyes as she continued, "And now?"

"True strength," Reggie began, stepping carefully forward, "isn't about flawless barriers." "It's in being brave enough to let someone see your cracks and trust them to stay anyway."

A gentle curve touched Penelope's lips as she gazed at him. "The transformation in you is remarkable, and there's such serenity about you now."

During their conversation, Penelope reached for and took Reggie's hand. The contact sent warmth spreading through his chest as their fingers intertwined naturally. A charged silence replaced their fading conversation as their eyes locked.

The shop seemed to grow still, the muted hum of the street outside fading into the background. Reggie took a hesitant step closer, his gaze never leaving hers.

"Penelope," he murmured, her name filled with equal parts hope and apology.

Her free hand lifted, brushing lightly against his cheek, and his breath hitched. This was it—the moment he had both longed for and feared.

Slowly, deliberately, Reggie leaned in, his forehead brushing hers, their shared breath mingling in the fragrant air. He paused, giving her the chance to pull away. But Penelope didn't move. Her lips curved faintly in the barest nod of permission.

When their lips finally met, it was like the world shifted beneath them. The kiss was tentative at first, a quiet exploration of unspoken words and unhealed wounds. But as Penelope responded, her hand sliding up to rest against his chest, the kiss deepened.

It was everything Reggie hadn't dared to hope for—an explosion of warmth and connection, the culmination of months of longing, and a promise of the future they could build together.

When they parted, their breaths mingled in the space between them, their foreheads still touching. Reggie smiled softly, his voice barely above a whisper. "You have no idea how much I've wanted to do that."

Penelope's laughter was soft, her tears sparkling like sunlight on water. "I think I do," she replied. "Because I've been waiting just as long."

They stood there for a moment longer, surrounded by the vibrant blooms and the quiet magic of the moment. For the first time, Reggie felt something he hadn't in years: totally in love.

Freud's contented purr provided a perfect accompaniment to the moment.

Penelope's smile could have outshone the sun. "We'll take it slowly," she reminded him, though her fingers remained linked with his.

"One day at a time," Reggie responded, his months-long burden lifted. So, shall we meet tomorrow? Reggie said. With a smile, Penelope responded, "Yes, see you tomorrow."

The afternoon sun warmed Reggie's office as he settled back into his professional routine, the lingering scent of Penelope's flower shop still clinging to his suit. Though seated again in his tiny leather therapy chair, Freud's perceptive golden eyes revealed he hadn't let go of the morning's events.

Reggie's first client of the afternoon arrived precisely on schedule, and despite the pleasant distraction of Penelope, his therapeutic focus engaged smoothly. Sandra Brown took her usual seat; her reluctance to be vulnerable and her trust issues demanded his complete attention.

"You seem different today, Dr. Fitzwilliam," Sandra observed, a slight smile playing at her lips.

"Perhaps I'm learning to practice what I preach about balance," Reggie replied, his professional demeanour softening slightly. Changing the subject slightly, how are you progressing in your exploration of vulnerability?

The session flowed naturally, his recent personal breakthrough lending unexpected depth to his therapeutic insights. Sandra's eventual self-discovery resonated deeply with Reggie's quest for authenticity.

Between sessions, his fingers found his phone almost of their own accord. Penelope's number appeared on the screen before he'd fully formed the thought.

"Miss me already?" Her voice carried a smile.

"I was considering," Reggie started, his characteristic professional fluency temporarily failing him. "Would you like to come over for dinner tonight? I make a decent coq au vin."

"Decent?" Her gentle teasing warmed his chest.

At least Freud hasn't complained.

Her laugh brightened the office. "Seven o'clock?"

"Perfect. I'll even light candles."

His afternoon clients benefited from his lightened mood, each session carrying a fresh energy that seemed to facilitate deeper connections and client success.

The afternoon progressed with similar successes, each session seeming to benefit from Reggie's newfound integration of personal growth and professional expertise. While seeing patients, he sometimes considered dinner and candles, but always refocused on his patients' needs.

His final client of the day, Michael Bennett, achieved a significant breakthrough regarding his own relationship patterns, the session's success feeling like a perfect culmination of the afternoon's work.

"You've helped me see that vulnerability isn't weakness," Michael said as he prepared to leave. "Somehow, it feels more real today."

"Because authentic healing happens in shared humanity," Reggie replied, the words carrying the weight of personal truth.

Silence fell over the office as Reggie collected his belongings, Freud seemingly pleased. The evening ahead held promise, but the afternoon's therapeutic successes felt equally significant——a professional validation of his personal growth.

Penelope's arrival at seven, in her floral dress, was breathtaking; her perfume a spring whisper, Reggie was momentarily speechless.

At his feet, Freud let out an inquisitive meow before weaving around Penelope's ankles, as if offering his approval. She crouched to greet him, her laughter soft and warm, and Reggie couldn't help but think the evening had already become unforgettable.

As Reggie and Penelope entered the kitchen, the rich aroma of their coq au vin—red wine, herbs, and slow-cooked chicken—filled the apartment. His stomach rumbled slightly, reminding him that he'd skipped lunch again, too caught up in his last session of the day to remember to eat. The familiar comfort of his kitchen, with its gleaming copper pots and organised spice rack, felt different somehow with Penelope's presence beside him.

"Allow me to assist," Penelope volunteered, relieving Reggie of the wooden spoon. Her fingers brushed his deliberately, sending a familiar warmth through his chest. Reggie couldn't help but smile as he watched her stir, her natural grace making even this simple task seem beautiful. The evening light caught the auburn in her hair, and for a moment, he forgot about the chicken browning in the pan.

"You're staring," she teased, not looking up from the sauce.

"Guilty as charged," he admitted, turning his attention back to the stove. The domestic intimacy of the moment struck him - how natural it felt to share his kitchen, his space, his evening with her.

Freud's sudden alertness was their first warning. His ears perked up, and his tail began to twitch - a sure sign of approaching disruption. The knock that followed seemed to echo through the apartment, shattering their peaceful bubble.

Reggie exchanged a glance with Penelope, noting the slight tension that had crept into her shoulders. "I'll get it," he said, wiping his hands on a kitchen towel.

The knock came again, more insistent this time. Freud had already positioned himself near the door, his posture suggesting he knew exactly who waited on the other side.

When Reggie opened the door, Cassandra stood there, her usual polished appearance somewhat subdued. Her eyes widened slightly at the domestic sounds and smells emanating from his apartment.

"Cassandra," Reggie said, his voice carefully neutral. "This is unexpected."

"Reginald." She swallowed hard, her usual sharp confidence notably absent. "I... I know I'm the last person you want to see."

From the kitchen, Penelope's quiet movements stilled, though she remained tactfully out of sight.

"My intentions are peaceful," Cassandra said rapidly. "I just... I owe you an apology. A real one." Her hands twisted together nervously.

"Would you like to come in?" He offered, the invitation slightly surprising even himself. Freud's tail twitched several times more, the cat giving protest.

Cassandra hesitated, clearly catching the domestic sounds and scents from the kitchen. "I don't want to interrupt your evening."

"You're not interrupting," Penelope's voice came warmly as she appeared in the kitchen doorway, wiping her hands on a dish towel. "The sauce needs to simmer anyway."

Something shifted in Cassandra's expression as she took in Penelope's comfortable presence in Reggie's space. A flash of old pain crossed her features before being replaced by what looked like acceptance.

"I've been doing some serious thinking," Cassandra started, her hands clasped. "And therapy," she added with a bitter laugh. "I've actually had quite a lot of therapy."

Reggie remained silent, years of professional experience telling him to let her find her way to what she needed to say. Freud remained a buffer between them, despite his tail having ceased its frantic twitching.

"What I did to you..." Cassandra's voice cracked slightly. "It wasn't just professional sabotage. It was a betrayal of everything we're supposed to stand for as healers."

The coq au vin continued to simmer quietly in the background as Cassandra gathered herself. Penelope moved closer to Reggie, offering steady, supportive company.

"I was jealous," Cassandra admitted, meeting Reggie's eyes directly for the first time. "Of your success, your integrity, the way patients trusted you implicitly. But mainly... she paused, swallowing hard. "I was jealous of how effortlessly you maintained boundaries I couldn't seem to respect."

As Reggie watched his former colleague grapple with her truth, he felt an emotional shift.

Cassandra went on, "I misled myself into believing I was revealing a hidden weakness in your methods, when really I was aiming to demolish something beyond my reach." And in doing so, I nearly ruined someone who had only ever shown me professional courtesy and respect."

Tears gathered in her eyes, surprising Reggie with their genuineness. "I am so deeply sorry, Reginald. For the pain I caused you, for betraying your trust, for manipulating Lily... for all of it. You deserved better from a colleague, and I failed not just you, but our entire profession."

The silence that followed felt weighted with years of complex history. Even Freud seemed to sense the importance of the moment, his golden eyes moving between them with careful observation.

"I don't expect forgiveness," Cassandra added quietly. "I just needed you to know how truly sorry I am."

Reggie felt Penelope's hand slip into his, offering silent support as he processed Cassandra's words. He was moved by the authenticity of her remorse, feeling unexpected compassion for her despite their professional rivalry.

"Thank you," Reggie said finally, his voice gentle but firm. "That couldn't have been easy to say."

"It wasn't," Cassandra admitted with a watery laugh. "But it needed to be said."

It's rare these days to see someone apologise so bravely and directly, making it impossible for me to refuse your apology. Reggie said, "So, I accept your apology, Cassandra." His voice was soft and forgiving. "We all have moments where fear drives us to actions, we later regret... The true measure is in how we face those mistakes and grow from them."

She turned to go, then paused. "I don't think I've ever seen you this happy, Reginald. You have a new peace about you." Humbly, Reggie replied, "Thank you, Cassandra. I wish you similar happiness." More tears appeared in her eyes as she departed.

As the door closed behind her, Reggie felt Penelope's arms slip around his waist, her chin resting on his shoulder. "You, okay?"

He covered her hands with his, letting out a long breath. "Yes. I think I am." He turned in her embrace to face her. "That was... unexpected."

"But good?" she prompted gently.

"But good," he agreed. "Though I think the sauce might be in danger of burning."

Penelope's eyes widened comically as she darted back to the kitchen, leaving Reggie to share a knowing look with Freud. The cat's tail had settled back to its usual contented swish, his own subtle signal that the evening's equilibrium had been restored.

Chapter 23

With his first client's arrival, Reggie settled into his leather armchair, bathed in morning light. Freud assumed his usual therapeutic posture, his golden eyes keen and watchful.

Sarah Matthews entered, immediately noting something different in Reggie's demeanour. What was once polished detachment had softened into something warmer—authentic.

"Before we begin," Reggie said, his voice carrying a new kind of confidence, "I want to share something with you. My experience with trust issues showed me that our greatest strength can be admitting our weaknesses.

Sarah visibly relaxed her shoulders. "You seem different today, Dr. Fitzwilliam."

"I've learned something important: being perfect isn't nearly as powerful as being real."

The session was remarkably open, with Sarah becoming less guarded as she responded to Reggie's sincerity. Freud's gentle purr seemed to approve of this evolved approach.

Michael Bennett's session followed, his usual defensive posture softening as Reggie shared insights from his own experience with perfectionism.

Reggie confessed he once believed excellence required concealing vulnerability, observing Michael's empathetic reaction. "Now I understand that true strength lies in acknowledging our humanity."

By the time James and Sarah Mitchell arrived for couples therapy, Reggie's new approach had settled into a natural rhythm. His expertise remained razor-sharp, but now it carried the weight of personal understanding.

"When we hide our vulnerabilities," he explained, watching them exchange glances, "we also hide our capacity for connection."

Freud's quiet observation added weight to every breakthrough, maintaining his therapeutic presence. The morning's sessions flowed with a depth that professional distance alone could never achieve.

Following the last client's departure, Reggie compiled his notes for the Sterling's final session. Across town, the old Victorian Terrace awaited. Freud padded alongside him as they made their way through the morning sunshine, both sensing the significance of the coming session.

The elegant Victorian Terrace was set against the late morning sky; its private gate ensured James and Veronica Sterling's secure entry to their garden. Reggie unlocked the entrance, Freud assuming his position in the carefully appointed therapy space. The room's warm tones and calm décor set the stage for their final meeting—one in which healing had gone both ways.

Punctual as ever, the Sterling's entered the Victorian sanctuary, instantly shedding their public facades. Veronica's designer suit and James's tech entrepreneur attire couldn't hide their nervous energy. Reggie noted how their hands remained clasped, a marked difference from their first session months ago.

"Welcome," said Reggie, indicating the comfortable leather chairs Freud had already occupied. "How are you both feeling today?"

Veronica's smile carried genuine warmth. "Different. Stronger." She gave James's hand a squeeze. "Together."

James nodded, his usual corporate mask completely absent. "We've been trying out the communication exercises you recommended. They're working."

Reggie sat down, reflecting on his path to self-discovery. "Tell me about a moment when you felt particularly connected this week."

"The board meeting," Veronica said, surprising them both. "Usually, I'd be so focused on maintaining the perfect image that I'd miss James's subtle support. But this time..." She turned to her husband, eyes soft. "This time I let myself feel it."

James's tech mogul facade melted completely. "Dr. Fitzwilliam, I finally grasped your meaning regarding vulnerability being a source of strength. When Veronica acknowledged my support publicly, it meant everything."

Freud's tail twitched in approval as Reggie leaned forward slightly. "You both realise that perfection is unattainable. Connection is."

"Like you did," Veronica observed quietly. "We followed your journey too, you know. The media crisis, the suspension and comeback. It showed us that even experts face their own battles."

"And win them," James added. "Not by being flawless, but by being real."

Reggie acknowledged their words with a slight nod, his own growth reflected in their progress. "Sometimes our greatest teachings come through our deepest challenges."

The session continued with natural flow, each moment reinforcing how far they'd all come. The Sterling's discussed connection strategies amidst public attention, and Reggie contributed personal insights.

As they prepared to conclude, Veronica paused at the door. "Thank you. Not just for the professional guidance, but for showing us that strength lies in authenticity."

James extended his hand. "You've changed more than our relationship, Dr. Fitzwilliam. You've changed how we view success itself."

Reggie shook James's hand, noting Freud's approving presence. "You've taught me as well. Every client does, when we're open to learning."

The Sterling's departed through the private garden entrance. Reggie's observation of their departure highlighted the parallel between their path and his own evolution—from a picture-perfect professional to an authentic healer.

Warm afternoon sunlight poured into Berkelouw Books through its tall windows, illuminating the assembled crowd. Reggie stood at the podium, his new book "Healing Through Authenticity: A Journey of Growth and Connection" displayed prominently beside him. Freud had claimed an elevated perch near the signing table, his regal presence adding gravitas to the occasion.

Seeing familiar faces like Marilyn, Mrs. Crumble, Pam, Anne, and colleagues from his practice filled Reggie with warmth. His publisher, Cheryl Penn, stood near the back, her satisfied expression reflecting the book's early success.

"Before I begin," Reggie's voice carried clearly through the space, "I'd like to introduce someone special." He extended his hand toward Penelope, who rose gracefully from her seat. "My journey to authenticity has been significantly aided by my partner, Penelope Winters, and her wisdom and love."

Penelope's hand found his, their fingers intertwining naturally as she joined him at the podium. Reggie's pride was evident as he looked at her, recalling their journey from her initial panic attack in the flower shop to the current shared success.

"This book," Reggie continued, his professional tone warmed by genuine emotion, "began as a traditional therapy guide. But life had other plans." A knowing chuckle rippled through the audience. "I learned that genuine healing arises from authentic connection, not flawless expertise, through personal and professional growth."

He shared carefully chosen moments from his journey - the suspension, the television show opportunity, the lessons learned through vulnerability. Each story resonated with the audience, their own experiences of growth and healing reflected in his words.

Reggie's sharing of how Mrs. Crumble's gardening advice helped him through hard times brought pride to her eyes. Marilyn laughed heartily at the mention of university, while Pam wiped away tears of emotion as he thanked her for her consistent support and the practice's growth. He also thanked his ever present feline companion, Freud, who taught him the finer details of chaos theory and that being ourselves, cat or human, is purrfectly, OK, which got a few laughs.

"And of course," he smiled, squeezing Penelope's hand, "sometimes healing comes through unexpected flowers and terrible coffee."

The crowd laughed warmly, many familiar with their story. Penelope's answering smile carried all the joy of their shared journey.

Reggie also announced his return to television - this time with a different focus that made his heart race with purpose. "We need deeper solutions, not superficial ones designed for popularity." Instead, he would champion genuine understanding of human struggles, exploring the messy, complicated journey of healing that he knew all too well. His vision of offering authentic growth rather than quick fixes or perfect solutions resonated deeply with the audience, and congratulations flowed freely. Several colleagues nodded in approval, understanding the courage it took to challenge the status quo of pop psychology and reality TV therapy. The bookstore hummed with celebration, each person there having played a part in his transformation.

Warm congratulations flowed as Reggie concluded his speech. Colleagues approached with genuine praise, friends offered heartfelt hugs, and family members expressed their pride. Penelope stayed with him throughout everything, showing the strength of true love.

Freud maintained his watchful position as the celebration continued, his golden eyes tracking each interaction with characteristic dignity. Bathed in afternoon sunlight, the book cover seemed to radiate hope and healing to those celebrating not just its publication but also a transformative journey.

The late afternoon sun cast long shadows across the garden of Reggie and Penelope's Southern Highlands home. The scent of blooming roses mingled with lavender as they walked hand in hand through the paths they'd lovingly created together over the past year.

Reggie felt a profound sense of peace, a stark contrast to his busy city life as a counsellor. His choice to divide his schedule between metropolitan and countryside locales had yielded a harmonious lifestyle he'd scarcely imagined. Two busy days of consultations in his Paddington practice, Monday and Tuesday, followed by his television work on Wednesday and slower-paced rural consultations in Bowral on Thursday and Friday, renewed his professional spirit and allowed him to help people in both settings.

"The delphiniums are particularly striking this year," Penelope observed, pausing to touch a vibrant blue spike. Her own contentment showed in her relaxed posture, the success of her second flower shop adding a quiet pride to her movements. The highland's shop had quickly become a community favourite, its window displays drawing tourists and locals alike.

"Your way with them is enchanting," Reggie smiled, observing her intuitive care for each plant. "Rather like your new shop - everything seems to thrive under your care."

Freud padded silently behind them, his dignified presence a constant in their shared life. He'd adapted beautifully to country living, claiming various sunny spots throughout the garden as his observation posts.

Penelope directed Reggie's gaze to a rose and clematis-covered bed, saying, "Look here." "See how they support each other? The clematis uses the rose for structure, while its delicate blooms soften the rose's bold statements."

Reggie squeezed her hand, understanding the metaphor. "Rather like us, wouldn't you say? Your natural warmth softening my professional edges."

Pausing by the herb garden, they noted the plants' imperfect, unplanned growth. Some plants had spread beyond their boundaries, others needed constant attention, but the overall effect was harmonious.

"That's what you always say about relationships," Penelope pondered, snuggling closer. "They need constant tending, but the imperfections make them real."

"Its authenticity enhances its beauty," Reggie reflected, remembering his past pursuit of flawlessness. Their marriage, like their garden, thrived not despite its imperfections but because of the care they took in nurturing growth.

Freud sat on a nearby bench, his golden eyes seemingly approving of the scene. The evening light illuminated Reggie's greying hair, its distinguished streaks mirroring the soft grey of Freud's fur.

"The salvias need dead heading," Penelope noted, her professional eye catching tasks even in their private paradise. "And the Japanese maple could use some gentle pruning."

"There's always work to be done," Reggie remarked, quite content with the thought. "Rather like how I still check in with Dr. Matthews for supervision, keeping my practice healthy."

Continuing their evening stroll, they noted surprisingly vibrant new growth and areas needing care. The garden, like their love, was a living thing - requiring care, offering beauty, and teaching them daily about the joy of growing together.

Freud followed at his own pace, occasionally stopping to inspect a particular plant or butterfly, his presence adding to the peaceful domesticity of the scene. He instantly approved of their highland life; his regal bearing seemed more fitting for the country than the city.

As the sun dipped below the horizon, casting a warm glow over the garden, Reggie and Penelope settled onto a bench, their fingers intertwined. At that moment, Reggie realised true love accepts flaws, cherishing the beauty born from shared imperfections.

Like the vibrant garden that surrounded them, their relationship was a tapestry of colours, textures, and ever-changing cycles of growth. There would be moments of pruning, of tending to delicate blooms, and of weathering the occasional storm. Season after season, their bond strengthened, their roots intertwining until inseparable.

Reggie knew that the path to fulfilment was paved not with pursuing flawlessness, but with the courage to be vulnerable, authentically human. As he gazed into Penelope's eyes, he saw the reflection of his own transformation - a man who had learned to trust, to love, and to find the greatest healing in the most imperfect of connections.

Please Leave a Review on Amazon

Loved the Journey? Your Words Matter.

If Love's Lifeline touched your heart, I'd be so grateful if you could take a moment to leave a short review on Amazon. If you are in America please use this QR code

amazon.com

Your feedback helps other readers discover the story—and it means the world to me. Just scan the QR code to share your thoughts. Thank you for being part of this journey. If you are in Australia please use this QR code

amazon.com.au

Other Great Titles Available From BiblioSky Publishing

www.bibliosky.com